ACELDAMA

JOHN HAZEN

BLACK ROSE writing™

ISBN: 978-1-61296-688-5
PUBLISHED BY BLACK ROSE WRITING
www.blackrosewriting.com

Printed in the United States of America
Suggested retail price $17.95

Aceldama is printed in Book Antiqua

To Lynn. Always. Always.

ACELDAMA

1

Circa 30 A.D.

Philemon Chayat, a young man in his upper teens with dark shoulder-length curly hair and a few thin wisps on his chin that passed for a beard, made his way through the crowded Jerusalem market. Practically all his worldly possessions were in the small cloth bag slung over his shoulder. The market's mass of humanity was thick as he weaved his way between vendors who noisily hawked their wares and their potential customers who ardently shouted back the maximum amount they would pay.

He had grown up on the outskirts of the city and was not accustomed to being jostled about like this but he did not care. He was searching for a specific address, hoping he could land his first job.

When six Roman guards marched in formation through the square, people stopped what they were doing and parted to let them pass. Many moved without comment but others whispered insults under their breaths. Although Judea had been part of the Roman Empire for nearly a century, the populace perpetually exhibited animosity towards their conquerors.

Philemon did not have an opinion about the Romans one way or another. He was so intent on locating the address he had been given that he walked right into one of the guards. Using his shield, the sentry gave him a hard shove to the side.

"Out of the way, you!" the soldier scolded in Greek, the lingua franca of the day.

Philemon mumbled an apology, backed off, and watched them pass through.

As he continued on his way, he noticed a billow of smoke emanating from a stone chimney at the far corner of the square. He surmised this was the location he was looking for.

He knocked on the door but heard nothing. He knocked again, this time more forcefully, but still he heard nothing. Trying the door, he found it unlocked and walked in.

Philemon saw the back of a muscular, shirtless man standing in silhouette before the yellow/white flame of an open furnace. The man's right foot was busy pumping a bellows, forcing air into the furnace making the fire even hotter.

Philemon called out in Aramaic.

"Excuse me."

The man, Amos Yahalom, turned around. He wore heavy leather gloves and a thick leather apron. His square-jawed face was bronzed from standing in front of this furnace for hours at a time. He squinted at Philemon until his eyes adjusted to the relative darkness of the room after staring into the fire.

"Excuse me, are you Amos Yahalom?"

"Yes, I am. How can I help you?"

"My name is Philemon Chayat. I'm here to see about a position. My uncle, Isaac Ben Abram, said you were looking for an assistant."

"Yes, yes I am. I had a helper who moved on. You know anything about making coins?"

"No, I don't, but I'm a hard worker and a quick learner."

"Well, if you're Isaac's nephew, that's good enough for me. You'll start as an apprentice. I can't pay you much of anything but I'll provide you a room above the shop here and I can feed you. I'll have the room cleaned out and you can move in tomorrow. Does that sound satisfactory?"

Philemon could not control his enthusiasm, "Yes sir, yes it does."

"Good, then let's start immediately."

Philemon threw his sack over in the corner and waited for instruction.

"I'm commissioned by the Roman provincial government to make coins that will be used in general commerce throughout Judea. Specifically, I produce shekels. Ever see one before?"

Philemon shook his head no. Amos reached into the bin on the rough-hewn oaken table and grabbed a shekel, which he then tossed over. Philemon looked it over and handed it back.

"We heat the silver until it melts. We pour it into little disks and then, while the metal is still malleable, we hammer it into coins using that stamp over there. After that we file away any rough edges, polish it up and inspect it. Got it so far?"

"You're on your own here?"

"Yes, just me, and now you."

Philemon nodded.

"One of your main jobs is to keep the fire very hot or else the silver won't melt thoroughly."

Amos pressed on the treadle, giving the fire another couple bursts of air.

"You can tell when the silver is ready by its color. Once it's ready, we pull it out, like this."

Amos extracted a ladle from the fire.

"And then we pour it into the mold up to the line. Once we've done that, we'll let it cool a bit and then it's ready for us to hammer each coin."

Using tongs, he extracted a disc and placed it into a nearby cast iron mold that looked like an anvil. He put the top piece on top of the mold and grabbed a heavy metal mallet.

"Now we hammer away until we know the coin is cast. Looking at your thin wrists, I'd venture to say you haven't done much hammering in your life, have you?"

Philemon shook his head no.

"Don't worry. In six months your wrists will be as thick as mine."

"How do you know when it's ready?"

"Well, for one thing, you won't see any gaps between the molds, but if you have any doubts, keep hammering. You can't over hit it."

Amos whacked away a dozen or more times. Then he tapped the side of the top mold, loosening it from the coin. Using an awl, he dug the coin out of the bottom part of the mold. He grabbed the shekel with tongs and dipped it in a bucket of water to cool it off. He smoothed out the edges of the coin with a file. Satisfied it was smooth enough he grabbed a smooth soft rag to polish it further. He then dropped it into the bin on the table.

"And there we have it: a shiny new shekel."

"Whose picture is that?"

"I have no idea. I just get paid to make the things, not to learn all about them. Somebody the Romans like, I'd assume."

Philemon nodded his head in return as Amos gave further instruction.

"With a little practice, you should be able to produce about 30 of these in a day, but we don't turn any more than 20 to the Romans. That's the number they expect. If you give them more, they'll come to expect the higher number all the time."

Philemon nodded his head one more time. The two returned to work.

Philemon tried his hand at the process, but he made a mess. Amos laughed.

"Looked simple, didn't it? You'll get the hang of it. Just takes some practice."

They worked together throughout the morning. Amos would stop to give Philemon some advice, but for the most part they were silent. The number of coins in the bin steadily increased.

The door opened and a beautiful teenaged girl with long auburn tresses walked in. She carried a small basket.

"Hi Abba! Mama sent me down here with your lunch."

The girl stopped short when she saw Philemon standing there.

"Esther, my darling. Meet Philemon. You know my good friend, Isaac; this is his nephew."

Esther did not hear her father as she and Philemon were entranced by each other. Amos smiled.

"Esther, my lunch?"

"Oh yes, Abba, here it is."

She handed it over but could not take her eyes off Philemon.

"I can run home and get more food. We didn't know you have someone else with you."

"No, no, don't trouble yourself. Thank you anyway," Philemon responded.

"It's no trouble, no trouble at all."

"Okay Esther," Amos remarked. "That will be all. My good wife always sends enough to feed a legion. Philemon, you can share this with me. Thank you. Don't you think you should head on back home?"

"Yes, yes I should. It was nice meeting you, Philemon."

Philemon, too tongue-tied to respond, mumbled something unintelligible as she left.

"That little whirlwind was my youngest. She means the world to me, you understand, right?"

"Yes sir."

"Good. let's have some lunch."

Lunch completed, the two got back to work. At one point, Amos finished a coin, inspected it and then tossed it into the bin. However, this coin bounced out and landed on the floor near Philemon's bag. Neither Amos nor Philemon noticed as they focused on their labors.

The end of the day arrived.

"That's enough for today," Amos remarked, "You did good work for your first day, Philemon. You'll work out fine."

"Thank you, sir."

At the same time Amos and Philemon were starting to put their tools away for the day, a self-important, menacing man, Matthew, flanked by two Roman guards, strode through the market. The crowd, which had parted to let the soldiers pass earlier, were a little less accommodating to Matthew and his guards. They could not pretend to hide their contempt for the man. One of the market's patrons spit on the ground in front of Matthew. A guard grabbed for his sword but Matthew waved him off and they continued their march.

"I'm going to head out," Amos said. "You finish cleaning up, okay? Be sure to collect any metal shavings; the silver is quite valuable. I'll gather the coins we finished and turn them in on my way home."

He counted the coins and put two in his pocket.

"Twenty-two. Not bad. Two will go toward tomorrow's count."

The door opened with a bang and Matthew strode in, full of his own importance. The two Roman guards remained by the door.

"Matthew, how nice of you to visit. Still the Roman's lapdog, I see."

Matthew did not respond but looked around, inspecting the facility. His eyes stopped on Philemon.

"Amos. Who is this?"

"An apprentice, he just started today."

Matthew shifted his gaze back to Amos, virtually ignoring Philemon.

"I thought I would save you a trip and come by to retrieve today's production."

Amos handed over the bag with the coins but as he moved, the two in his pocket jangled, which Matthew heard. Pointing at Amos' pocket, "And those?"

Amos innocently pulled them out of his pocket.

"With an assistant, I was very productive today. These are to go towards tomorrow's count. You have the twenty for today."

"Or perhaps you are looking to make a profit for yourself. Men, seize him. You can explain your actions to the magistrate; perhaps you can be more convincing in court."

The guards grabbed Amos, who initially struggled but then resigned himself. Matthew turned to Philemon.

"And I'll be back for twenty-two shekels tomorrow. You better have them for me."

The guards escorted Amos out. Matthew turned and shot one last malevolent look at Philemon as he departed.

Philemon was shaken badly, but he was also angry. Picking up his sack, he noticed the stray coin that had bounced from the bin. He placed it in his bag and departed.

Walking through the streets heading home, Philemon was distraught and concerned over the fate of Amos. The streets were relatively deserted when he came upon a haggard old woman sitting on a stoop, begging for money.

"Alms for a poor woman; alms for a poor woman."

Philemon, momentarily considering giving her the shekel, reconsidered and moved on. The old woman gazed upward, her eyes meeting his. She pointed at him with great urgency.

"Evil! There is a great evil about you!"

"What are you talking about?"

"Evil! Evil! "

Agitated and disturbed, Philemon moved on. "Stay away from me you hag! Leave me alone!"

Philemon hurried away down the street, leaving the woman shouting after him.

"What can I do?" he asked himself. "Uncle Isaac is away and not due back until tomorrow. I'll have to wait until then to see if he can help Amos."

He soon found himself by the doors to the Great Temple. Inside, a group of men stood in a circle, saying their evening prayers. He joined them but, wracked with anxiety, his participation was half-hearted. The prayers ended shortly thereafter and, as Philemon left, he noticed a priest standing off to the side. He approached the priest.

"Good evening my son. How can I assist you?"

Philemon pulled the coin from his sack. He was still visibly shaken.

"I have a friend who is in trouble. He made this shekel. Perhaps God will look favorably upon him in his time of need if I gave it to the temple instead of to the Romans."

"That's very nice of you. I'm sure I can help you with that. Your act will not go unnoticed in the eyes of God."

Once Philemon handed the coin over, he looked as if a great weight had been lifted from his shoulders. He walked through the temple door out onto the street. Someone yelled out but it was too late. A runaway horse with an empty wagon trailing behind bore down on him. He could not react in time and the horse trampled him under its hooves. People ran to help, but he was dead by the time they arrived.

The priest, having heard the commotion, headed outside the temple and saw Philemon's body. Still holding the coin, he said a silent prayer, shook his head at the boy's death, looked down at the coin in his hand and turned to head back inside.

2

Sister Marguerite, a middle-aged nun in her full religious habit and wimple, stumbled about with a flashlight in the attic of her convent, L'Ordre de la Tour. The order was started in the late eighteenth century but had fallen on very hard times. It now consisted of twelve nuns and one novice. The building that housed the order in St. Denis, a suburb north of Paris, was as old as the order and in need of many repairs.

The Sister's objective was to locate a leak in the ancient roof to see if the nuns could do a makeshift repair themselves or whether they needed a roofer to come in. If the latter, Mother Superior Angelique would need to appeal for assistance to her superior, The Most Reverend Emile Lachaille, the Monsignor of Notre Dame. She would not relish this task since similar appeals made in the past for funds to help her small order had always fallen on deaf ears.

Sister Marguerite could hear the voice of Sister Dominique calling up to her in French. "Sister Marguerite, did you find the leak yet?"

"No Sister, I have not! It's rather difficult going up here so I'd rather not be asked such questions until I'm done. Ouch!"

"What happened?"

"I bumped my knee on a damn beam."

"Sister Marguerite, please. Your language!"

Sister Marguerite said nothing in response but continued on, pointing the flashlight toward the rafters to see if she could locate the leak. As she proceeded on, she did not see another beam; this time she tripped. As she fell, she reached out to brace herself on the wall. Instead of supporting her, some loose mortar gave way and her hand punched through the wall.

"Sister! What happened! Are you alright?"

Sister Marguerite pulled her arm out of the hole and began brushing the dust and mortar off of her sleeve. As she was about to respond to her fellow Sister, she shone her light into the newly created hole. Excitedly, she retraced her steps back out of the attic, calling out to Sister Dominque.

"Sister, get Mother Angelique! Get her now!"

Three of the younger, more fit, nuns and the order's young novice struggled as they lowered a heavy chest down the steep steps from the attic. The chest was about five feet long, three feet high and three feet wide. It was made of solid wood, perhaps oak, with metal bands around it. The chest was kept shut with a cast iron lock. The other nuns of the order, including Mother Superior Angelique, were crammed in the room, looking on expectantly.

Two steps from the bottom, the nuns lost their grip as the chest slid down the ladder and landed with a thud on its edge.

"Careful Sisters! Don't damage it!" Mother Angelique admonished them.

The Sisters maneuvered the chest onto the floor and moved it to the center of the room. At that point, the novice, Marie, a beautiful raven-haired woman in her early twenties, took her natural place, standing behind everybody else, outside of the small room and unable to see anything.

Sister Marguerite was the first to notice the lock. "Oh dear, look at that lock! We will have to hire a locksmith to open it, I'm afraid."

On hearing this, Sister Geneviève departed. Less than a minute later she returned holding a small tool kit. She knelt down in front of the chest.

"Sister Geneviève," Mother Angelique remarked, "little did I know the skills you learned on the streets before God brought you to us would be of use once again."

Sister Geneviève looked up guiltily but, once she saw the Mother Superior smiling, she continued with her work. As she poked at the lock, one of the older nuns, Sister Félicité took the Mother Superior aside for a word.

"Mother, do you suppose the rumors we had always heard are true and it is in chest."

"We should not put too much stock in rumors, should we Sister Félicité?" Mother Angelique responded rather gruffly.

"No, Mother Superior."

Realizing she had been too severe with the Sister, the Mother

Superior tenderly placed her hand on the Sister's arm.

"If it is indeed there, God will reveal it to us in His time."

As she said this, the sound of the locking mechanism springing open could be heard. The Mother Superior walked over to the chest.

"Well done, Sister Geneviève, well done indeed. Shall we see what's inside?"

Not a word was spoken as the Mother Superior attempted to lift the cover. Seeing that it was heavy and she was straining, Sister Geneviève and Sister Dominica rushed to help. Together they lifted it and the cover fell clumsily back. There was a collective gasp as on top was an ornate gold pitcher and an etched silver platter. Under those items was an exquisite tapestry, neatly folded to fit into the chest.

Mother Angelique lifted the silver platter and held it up in the light. Despite a heavy centuries-old tarnish, the nuns could discern a crest with three parallel keys from top to bottom.

"What is that?" asked Sister Gertrude.

"That," responded the Mother, "is the crest of Avignon. This platter and all of the contents of this chest, I believe, belonged to our order's founder, Sister Catherine, who was once known as the Countess of Avignon."

A collective *Ahh* went up from the group.

"That is of no matter to us. What this means is that God has answered our prayers. We shall sell the contents of this chest to fix the roof and make other repairs that are needed to keep our order alive.

"Sister Félicité, please find me the name and address of the man who helped us so kindly last year. I think his name is LaFleur, but I am not positive. Perhaps he can help us again to sell these items. Sister Marguerite, I want you to go through and catalogue every single item that is in this chest. Every item must be accounted for. Do you understand, Sister?"

"Yes, Mother Superior."

"Very well. Now everyone else, the excitement for the day is over. Let's get back to our duties."

Everyone except Sister Marguerite left the room as she pulled the contents out of the chest one by one, organizing them into categories around her on the floor.

A few hours later, Mother Superior Angelique, alone in her spartan room reading her bible, heard a knock on her door.

"Come in."

Sister Marguerite walked in and handed over a piece of paper with a list on it. Before Marguerite could say a word, the Mother Superior snatched the sheet and scanned it with her utmost concentration.

"Mother, as you requested, I have catalogued every item in the chest."

"Are you sure this is everything?"

"Yes, Mother. I went through it three times to make sure I included everything as you directed."

"Thank you Sister. I am sure you did your usual thorough job."

Sister Marguerite bowed and departed, leaving the Mother Superior staring out the window onto the courtyard.

"Thank you God," she prayed, "thank you that the rumors were not true."

•   •   •

Later that same night, the door to the room containing the chest opened a crack. The contents were still neatly arranged in piles on the floor, just as Sister Marguerite had left them. Novice Marie peered in through the crack. Satisfied she was alone, she sidled in and closed the door behind her. Once in, she knelt down and turned on a flashlight, illuminating the treasures around her. A look of wonderment spread across her face.

Glancing in the empty chest, she noticed a very small indentation in the bottom board. She reached down to see if the board would move. When it did, she used her fingernails to pry open the board revealing a small compartment underneath. In the compartment she noticed a sheaf of yellowed papers that she proceeded to take out and examine. Reading softly to herself:

"I owe my life as Sister Catherine to my late husband, Guillaume de la Tour, Count of Avignon. The gift he gave me opened my eyes."

Leafing through the pages, she read a couple more lines:

"The coin has been a curse to the others who have possessed it, but to me it has been a true gift."

She went to the last pages:

"Please Dear God, release him from Aceldama," she looked up

from the pages. "Aceldama? What's that?"

She glanced back into the chest and noticed something else in the compartment: a small purple velvet sack. As she was about to reach in to see what was in the sack, she heard a noise and a voice calling out.

"Who's there?"

It was Sister Marguerite. Marie liked Sister Marguerite but she could be a little gruff and could be a stickler, requiring everyone to adhere to the rules of the order. Marie already had several minor infractions against her. Being here without authorization would be viewed as more serious. A novice should not be up and about at this late hour; she certainly should not be here handling these artifacts. She could be expelled from the convent for an infraction such as this. She panicked.

She attempted to place the papers back in the compartment but they fell from her hand onto the floor. Sister Marguerite's footsteps were getting closer so Marie gathered up the sheaf and hid them under her blouse. She reinserted the board back in its place just seconds before the Sister opened the door.

"Marie? What are you doing here? You know you shouldn't be here! You shouldn't even be up at this hour!"

"I'm sorry, Sister Marguerite. I couldn't see anything when all the sisters were here before. I just wanted to take a glance at the treasure."

"Marie, Marie. One of these days your curiosity and inability to abide by the rules are going to get you in a lot of trouble."

Marie looked troubled but Sister Marguerite reassured her with a warm smile.

"Don't worry, Marie. I won't tell Mother. Your secret's safe with me. This all is quite amazing so I understand your curiosity.

"Mother wants all this packed back into the chest so Mr. LaFleur can pick it up tomorrow. You can help me put it all back in."

Marie felt a wave of relief wash over her as she and the Sister put the artifacts back in the chest. Marie felt the papers tucked in her blouse and at one point contemplated telling Sister Marguerite about the papers, the compartment and the velvet sack, but in the end she decided against it. Better to let things be.

3

Eleanor Fitzgerald, director of the Hoboken, New Jersey chapter of Center of Hope Charities, was very happy. It was the Center's best fundraiser ever. She had never seen so many activities going on at once. The entire community was involved. A car wash, a raffle, a bake sale, finger-painting for the kids—these were just a few of the multiple events taking place that day.

Elly, as she liked to be called, was a tall and slim middle-aged woman with long silver gray hair pulled back into a pony-tail. Her face had a well-tanned, healthy look that belied a love of the outdoors. Her usual uniform consisted of a gray T-shirt, khaki cargo pants, and heavy work boots.

She was widely known as the saint of the neighborhood. Even the most hardened gang members would part to let her pass as she walked down the street. She was a tough, fair, kind-hearted, and indefatigable saint.

The exhausting day completed, about ten people remained in the Center's main hall. She walked over to Tim and Anna Harrington, who were busy with the cleanup. Tim had neatly trimmed wavy dark hair, prominent eyebrows and handsome features. Anna had short blond hair parted in the middle that framed a face with beautiful translucent skin and great cheekbones. She had dimples at the ready and full, although not overly so, lips. Her head was perched on an elegant neck that complemented a perfectly proportioned body.

Elly and Anna had been close friends for over two years. Elly was originally from Ohio. After her husband passed away, she hooked up with the Center of Hope Charities and was asked to move to Hoboken, New Jersey to breathe life into the struggling center there. Originally reluctant to leave her lifelong home, she later conceded to Anna that it was the best thing she had ever done; she knew she would wake up every day and make a difference.

Elly had been working at the Center for two weeks when a homeless family arrived, looking for help. Their young boy was having a terrible asthma attack. One of her fellow workers told her the best place to take the boy was the Childcare Pediatric Clinic, just up the street.

She packed up the boy and his mother and off they went. Anna, a pediatric nurse at the clinic, was on duty when they walked in. Anna took one look at the boy and without waiting brought him back to see Dr. Holt. The doctor gave him a shot of adrenaline and an antihistamine inhaler. The boy's breathing soon recovered and he was fine.

Elly was impressed that Anna did not ask bureaucratic questions or give them trouble because of a lack of insurance. Instead, she took the boy right in for treatment.

After that, Elly would periodically come by with similar cases. The lead physician, Dr. Richardson, made it clear he did not like it, noting the clinic was not a charity ward, but Anna would bypass him and bring the case to either Dr. Holt or Dr. Cohn. Together, they would figure out the paperwork, after the fact.

Once when Elly was in, Anna invited her to join her for lunch. They had been friends ever since. Over time, Elly had gotten to know Tim as well.

Both Anna and Tim felt guilty when Elly had asked the inevitable question—How did the two of you meet?—and they had to tell her the pat answer they always gave: We met in church. They just did not feel they could tell her or any of their friends the truth that they had met when Anna worked as a stripper and she gave Tim a lap dance. Although someone like Elly would understand, Anna did not want to take the chance that her past would come back to haunt her. Somehow, the truth would inevitably work its way back to one of the less forgiving parents of a child at the clinic and she would be through at the clinic, kept away from working with children, doing what she loved.

Tim had cringed the first time Anna blurted out that they met in church; he had not been inside a church in over twenty years. But it was the first thing to pop in Anna's mind so that's what became the new truth.

"I can't thank you two enough for all you've done," Elly noted to Anna and Tim as they were cleaning up after the fundraiser. "Tim, thanks to you for suggesting this day. The neighborhood needed something to bring it together."

"Be honest now, Elly. You were skeptical at first, weren't you?" Tim responded. "You didn't even know who it was when I called. And we've known each other for what, two years now?"

She laughed. "That was your own fault. You identified yourself as Tim Harrington. I know you by one of two names: either 'Tim-and-anna' or 'Anna-and-tim'. I don't ever think of the two of you as being separate people."

Anna drew Tim close to her.

"And if I have anything to say about it," Anna noted, "it's always going to stay that way."

Tim hugged Anna even closer.

"Oh Tim," Elly added, "you mentioned that you're into collecting coins. My brother's son is a fledgling numismatist."

"I understand they've discovered a vaccine to combat that malady," Anna joked.

"Ha, ha, very funny," Tim responded. "Give me his number, Elly, I'd love to talk with him to compare notes."

"Will do. I take it you're not a fan of this worthy pastime, Anna?"

"I have only two words to describe coin collecting: *bo* and *ring*."

"One of these days," Tim interjected, "she'll come around and appreciate the appeal of a truly rare coin."

"I doubt it," was Anna's retort, "but I somehow think you'll keep trying to convince me otherwise."

Tim just smiled.

"Why don't the two of you get out of here? You've done yeomen's work already. We've got enough here to clean up."

"Sounds great. We have some packing to do."

Anna turned to Tim with a confused look on her face.

"Packing?"

"You'll see. Let's go. Bye, Elly."

•　　•　　•

Tim pivoted to his left and surprised Anna with a kiss on her lips. In response, she placed her hands on both sides of his face, pulling him close. They embraced even when the spotlight from below shown on them. After a few moments, when the *bateau mouche* full of tourists had progressed under the Pont Neuf as it plied its way along the Seine, the two lovers were again alone under the streetlamp on the bridge. They stood there gazing into each other's eyes, oblivious to a constant stream of motor scooters roaring by.

They presented a nice picture on the streets of Paris. Tim remarked how proud he was when he noticed the heads of Frenchmen turning as she passed by. Anna could not help but notice it herself, although for the record she stated that they were staring at the two of them, impressed by how much in love they were.

"Tim, thank you so much for this. I couldn't think of a better tenth anniversary present. I still can't believe you kept it a surprise up to the day we arrived at the airport."

"Do we have to go back day after tomorrow? How about if I call Peter and tell him I'm going to work here for the next year or so? You call the clinic and tell them the same. I'm sure there's a desperate need for English-speaking pediatric nurses in Paris. Whaddya say?"

Anna laughed.

"I love it. You'll bring a new European flair to the homes you design. New Jersey needs more of that. And I can tell the doctors that I need a year to study the French health care system. Yeah, that's the ticket. I can just imagine the look on Richardson's face."

She held him close and cradled his face once again in her hands as she stared into his eyes.

"I don't care where I am, as long as I'm with you."

They kissed and continued their walk along the bridge toward their rented apartment on *Île de la Cité*. After the boat's wake had subsided, the Seine, which was curiously tranquil for this time of night, reflected the lights of Paris, further intoxicating them with the beauty of this city. They took a last glance at the river and then strolled arm-in-arm onto the island.

As they entered *Place Dauphine*, he again hugged her close.

"Do you know what happened on this spot?"

Anna surveyed the dimly lit triangular square with its sand bocce courts, park benches and rows of enormous shade trees.

"I have no idea."

"During the French Revolution, a family was burned at the stake on this very spot."

"How charming."

"It gets better. First, a priest tried to get the mob to stop so they threw him onto the fire. And then, after a man takes pity and shoots the family's teenaged girl who is screaming as flames start to envelop her, he gets tossed onto the pyre."

"Sometimes I worry about the things that clog up your brain. I'm sure those synapses could be put to far more productive use."

"Well, maybe you should pay more attention to history, but that's neither here nor there," he noted. "I actually did have a point to all this. It's that I would march through the flames of hell to get to you. The most wonderful part is that you'd do the same for me without hesitation or question. Knowing that someone as special as you could fall for me makes me feel special. It makes me feel like a king, which maybe is not the proper simile to use, given I was just talking about the French Revolution. But you know what I mean."

"Yes I do."

They kissed again and proceeded up the stairs to the second story apartment.

The following morning, Tim ventured out on his own, without Anna. Although her birthday was not for another three and a half months, he wanted to buy her present in Paris that would be difficult if they were together. Anna decided to do some clothes shopping. They agreed to meet back at the apartment around 4:00 to get cleaned up for their dinner at an upscale restaurant on *Île St. Louis* where their friend, René Bouvil, would join them

Anna had limited success shopping, although she did find a nice lightweight blue raincoat at a small boutique in the Marais. What she enjoyed most was ordering two glasses of champagne at a café on the edge of the *Place de Vosges*. She sat for an hour, watching a group of children in the park playing a game whose rules were unknown to her. She wondered if there were any rules at all or whether they made the game up as they went along. She finished her drink and headed back to the apartment.

When she returned, Tim was waiting for her. He could barely control his enthusiasm.

"Look what I found!"

He held up an old coin. It was so tarnished that it was hard for Anna to discern at first what it was. She noted that it had a hole punched in it.

"Not in very good shape, is it?"

"The hole? That reduces its value of course but it'll make a great medallion, won't it?"

"I suppose so. Um, Tim, this isn't what you envisioned as my birthday present, is it?"

"No, silly. This is for me. Don't worry; I have your present safely packed away. You'll get it on your birthday."

Anna was relieved. She couldn't imagine herself wearing this thing and then having to pretend to be pleased about it in front of Tim.

"I'm guessing you used the word "found" in a figurative sense, right?"

Anna supposed he spent an extravagant amount, but since it gave him such joy, she did not pursue the topic. Nor would she begrudge him a run to Galleries Lafayette first thing the next morning before their flight to pick out a new silver chain to hang it properly around his neck.

"I was over in a neighborhood near the *Arc de Triomphe* and I came upon this market. There were booths of all sorts, some selling antiques, others books, others stamps. I found one that was selling old coins and when the guy showed me this one, I had to have it. He said it was a shekel."

Anna took the coin from Tim to inspect it. It was about an inch and a half in diameter. For the most part, it was thoroughly covered in black tarnish. When Anna off-handedly suggested polishing it, Tim shot her a disdainful look asking how she could even think of such a thing. Polishing old coins was just not done. It reduced their value. She gave her best, "Well, excuuuse me," response and they both laughed.

Though it was worn and had a few pockmarks from weather and time, Anna could clearly make out the profile of a man on the front.

"That's the god Melqart," Tim explained with a newfound air of authority.

Anna turned the coin over. On the other side, also quite discernible, was an eagle and some writing, but she had no idea which alphabet it was. When she referred to it as the backside of the coin, Tim corrected her, saying that it was known as the 'obverse' not back, side. She rolled her eyes and handed it back to him.

When they arrived at the restaurant, René was standing outside waiting for them. When Anna had first met him at Orly Airport ten days earlier, she kept telling herself *I'm a happily married woman, I'm a happily married woman.* He was tall and slender, with short cropped black hair, a Gallic nose and deep set eyes. Together these features created a look that could be nothing else but French. To top it all off, the first impression he made on her was in uniform, being a captain in the French *Gendarmerie*, the arm of law enforcement that handles security at airports and federal facilities as well as police duties in rural France.

He ushered them through airport security and customs and then drove them to their hotel. Unfortunately, he was not able to spend any time with them during their stay until they met for dinner. Anna was somewhat disappointed he was not in uniform but she was still taken by how dashing he was, even in a casual suit and turtleneck shirt.

He gave them both big hugs and the traditional kiss on both cheeks and then they entered the restaurant.

"How many years had it been since you two last saw each other?"

René answered. "Twenty-one years. We were both in what you call high school when I come over for a month. We have great time, but then on last day of my trip, Tim's father, he dies in accident."

A pall descended on the three at the mention of the accident.

"Since then, your husband and I write letters but never a chance to get together again. When Tim telephone to say you come to Paris, I look forward to show you the sights, but *Gendarmerie* work with NATO and I do not have time. *C'est la vie*, as we French say."

"Well, I'm glad you could join us for dinner tonight."

"And I am so happy to meet you, Anna. Tim, he is very lucky man."

"Yes, I am," Tim replied as he reached over and took Anna's hand.

"Me, I will be a bachelor all my days."

"You fly to Turkey tomorrow?"

"Yes, for one week."

"You remember when we went to see a baseball game, and how lost you were?"

René laughed. "I will never understand that game. I take rugby or futbol any day."

They finished their meals and when it came time to go, Anna could see both Tim and René's eyes welling up. They said their goodbyes and then Tim and Anna took a leisurely walk back to their apartment.

"He's quite a guy," Anna observed.

"None better," Tim replied. "I'd like you to get to know him. He's quiet and serious on the outside but once you get to know him, he has a wicked sense of humor. He was so supportive of me after Dad died. He stayed on an extra week and then called me every day for a month after he went back home. I would have kicked myself if he was gone when we were here and didn't get to see him at all."

When they returned, Anna could sense something different about their apartment. Nothing was missing but various items seemed in a slightly different place than they had been. She mentioned this to Tim, but he did not notice anything amiss.

Anna went to the kitchen to wash and put away the dishes they had used earlier in the day. She noticed there was one glass missing.

"Tim, did you break a glass?"

Receiving no answer since Tim had already fallen asleep, she shrugged. Perhaps her memory about the number of glasses was incorrect. She hoped they would not get charged for it. She joined Tim in bed.

•　　•　　•

The following day, they were sitting on their plane waiting to take off to head back to the states. Anna could see the new silver chain peeking out from under Tim's shirt.

"Tim, promise me we'll come back some day."

"You better believe we will. If nothing else, René made me promise. He wanted to do a better job of showing us the town."

"Where did he say he was going?"

"Turkey. Some NATO stuff the *Gendarmerie* is helping on. He'll be back in a week."

They sat holding hands as the plane took off from Charles DeGaulle Airport. Looking out the window, Anna swore she could make out the Eiffel Tower through the haze.

"Yes, we need to come back soon, real soon."

"We will, my love, we will."

4

Unaccustomed as she was to leaving the safe confines of the convent in St. Denis, Mother Angelique had to make the trip into the heart of Paris. She received more than a few astonished looks as she quietly sat on the Metro making her way to the Hotel de Ville station, which was a short walk to Notre Dame Cathedral.

She could not help but fidget while she waited to be received by her superior, The Most Reverend Paul Lachaille, the Monsignor of Notre Dame. The anteroom, like the Monsignor's office she was about to enter, was ornately appointed with pieces of fine art, teak wood paneling, and rare volumes of religious texts. The door opened and the Monsignor walked out to greet the Mother.

"Angelique, what a lovely surprise. We don't get together nearly often enough. Please, why don't you come in?"

The Mother Superior, scarcely acknowledging the greeting, walked into his office. The wimple and habit she wore emphasized the look of grave concern etched on her face. The Monsignor followed behind, closing the door. He took his seat behind his desk and she sat a chair in front of the desk.

The Monsignor, smiling and somewhat condescending, tried to open the conversation in a light vein. "Now, what was so urgent that you had to meet with me but was so sensitive you couldn't tell me over the phone?"

The Mother Superior's face was downcast, as she was unable to respond or even look her superior in the eye.

"Angelique, it can't be as bad as all that. You can tell me; we're old friends."

Still unable to lift her eyes from the floor, she speaks. "The rumor, the legend, it's all true."

"I'm sure I don't know what you're talking about, Angelique."

The Mother Superior looked up. "The silver coin, it was at the convent all this time."

The Monsignor eyes opened wide and his face blanched. "What? You have it?"

"No, that's why I needed to see you immediately. It was in a secret drawer in a chest we found in a hidden room in the attic. We sold the chest and its contents to pay for our new roof. I found out afterwards when I went over the bill of sale with the man who was helping us. He sold it."

Mother Angelique looked back down at her lap.

"You fool! Don't you see what you've done? You have no idea the damage you may have caused!"

The Mother looked into the eyes of the Monsignor. Her face grew stern as her eyes narrowed.

"Perhaps if you had responded to just one of my pleas over the past ten years to assist our convent to make necessary repairs, we would not have been desperate to sell off our legacy."

The two tensely stared at each other for a few seconds until the Monsignor sighed and relaxed.

"I apologize, Angelique. The news caught me by surprise. I should not have lashed out the way I did.

"We need to figure out where to go from here. We have to get the coin back. What was the name of the man who helped you?"

"LaFleur. Etienne LaFleur."

He pressed a button and soon his receptionist came in.

"Alice, please call William Canford for me. Ask him to go the Ordre de la Tour convent this afternoon. Angelique, would 3:00 be convenient for you?"

The Mother Superior nodded.

"Tell him he is to speak with the Mother Superior and nobody else. She will tell him all she knows. He'll take it from there and know what to do."

"Yes, Monsignor."

The Monsignor scrutinized the Mother Superior.

"So, Angelique, how much do you know about the coin?"

"That the founder of our convent had it in her possession up to the time she died."

"There's much more to it than that, Angelique, but for now that will suffice."

"Yes, your eminence."

5

Stephanie LaFleur inserted the key into the lock on the door of her ex-husband's apartment on Rue de la Paix in Paris. Although divorced for three years, they were still very close. If her husband, Etienne, had his way, they would still be together. She was the one who needed her space.

"Etienne," she called out as soon as she stuck her head in the flat, "are you here? Where were you last night? Did you forget you were supposed to meet me for dinner? Why didn't you call?"

Hearing nothing, she went further in. She shook her head as she surveyed the mess. Papers were everywhere. Drawers were opened or pulled out. It looked as if a fight had taken place but she was not alarmed. When it came to his business, Etienne was scrupulously organized but in his private affairs, he was sloppy or even slovenly. It was one of the reasons she divorced him after twelve years of marriage.

She checked the living room and kitchen and then walked to the bedroom. Upon opening the door, she let out a piercing shriek. Her former husband was there, hanging from a rope attached to a beam on the ceiling.

Stephanie ran to the kitchen, grabbed a sharp knife and hurried back. Climbing up on a chair, she cut him down. His body fell, flopping onto the bed below.

An hour later, Inspector Albert Archambaut of the French National Police entered the apartment. A fit man in his early fifties, gray had started to appear on his temples while his neatly trimmed mustache was still a dark brown. People often wondered aloud—but never to his face—whether Archambaut went to bed wearing a bow tie as they had never seen him without one.

He surveyed the apartment. Stephanie LaFleur was on a couch in the living room, head down, a handkerchief in her hand. Crime scene investigators were milling about, dusting for fingerprints and collecting other pieces of potential evidence. Sitting in a straight-back chair off to the side was a young woman with stringy blond hair and dressed in a long loose-fitting bohemian dress. She sat there, staring off into space and clutching a beaded fabric purse.

Archambaut glanced into the bedroom and could see the feet of Etienne LaFleur's body that lay on the bed.

"Albert, come on in," Archambaut's assistant, Officer François Dubois, called out from his position kneeling next to the body.

"What do we have here?" Archambaut asked as he walked into the bedroom.

"This is Etienne LaFleur, the owner and resident of this apartment. His ex-wife, Stephanie, arrived an hour ago and found his body hanging from the rafter there. She cut him down but he was already gone. That's her out there sitting on the divan. We got her statement but I wanted her to stick around in case you wanted to talk to her."

"I take it you've already deduced this was a homicide, not a suicide."

"Yes, the ligature lines around the neck indicate post-mortem trauma. There was a blow to the head that the medical examiner believes is what killed him. He was then hanged to throw us off. The medical examiner puts the death from between seven and eleven last night."

"Who is the other young woman sitting out there?"

"Her name is Sophie Alain. She wandered in about five minutes ago claiming she had some information that may assist our investigation. I haven't had a chance to interview her yet but I have my doubts about her."

"Why?"

"Well, her pupils are the size of ten euro pieces. She's high on something. Plus, her timing seems suspicious."

"Thank you, François. Good work."

Archambaut headed over to Stephanie LaFleur.

"Madame LaFleur, I am Inspector Archambault. I am very sorry for your loss. I understand you are the former wife of Monsieur

LaFleur."

"Yes, but we have remained close. We were supposed to get together for dinner last night. He'd sometimes stand me up because of work, but he'd always call me to let me know. When I didn't hear from him last night, I tried reaching him but there was no answer so I went home. I tried calling him again this morning and when he didn't answer any of his numbers, I became concerned and came over. That's when I found him, hanging in there. I cut him down and put him on the bed as best as I could, but he was already dead."

"Had he been depressed or upset lately? Any health, financial or personal issues that could have led him to this?"

"Far from it, his work was going well. He's a very good father to our two children. He wished we were back together but he was moving on. He was very active in his local church as well. I don't understand him taking his own life."

"What did he do for a living?"

"He was a estate broker of sorts. He would act as a go-between, connecting people who had works of art, jewelry, and things of value with those who would buy them or those who could sell them for him."

"And business was going well; no financial difficulties?"

"None that I know of, although Etienne could at times be a very soft touch."

"How so?"

"His latest job was helping out a convent that had fallen on hard times. My guess was that he was not making any profit at all helping them out."

"A convent?"

"Yes, he never told me which convent but he was helping them raise money."

"How so?"

"They'd discovered a chest full of artifacts hidden away in the attic."

"I see. The apartment, it's quite a mess. It looks like someone was looking for something."

"I noticed it was a mess but I didn't think anything of it. Etienne was never one to do much in the way of housework."

"Is there anything else you can tell me? Did he have any enemies?"

"Why do you ask? Do you think this is not a suicide?"

"I'm just trying to cover everything before we come to a conclusion."

"In answer to your question, everyone loved Etienne. I can't imagine anyone wanting to hurt him."

Stephanie LaFleur choked up a bit before continuing.

"If it's okay, I'd like to get back home. I've been here hours and I left the children with a neighbor. I need to break the news to them."

She broke down again.

"That's quite alright. I believe we have your contact information in case we have any further questions. Would you like one of my staff to take you home?"

"No, I'll be alright. I don't live very far. But thank you."

"Again, my condolences for your loss."

Archambaut helped her up and walked her over to the door. He then turned to Sophie Alain.

"Ms. Alain, I am Inspector Archambaut. I understand you may have some information that can assist us in this investigation?"

"I'm not sure but I may have heard something relevant."

"What did you hear?"

"I heard what sounded like a man loudly arguing with a woman and then it was quiet. They were arguing in English but it was obvious the man was French while the woman was American."

"American you say?"

"Most definitely American."

"Could you hear what they were arguing about?

"A coin. Definitely about a rare coin."

"When was this?"

"Around seven thirty last night."

"Do you live at this building or were you visiting someone?"

"Neither. I solicit contributions for the WEF, The World Environmental Fund, and was about to knock on the door when I heard the shouting and I moved on down the hall. Then a man and a woman burst out of the apartment. I did not see either of their faces before they ran to the stairs."

"Why did you come back today?"

"I hadn't finished canvassing the building last night and then when I came back today and saw all the police, I put it together with what I heard last night."

"I see. You could tell it was an American accent, even through a closed door?"

"They were arguing very loudly."

"You saw a man and a woman leaving this apartment. Do you think you could describe what they looked like to our sketch artist?

"I'm not sure but I'll try.

"That would be very helpful. Is there anything else you can think of?"

"No, I don't think so."

"I'll have one of my men take your complete statement and arrange for the artist to come over here. Then you can be on your way. Thank you very much for coming in."

Archambaut walked Sophie over to a crime scene investigator who led her into the kitchen to take her statement. Dubois headed over to Archambaut.

"What do you think, boss? Anything here worth tracking down?"

"A nut case. Strung out, too. Probably nothing useful but you never know."

6

Circa 32 A.D.

Marcus Carolis, accompanied by twenty-nine of his fellow soldiers, traipsed along a dusty road out of Jerusalem. Marching solemnly beside him was a lad of no more than eighteen, less than half Marcus' age.

"Nervous?" Marcus asked, but the boy stared stonily ahead.

"Never killed anyone before, have you?"

The young soldier remained silent.

"Well, once the action starts you'll get used to it. Part of the job."

The soldiers arrived at their destination, the small village of Michaelia, and proceeded to carry out their orders: eradicate a suspected revolutionary band and anyone suspected of harboring these insurgents. The rebels were not a real threat, just a minor annoyance, but they gave the Romans an excuse to send a clear reminder to the Judean populace that they had in fact been conquered and were under Roman rule. To send this message, the squad was to wipe Michaelia off the map.

With typical Roman efficiency, they executed one hundred twenty people in under an hour. Marcus would not let his ears take in any screams or cries for mercy. Neither was he concerned that they encountered little armed resistance nor did they find any evidence of an insurgency.

As the squad was departing, a moan emanated from the center of the village.

"Carolis, go back and eliminate that confounded noise!" the unit commander barked.

Retracing his steps, Marcus came upon a boy of no more than thirteen, drenched in blood, struggling to pull himself up to the community well. He had a deep wound in his abdomen. There was a gash in his right leg and his left arm dangled by a strip of sinew. Marcus was astonished the boy was still alive; killing him would be an act of mercy, he reasoned.

The boy had not noticed the soldier's approach. He was intent on getting some water, although how he was to accomplish this feat with only one arm and no strength was a mystery. Marcus walked up close and drew his sword to deliver the fatal blow. As he did so, the boy looked up into his eyes and smiled. Marcus did not know what to make of the smile. It was not one of defiance but instead expressed inner peace, acceptance and even forgiveness.

Marcus plunged the blade into the youth's neck, finishing the job.

He rejoined his unit and they headed back into Jerusalem, marching through a bustling market for everyone to see. Rome needed to send an unequivocal message. Why erase a village from the face of the earth if nobody knew about it?

The anxious shoppers parted and re-formed as the soldiers passed through. Despite having spent a great deal of time in this very market and cordially interacting with its merchants, Marcus felt no mixed emotions as he proudly paraded along, still sporting the blood of the victims on his body and armor.

Marcus returned to his quarters to clean up, content he had performed his duty well. That night, he fell into an untroubled sleep.

The next day, he resumed his more mundane responsibilities of patrolling the neighborhood around the temple. At this stage in his life, after surviving hard-fought battles in Gaul and Macedonia, peace-keeping duties suited him just fine.

He had been stationed in the Roman province of Judea for five years. He had hoped his previous deployment on Crete would have been the final posting of his career. He could still feel the gentle breezes blowing off the Mediterranean. In his estimation, that isle, not this patch of scorched earth, was the Promised Land. But he now found himself in Jerusalem and he made the best of his situation.

As a Roman soldier and citizen, Marcus knew he was naturally superior to the people around him, but still he had pleasant interactions with a number of Jews. One such friend was Yakov ben Aron, who sold earthenware pottery in the same market through which Marcus had marched.

Marcus was not an educated man, but he was curious. He was interested in learning about the myriad religious beliefs throughout the empire. He could not comprehend, for example, why the Jewish people steadfastly held onto their worship of a single god. His friendship with Yakov developed out of his quest to expand his knowledge on this subject, although their initial encounter could have been disastrous for Yakov.

Less than a year after Marcus had arrived in Jerusalem, he and a fellow soldier, Cyrus, were standing at the edge of the market. In this spot, the two soldiers could feel the energy of the constant haggling and hawking but not be overwhelmed by the crowd. Marcus also enjoyed the pungent, but thoroughly pleasant, aromas of the nearby spice merchant's stall.

When an attractive teenaged girl walked by, Marcus turned to his comrade and commented about how he would like to make that one "kneel down and worship his single god." Cyrus chuckled at his friend's turn of phrase.

Without opening his eyes, Yakov, whom neither soldier had noticed resting on a nearby bench, replied, also in Greek: "Jews don't kneel. And even if she did, it would take a lot more than what I imagine you have to bring her to her knees."

Marcus and Cyrus looked down on the diminutive fellow.

"You know," Marcus stated, "I'd have every right to run my sword through you for your impudence."

"Yes, but think of the mess. Your sword could get wedged in my ribs. And what if you missed? I'm small and wiry. How embarrassing would it be for you if I dodged your parry? It's better if both your swords remained sheathed."

Marcus thought for a second about both the logic of the man's argument and the double entendre he employed. He burst into laughter.

"I guess you're right, my little friend. So, Jews don't kneel to their god?"

"No, once a year during the high holidays will the priest throw himself on the floor as a sign of utter subjugation to the most Holy One, blessed be He. Otherwise, we sit or stand. We stand an awful lot."

With that, Marcus sat beside Yakov and began a conversation on Jewish vs. Roman religion. Cyrus shook his head and walked away. After about thirty minutes, Marcus excused himself to continue his patrol, but he returned the following week to resume their discussion, and the week after as well. This dialogue would continue over the course of the next four years. A typical conversation went something like this:

"Morning, Yakov."

Yakov would imperceptibly nod to acknowledge Marcus' presence but make no other comment or gesture. Marcus would then put forward his challenge.

"The Roman religion is superior because it is flexible. Sometimes an event or situation occurs that cannot be explained. We would then turn to our priests who'd announce the discovery of a new, previously unknown god that explains all."

"I'm not exactly sure that's how your religion works, but I will have to admit that you do have hundreds of local deities that had to come from somewhere. For the Jew, our God does not change just because the situation is unexplainable. Even if we can't explain it, we know God can. We are content with that."

"But you can't just have one god that creates everything and is at the center of all from birth to death."

"And beyond."

"Yes, and beyond. It doesn't make sense."

"It makes more sense than inventing a new god every time you can't explain something."

"I said the priests discover a new god, not invent one."

"Yes, you did say that. But these gods can't be very powerful, can they? They've been quiet all these years and come to life when they eventually get discovered. Our God makes himself known to us every single day."

Since Yakov was far more learned than his friend, he would win the debate for that day but Marcus would not relent. He would go away, mull over the conversation and return the next time with a fresh argument, which Yakov would in turn debunk.

The day after the Michaelia massacre, Marcus arrived at the market as if nothing had happened, hoping to resume their discussion. He had a fresh idea he was certain would stump Yakov but, when he arrived, Yakov was not in his customary spot on the bench. He was at his stall, dealing with customers. Marcus waited until Yakov was done with them and walked over, greeting him in his usual friendly manner. The response he received was unexpected.

"Marcus, I have always accepted that you were a Roman soldier and had to perform your duty. I knew full well that sometimes the things you did were immoral and even repugnant, but still we became friends. I know that, in your mind, you feel you had every right to kill those people. I am not one to judge. But to then triumphantly march through this market, through my home, with the blood of these poor souls still wet on your hands, this I cannot forgive. You once asked why, if our God were so powerful, would He let us be conquered by the Romans. I, of course, answered you but, to be honest, I've

asked the same question myself many times. I didn't know the answer either. Until yesterday, that is. Seeing you like that made me realize how superior I am to you and how superior my God is to the hundreds of deities you Romans kneel to. I can no longer be your friend, Marcus. Goodbye."

With that, Yakov turned back to his stall and to his work. Marcus, unclear in his mind what had gone wrong, meandered away toward the temple.

As he passed a side entrance, he heard a disturbance going on inside the edifice. A man he had seen around but did not know well was in a heated argument with several of the priests. When the quarrel started to get physical, Marcus contemplated going in to break it up. Normally, the Romans did not interfere with anything inside the temple, but he was angry at Yakov. He went in with the intention of butting a few Hebrew heads together. However, as he entered the main hall, the situation resolved itself. The shouting stopped. The man turned to storm out, but before he did he angrily threw a small bag to the floor, scattering its contents throughout the hall. The priests' assistants scurried to gather in everything, but they missed a coin that had rolled until Marcus stopped it with his sandaled foot.

It was a shiny silver shekel, a local currency of moderate value. Marcus felt justified snatching up the coin; he deserved to be compensated by the Jews for Yakov's disrespect. He stuffed it into the pouch that hung around his neck.

That night, the nightmares began. They did not come every night but recurred often enough to be deeply disturbing. His first thought was of the boy he had killed. The boy and his smile, they were to blame for these dreams. Yakov and his speeches strengthened this image in his mind.

"Well, in that case, damn the boy and Yakov, too. Damn them both to whatever hell they believe in!"

He had heard of things like this happening to other soldiers. They went soft. Maybe it was just time for him to retire. His father's estate outside of Rome now belonged to him. All he had to do was return home. Perhaps the gods had sent the boy to tell him it was time to live out his days in comfort as part of the landed gentry.

But Marcus Carolis was a career soldier. He did not know anything else. He always envisioned himself dying as a soldier, preferably in glorious battle. He was surprised he had lived this long.

When the nightmares became a regular occurrence, he began to neglect his duties. His appearance grew haggard and his mood irritable, but he still he could not bring himself to leave soldiering. He decided to outlast whatever was vexing him. He hoped the dreams would go away some day. They never did. In fact, they became much more frightening and vivid.

Each night over the course of next three months, he had the same vision. He was being steadily drawn into an abyss, a nothingness, and could not resist its pull. A voice, speaking the language of this conquered people who did not realize they were conquered, called out to him from the void. The voice was simultaneously plaintive, pleading, and commanding. Inevitably, he would wake up in a cold sweat, deeply troubled about what he had just dreamt.

Often after he had awakened, he would lie in his cot and stare off into space, hoping fresh, untroubled sleep would overtake him. If that did not work, he would go for a walk to clear his mind. On one of these walks, he heard rustling behind him. As he turned to investigate, a club flew out of the darkness, hitting him square between the eyes. Four figures converged on him from the shadows; he was being robbed. The men groped around to locate anything of value on the prostrate soldier.

Perhaps if he had not resisted, they would have taken his possessions and fled, leaving him with his life. He could not, however, endure this ignominy. It was not the money; money did not mean a lot to him. The military had always taken care of his basic needs and he was not one to buy any luxuries. Whenever he came across any cash, the coins would find their way into the leather pouch hanging around his neck, residing there for months or even years.

He fought back because he was a Roman soldier, part of the greatest military force in history. He was determined to fight even though the odds were incredibly against him. He was outnumbered. His abilities were severely limited. The initial blow had been well placed and effective. His head was not clear. His vision was greatly impaired.

It soon became apparent he would lose and would most likely die. What upset him most was he was not going to be killed on the field of battle. He would instead perish at the hands of hoodlums, of common criminals. His impending death was confirmed as one of the assailants pulled out a rusty knife and drove it deep into his gut. While the pain was excruciating, Marcus was impressed with his assailant's technique. After that, he could summon forth no more strength.

He lay there a few minutes, life ebbing from his body. There was only one thing left to do: he smiled. As the last breath was departing his body, he heard a voice, the voice of his dream, beckoning for him to come. His smile vanished.

The four descended and cut the purse off Marcus's now still chest. They ran off to divide the spoils. It did not take long before all the gold and silver coins were spent on wine and women.

7

"Tim, I've had it. You need professional help."

Tim mechanically turned to look at Anna. A dull yellow radiance from the streetlight outside the window filtered through the slats in the blinds. Even in the gloomy darkness of their bedroom, he could make out the concern in her hypnotic blue-gray eyes. Normally, he loved to gaze into those eyes, to dive in and lose himself there forever. To him, she was the same vital, intelligent beauty who had captured his heart so long ago. Over the past decade they had been married, she had not succumbed to the side effects that often accompany a satisfied and successful urban lifestyle. Neither had he, he was proud to acknowledge. Many of their friends, both male and female, led too sedentary an existence, resulting in weight gain, boredom, divorce, or all three.

On this night, as it had been every night over the past three months since they had returned from Paris, he did not see her beside him. Instead, he looked past her and saw only the terror from which he had just emerged.

On those nights that Anna did not wake up, he would pad downstairs in their Hoboken brownstone to be alone with his thoughts. Sometimes, he would walk down to the pier and gaze at the New York skyline. As an architect, the sight would fill him with awe and transport his mind far away.

Most nights, though, Anna would awaken and they would talk. She had endured having her sleep disrupted for as long as she could, but after three months her patience had run out. More to the point, her level of anxiety had reached its limit.

"Sorry, hon. I was dreaming again."

"Same dream?" she asked, knowing full well what the answer would be.

"One of the variations, yeah."

"Don't you think it's time you went to someone for help?"

Tim gazed tenderly at his wife, his best friend. He had resisted the idea of going to a psychologist or therapist, but he realized there were no other alternatives. Still, he said nothing.

Anna broke the brief silence.

"You remember Joan went for counseling after Bill died. The therapist was a little off-the-wall but she really liked him. And, he helped her. I remember his name, Philip Mordecai. He's both a psychologist and a medical doctor. You could make an appointment. If he can't help you, maybe he can refer you to someone else."

Her voice began to quiver.

"Please, Tim. I'm very worried."

Tim held his dear wife close. He felt her gently sobbing. He patted her head and tried to reassure her but, to be honest, he was worried himself. He had noticed how gaunt he had become and how the disturbances in his sleep were interfering with all aspects of his life. He was not productive at work; he did little around the house; they had no sex life to speak of anymore. It was like he had aged ten years in three short months.

"I'll call him in the morning."

Gradually, Tim and Anna fell asleep in each other's arms.

•　　•　　•

With trepidation, Tim went to see Dr. Philip Mordecai. He had ample reason to mistrust therapists, psychoanalysts and their ilk. Maybe Dr. Alan Stewart was capable in helping a 50-year old get through a mid-life crisis, but he had been in way over his head guiding sixteen-year old Tim through the tragic loss of his father in a boating accident. The treatment proffered by Dr. Stewart did not help him deal with his situation; if anything, it reinforced negative feelings Tim had about himself. It was the love of Anna and the healing quality of time—but most definitely not Dr. Stewart—that helped Tim cope with the loss and the guilt.

Now, years later, he was again in need of professional help. Despite his anxieties, he was determined to force himself through Dr.

Mordecai's front door if for no other reason than to remove the grave concern that marred Anna's lovely face. He walked in.

The waiting room was not what Tim expected. Trying as hard as he might to cleanse his memory banks, the stuffy, stodgy office of Dr. Stewart with the months-old copies of *People* magazine, the purported calming effect of a fish tank, and the 'payment is expected upon delivery of services' notice crept into his mind. None of these were to be seen here. Instead, it was a shrine to baseball.

Autographed pictures of Carl Yastrzemski, Hank Aaron, Johnny Bench, and other baseball immortals adorned the walls. On the coffee table was a cast iron bank where a mechanical pitcher zoomed a penny past the batter into a catcher receptacle. A bowl of pennies accompanied the bank. Various bats, balls, and pennants were positioned around the room. Against the far wall was the *pièce de resistance*, a vintage pinball machine appropriately named World Series Baseball, similarly accompanied by a bowl of coins. Tim expected to see a retired ballplayer, in full uniform and a chaw of tobacco in his mouth, at the receptionist desk, but the chair was empty.

He was tempted to play a game of pinball but thought better of it, so he walked around to admire the photos. After a few minutes, the door to the inner office opened. A man emerged and extended his hand.

"Tim Harrington, I presume. I'm Philip Mordecai."

Tim did a first impression appraisal. *About my age, between 35 to 38. Rather good looking. Medium build and height. Sandy brown hair. Decent, friendly-looking guy. Neatly dressed in a casual nice sort of way. Down-to-earth.* Tim appreciated it when doctors or other professionals introduced themselves by their real names. He always found it pompous when somebody referred to himself as 'Doctor So and So.'

"Yes, doctor. I'm Tim Harrington."

"Sorry there was no one here to greet you. I had a wonderful assistant for about ten years but her husband went and got a job in London. I begged and pleaded but even my inestimable charm wasn't enough to keep her on this side of the pond. Since then, I've gone through two assistants who just didn't work out."

"That's okay. I just got here."

"Would you like to come in?"

They walked into his office, which was definitely more run-of-the-mill than the waiting area. An array of diplomas indicating extensive training in both medicine and psychology adorned the walls. There was mahogany paneling, a large mahogany desk, two black leather upholstered chairs, and a couch. Everything was strategically placed. After the waiting room, Tim felt this was somewhat of a letdown.

"Where do you want me?" Tim inquired.

"Wherever you'd be most comfortable."

Tim sat in a chair, Phil in the other.

"I like to get to know a little about my patients before I delve into their subconscious. Why don't you tell me about yourself? Are you a baseball fan?"

"Why yes, I am. Do you refuse to treat non-baseball fans?"

"Of course not. But with patients such as you, I know I have a stronger foundation on which to build. Go ahead."

Tim had difficulty discerning whether the doctor was serious or joking, so he plowed ahead.

"Well, Dr. Mordecai,"

"Please, call me Phil."

"Okay. I'm an architect, married with no children. My wife, Anna, is a pediatric nurse. She works in a clinic not far from here. She could have done even more; she's so intelligent and good with people, especially kids. I run into parents of children who are patients at the clinic and they just rave about how she is with their kids."

Tim looked over to see the doctor smiling.

"Why the smile?"

"It always earns points in my book when a patient goes on and on about his or her spouse. Shows a strong interpersonal relationship. However, I was asking about you. We can get to her in a bit. You're an architect. What do you design?"

"Primarily residential. We have a small firm, just three of us. Mostly single-family homes. We cater to upper-class tastes, but over the past few years we've gotten involved in quite a few affordable housing projects."

"That's noble of you."

"Anna's influence, I'm afraid. I see how much good she does on a daily basis and here I am dealing with people who bitch because their BMW is in the shop and they're stuck driving their Lexus. It just dawned on me that I could be doing more."

"It seems we're not going to stray too far from talking about your wife, are we?"

"No, I guess not."

"How did you two meet?"

Tim evaluated the doctor for a second.

"We met in church."

In turn, Phil regarded Tim without saying anything for a brief period before proceeding.

"I see. Why are you here and what do you think I can do for you?"

"I don't think you can help me. I'm here because I promised Anna."

"You don't have much use for psychology, I take it."

"No offense but, been there; done that."

"No offense taken. I'm not crazy about spilling my guts to a stranger either. To be fair, you've provided info about yourself but you know practically nothing about me. My original training was to be a surgeon, a brain surgeon to be exact. I was following in my father's footsteps. That changed when my sister, Jennifer, committed suicide a decade ago. I blamed my father—and the lack of attention he paid her over the years—for her killing herself. I switched professions mainly to spite him. I haven't spoken to him in all that time."

"And I'm the one that's seeing a shrink?"

"At least I'm able to face my problems out in the open and discuss them. How about you?"

"Okay, you got me there."

"Shall we start again? Why are you here? And please no more bull, such as 'I met her in church'. I can't help you if you don't tell me the truth."

"I've been having nightmares, actually a recurring series of nightmares. They started three months ago, the day we left Paris."

"Tell me about your dreams."

"There is nothing, a void, except for three people: two men and one woman. They seem to take turns in the dream."

"Do you know these people?"

"No, I don't know any of them. They're all dressed in old-fashioned clothes. Kinda like they're characters in a play, or several plays going on at the same time."

"Go on."

"The woman is dressed as a nun, in an old-fashioned, conservative habit. One man is scruffy and disheveled; looks like a sailor's outfit from a long time ago. The other man is a Roman guard."

"Roman as in Julius Caesar, Ben Hur times?"

"Yes."

"Anything more?"

"They're all speaking in languages I don't understand. The woman is definitely speaking French; that much I can recognize. I have no idea what the sailor is speaking. The Roman gentleman, I've kind of assumed, is speaking Latin or Greek."

"I see."

"I don't speak any of these languages. They seem to understand each other quite easily. I'm the only one who doesn't understand."

"Anything else?"

"They hurt. There's such grief and anguish in their voices. I feel intense pain.

"I'm normally a person who never remembers my dreams. These nightmares, on the other hand, are so vivid I have trouble keeping track of whether I'm asleep or awake. I'm worried about my sanity.

"In addition to the three people, I see other images. They are people, but they're almost transparent. Hundreds of them, walking about aimlessly. They make collective sounds as they talk, but you can't make out any individual words.

"I feel another presence, someone or something I don't see but definitely feel. Everybody is petrified of whoever or whatever this other being is.

"There's another thing, too."

"What's that?"

"They're demanding I do something. Help them. Do something to lessen their pain. There's a specific act I must perform, but I haven't a clue what it is. Then they hold me personally responsible when I can't help them. I wake up not only spooked but utterly helpless."

"And this is recurring, night after night?"

"Yes, every single night."

"We'll see what we can do to figure out why you are having these dreams and what significance they may have. In the meantime, let me write you a prescription that should help you sleep undisturbed through the night. You say you always wake up after these dreams?"

Tim nodded.

"Have a little pad available by the bed. In case these pills don't do the trick, write down all you can remember that your uninvited guests say or do."

"But they speak in languages I don't know."

"Then write it down phonetically. We'll try and sort through them later. Just the act of writing these thoughts down will help you to focus. It might help you gain some insights that would be lost as you go back to sleep."

"Any idea what could be causing these dreams?"

"I haven't a clue. It would be idle speculation on my part. Unless you're bonkers, dreams are often rooted in your reality. Since my clinical judgment is that you're not bonkers, we'll have to dig to uncover that reality. Maybe it's linked to the reason you have such animosity towards my profession."

Tim and Phil chatted for another half-hour or so. Tim related the story of his father's death and his sessions with Dr. Stewart. Periodically, Tim would recall another detail about his dreams, which the doctor would scratch down in his pad. The session came to a close.

"I think we'll end here," the doctor noted. "It may take a little time, but I do think we can get to the root of the problem here. Your dreams do sound like something out of Dante, if you don't mind me saying. Next time I'd like to go into a little more depth about your father's death and how to this day you still feel responsible. Who knows, maybe you'll even tell me the real story about how you and your wife met."

Tim smiled.

"Maybe I will."

"So, here's the prescription. Shall we meet again next week, same time?"

"That sounds fine."

"Oh, by the way, what team do you pull for?"

"Team?"

"Yeah, baseball."

"Oh, I'm a lifelong Red Sox fan."

"Then we shall get along splendidly as I'm a diehard Yankee devotee. I hate it when I'm in perfect agreement with my patients on the things that matter most. A little controversy helps to keep things spiced up a bit. Plus, this way you have to say one simple thing if I overstep myself."

"What's that?"

"2004."

8

"Dr. Cohn, are you ready for your next patient?" Anna asked. "It's Eddie Wilkerson."

"Shit. That little bastard again."

Anna stood there dumfounded. Of the three doctors at Childcare Pediatric Clinic, the kindly gray-haired septuagenarian physician was her favorite. She had never heard him so much as utter the word 'damn' in the five years she had known him. The doctor started to blush after his outburst.

"Anna, I'm so sorry for that display. He's a handful for anybody but for some reason we're like oil and water, and I'm his pediatrician. You've never had the pleasure, have you?"

"No, doctor. I've heard the horror stories so whenever he's due to come in I conveniently find something else to do."

"Smart girl. Last time he was here he nearly tore my ears out when he yanked on my stethoscope. Time before that, he pulled the blood pressure monitor off the wall in the split second I turned my back to get a tongue depressor. Kid's a bear at nine years old. All this happened with his mother sitting right there thinking her little precious is so clever.

"Hilda's off today. You think you can help me with the little beast—I mean little darling?"

"Of course, doctor."

Anna went out to the waiting room to find Eddie standing on a chair. He was reaching into the aquarium, trying to snag any fish that swam by, ignoring Mrs. Wilkerson's mild admonishments to stop doing such things.

Anna walked up to Eddie.

"Hi, Eddie, my name's Anna."

Eddie pulled his arm out of the water and smiled.

"Hi, Anna. Do you like the fish?"

"Why yes I do. Maybe we should just let them swim on their own, okay?"

"Okay, Anna."

"Let's go see the doctor."

"Okay, Anna."

"Mrs. Wilkerson, would you like to join us?"

"Um, no. That's alright. You seem to have it under control. Thank you," responded the woman who was too flummoxed over the change in her son's behavior to make sense of anything.

Anna led Eddie into the examination room and stood there while Dr. Cohn conducted his examination. At one point, Eddie started to fidget and Anna cleared her throat. Eddie gazed in her direction. He smiled and became still again. When the doctor concluded his checkup, Anna escorted Eddie out, depositing him back into his mother's waiting arms. Anna returned to the office area. She heard Dr. Cohn call to her from his office.

"Anna, I've never seen anything like that. That kid sure drank whatever Kool-Aid you slipped him."

"We just seemed to hit it off, I guess. He's not such a bad kid. Just needs a firm hand."

"You're our office's Father Flanagan, seeing good in these kids where no one else does."

"I wouldn't go that far."

"Well, you have a gift that I can't explain. Remind me when he comes back that I'm to have you in the room while I examine him."

"Yes, doctor."

"Anna, are you doing okay?"

"Yes. Why do you ask?"

"You've seemed so listless lately. You look exhausted. Everything alright at home?"

"I...It's...nothing. Tim hasn't been sleeping well and it's keeping me up, but we're okay."

"Has he been to see a doctor?"

"He's going to see a psychologist at five."

"A psychologist?"

Anna could not decipher whether the doctor's tone indicated

surprise, alarm or some other emotion but, before she could dwell on it, Dr. Cohn continued.

"Well, I'm sure they'll get to the bottom of whatever is bothering him. If you want to clear out of here early to be with him, go right ahead."

"He's had bad experiences with therapists in the past. It was something he had to do on his own."

"If you need to get out of here, if not for him then for yourself, feel free."

"Thank you, doctor, but if I weren't here I'd just be sitting at home worrying, so I think I'll stick it out."

"As you wish, my dear. You two take care of yourselves…and each other. You hear me?"

"Yes, doctor. We'll try."

At 5:00 she went straight home. She needed to put her feet up, have a drink and relax before she could think about starting dinner. To make things worse, after his session Tim had an appointment with a client to go over some designs and would not be home until after ten. He had been so erratic at work lately, including being personally responsible for losing David Ellis, one of their biggest clients. He could not afford to irritate another paying customer.

She had an hour or more before she would get any news from Tim. She opened a bottle of *Côtes de Rhone* to help pass the time. Maybe Mags was home, she hoped. She detested talking on the telephone but, for her sister, she always made an exception. Magda could bring anybody out of a funk, especially Anna.

Whereas Anna was practical and reasoned, her older sister by three years was wild and unpredictable. If Magda had a date with one man over the course of a week, it was considered to be very slow. She was funny and alive. She spoke her mind. Despite their difference in age, Magda had always included Anna in things when growing up. They were the best of friends.

Magda lived in Nashua, New Hampshire. The last time they had met up, about two months earlier, they reminisced about Anna and Tim's wedding. Magda, who had been maid of honor, made a wisecrack that being in proximity of Anna's pure white wedding dress would turn it yellow. Anna meekly protested that her past was not so pure either. She could yellow the dress on her own, thank you very much.

When the subject turned to Magda's short-lived marriage to Marty, the best they could do was heave a collective sigh. It had been doomed from the start. Anna had warned her sister not to proceed with this ill-fated union, but Magda was not one to take such advice.

Anna had a bad feeling about Marty from the first instant she met him. On those occasions when she found herself alone with him, his conversation would be laced with plenty of innuendo and double entendres. There always seemed to be a sexual undercurrent in any comment he made. It was never blatant enough for Anna to have proof he was indeed hitting on her, but she was convinced he would jump at the opportunity to go to bed with her if he had even nominal assurance that Magda would not find out.

Anna expressed her concerns to her sister, who in turn brushed them aside. Anna did not press the issue. She convinced herself that it was all in her imagination. Magda appeared to be very happy.

Anna and Tim were in Nashua spending some time with Magda and Marty. Magda announced that she and Marty were getting married. That night. Even Marty seemed startled at the proposition but within a few moments he mumbled, "Sure, why not?" Despite severe misgivings about the entire enterprise, Anna and Tim agreed to be witnesses. Anna was quite sure her sister had not done the blood tests or waiting periods or any of the preliminary formalities. Those were details and Magda was not into details.

Magda tore the page out of the phone book containing justices of the peace and off they all went, looking for someone who would perform the ceremony late at night on a moment's notice. They located a retired judge just over the border in Maine who must have been in his nineties. Initially, he had Marty marrying Anna. Once that was straightened out, he started to marry Magda and Tim. In the end, they got tired of correcting him and technically, Anna was pretty sure she ended up marrying Magda.

Anna's misgivings proved to be on the mark. Magda and Marty's marriage lasted less than a year. Anna was correct about his tendency for philandering. He had also hidden a drinking problem pretty well in the past but, once he was married, he felt he had the right to drink without cessation or censure. Once drunk, he had little tolerance for a wife as willful and independent as Magda. When they broke it off, Anna was more devastated than Magda. She was glad her sister had rid herself of this miscreant, but she so wanted Magda to find the happiness she had found with Tim. Magda, for her part, was philosophical about the whole affair and started dating even before the divorce was final.

Now, as Anna sat alone in her brownstone, she needed Magda one more time, not that she expected any concrete or useful advice. Instead, she would be there, listen and then say something inappropriate or off color. However, as all she got was her voicemail. That in itself, with Magda's trademark off-the-wall comments punctuating the message, made Anna smile, but it did not have a lasting effect. Her feeling of worry soon returned.

She sat and stared out the window, hoping for Tim to call with good news, or any news whatsoever. She needed to hear the sound of his voice so badly. She wanted him to hold her but that would not happen until very late that evening. The bottle of wine slowly disappeared.

9

Tim called Anna as soon as he left the doctor's office. Although there had been no earth-shattering breakthroughs, the excitement in his voice was palpable. Both wished he could postpone or cancel his evening meeting, but both knew full well he could not. This contract was at a crucial juncture. After letting so much slide over the past three months, he could not fail on this one. They would have to wait a little longer to be in each other's arms.

When he walked through the door, Anna could see the noticeable change in him. She could not shut him up as he described his session with Dr. Philip Mordecai. Nor did she want to shut him up. She did have to caution him, though, not to perform self-psychoanalysis when he speculated that perhaps the repercussions of his father's death were only now emerging, twenty-four years later. She did not want him to get far ahead of himself and be disappointed but neither did she want to dampen his enthusiasm. It had been way too long since she had seen him this positive about anything. She too was feeling his optimism that before long this would all be behind them.

He had picked up the sedative at the pharmacy on the way home, but taking it could wait. He sat down beside Anna, took her face in his hands and started kissing her. First, the kisses were almost tentative. He had not shown her any attention since Paris and was a little apprehensive as to how she would react. He need not have been. Starting deliberately but soon giving in to the passion that had been denied them for months, they made urgent love on the living room floor. They rediscovered each other's bodies and became one again, although they both knew in their hearts that they had never been, nor would they ever be, apart.

Exhausted, they trudged up the stairs. Tim stopped by the kitchen to take his prescription. In the bedroom, they took up where they had left off, although before long he drifted into a deep sleep. Anna held him close, her limbs intertwined with the person she loved the most in the entire world; she could never remember being this happy. She was satisfied on so many levels that she found it difficult to believe that this itself was not a dream.

.   .   .

That first night, the prescribed sedative did its job. Tim did not stir once. Anna kept waking up because she was anxious about him as he moved or shifted positions. She did not mind at all holding him for a few minutes before drifting back to sleep.

The next morning, Tim went to work rested and with a smile on his face. Anna was exhausted but happy. They believed this whole episode was behind them but the next night the nightmare returned. When she awoke in the morning, she found Tim withdrawn and frightened.

When she asked him what was wrong, he responded that he could not tell her. She pressed for more, but he remained silent and stared fretfully into space. For perhaps the first time ever in their relationship, Tim did not open up to her about something that was bothering him. Normally, they could and would talk about everything without hesitation. Despite her pleas for Tim to talk to her, he sipped his coffee without uttering a word.

Tim got up, saying that he would call Dr. Mordecai for an immediate appointment. He kissed her on the forehead and then left. Anna sat alone at the breakfast table with her coffee and took over for him staring off into space.

Once he got to work, Tim left a message for the doctor. Phil called him back an hour later and advised him that he was out of town but would be returning late the following day and could meet with him at six.

That night, Tim tried not to fall asleep, but exhaustion overtook him. So did his dream. Like the previous morning, after hardly saying a word to Anna, he went to work looking like a wreck.

Promptly at six, Tim walked into the doctor's waiting room. Phil invited him into his office and Tim walked in.

"So, you're still having the dream."

"I took the prescription the first night and I had a great night's sleep. I took it again last night."

"But the dream returned anyway."

"More frightening than ever."

"What was so different?"

Saying nothing, Tim stared at the floor.

"Tim, you came back here because you trust me and think I can help. What was so different about this dream? Were there different people involved? Were they threatening you?"

"For the most part they were the same. They seemed mad at me, like they knew I was trying to get rid of them by taking the drug, but that's not what frightened me."

Receiving only silence in return, Phil waited him out.

"That other being, the one that the three of them are terrified of, made himself known."

"What did he do?"

"His voice was like the wind. He issued a threat that cut me to my very soul."

"What did he say?"

Tim hesitated.

"What did he say? It's a dream. No matter how real it may seem, it was a dream. This being or whatever you call him has no power over you. You have to realize that you have power over it. What did he say?"

"He said only one word, but his meaning was very clear."

"And that word was?"

"Anna."

10

Inspector Archambaut was sitting in his office fuming. He did not like it one bit when any of his cases went cold. It had been three months since the LaFleur murder and they were no further along than they were on day one. In fact, they had taken several steps backward.

All of Mr. LaFleur's records for the month leading up to his death were missing. The police had a drinking glass from LaFleur's kitchen with a set of unidentified fingerprints that were nowhere in the French or European database. When they tried to track down Sophie Alain to ask her some follow-up questions, they discovered the contact information she had given them was bogus. When they tried to locate her through the World Environmental Fund, they discovered that there was no such organization. They tried other similar organizations, figuring they may have misunderstood her, but nobody had any record of Ms. Alain or that they collected funds in this manner.

Archambaut was reviewing the file when Officer Dubois stuck his head in.

"What is it?" the Inspector snapped, but then he relented.

"I'm sorry, François. This case is so frustrating, but I shouldn't take it out on you. What do you have?"

"Well, it's not much but we were able to track down the convent LaFleur was helping. It's an obscure, shut away order of about a dozen nuns up in St. Denis called *l'Ordre de la Tour*. I'm not sure what a bunch of secretive nuns can tell us but it's more than we had ten minutes ago."

Archambaut laughed.

"You're right on that one. See if you can contact them to arrange a time for me to go up and meet with them."

"Sure thing boss."

Twelve years of Catholic schooling prepared Achambaut to sit still in an uncomfortable straight back wood chair as he waited for Mother Superior Angelique to enter and meet with him.

A large painting of Jesus delivering the Sermon on the Mount hung on one wall; a statue of the Virgin Mother was on another. There was a big oaken table with five straight back, uncomfortable looking chairs around it. The nun who had escorted him into the convent did not say a word the entire walk to the Mother's office. After motioning for him to take a seat, she left the room. Five minutes later, Mother Superior Angelique entered. Archambaut rose to greet her.

"Mother, thank you so much for seeing me."

"In your message, you said you wanted to talk about Mr. LaFleur. Did something happen to him? Please tell me you have recovered the coin. Please tell me that."

"I am afraid not, Mother. I know nothing about a coin but I do have much graver words to impart."

Arachambaut noticed a look on the Mother's face that he could not discern. It was almost as if she doubted that any news could be worse than not finding her precious coin.

"I know that you had had dealings with Etienne LaFleur. I'm sorry to have to tell you that Mr. LaFleur is dead. He was murdered. You may have been the last person to speak with him so I've come to see if you have any information that could help us in our investigation."

"Oh that poor dear man. I hadn't heard. We get so little news of the outside world. Why would anyone do such a thing?"

"That's what I'm hoping to find out."

"I don't know what I can tell you. We discovered a chest full of old artifacts hidden in our attic and Mr. LaFleur was very helpful in selling these artifacts to help us do repairs to the convent building. Our roof was in terrible condition."

"When did you last see or speak with Mr. LaFleur?"

Mother Angelique put on her glasses and pulled a small calendar out of her pocket. She flipped the pages.

"Let's see, he came here on the thirteenth of April to take away the chest. On the seventeenth, we received a check from him for the sale of the goods. Included with the check was a full inventory of the items that he sold. It was then that I noticed a silver coin on the list of items. This never should have left the convent but it was in a secret compartment. I called him that day to see if I could get the coin back but he advised me that he had already sold it to a coin dealer. He had heard that the coin dealer sold it within hours, I think to an American."

Archambaut perked up. Perhaps the mysterious and elusive spaced-out bohemian girl was telling the truth. She had mentioned a rare coin and an American.

"Did he happen to mention the name of the coin dealer?"

"No, and I was so distraught at that point I didn't think to ask. I'm sorry."

"No, you've been very helpful, Mother Angelique. You've confirmed a few things that I was skeptical about. Yes, you've helped a great deal. Thank you."

When Archambaut returned to the precinct he summoned Dubois.

"Yes, boss," he answered. "How were the nuns? Anything helpful there?"

"They were very helpful, François. Let's get those fingerprints over to our friends at the FBI. They still owe us for our help on the drug ring case, although they do tend to have very short memories when it comes time for us to ask them for something."

"FBI?"

"Yes, it may be that our elusive friend Ms. Alain may have been telling us the truth about some Americans and the rare coin. Maybe the FBI will get a hit."

"On it."

11

After Tim had left that morning, Anna sat around for a few more minutes. She pulled herself together and headed to work. She went through the motions at the clinic, however. Her mind constantly returned to the look of pain, worry and exhaustion on Tim's face.

In the evening, she went home to a dark house and waited to hear news from him. She hated it when Tim was not there during the evening. In addition to missing his company, she also despised the telephone. Without him there, she would be forced to pick up the receiver.

When she was six, the phone had become a source of lies, anger and, ultimately, divorce. Her father would call with news that he was working late. At first, her mother accepted these calls calmly and with dignity. Then, as her parents' relationship deteriorated, the phone never seemed to be used to exchange pleasantries or harmless gossip. Rather, it was the source of recriminations, harsh words and barbed, sarcastic exchanges. In the end, it was the vehicle through which details of the divorce were worked out. Using a six-year old's logic, it was clear that, if one wanted to avoid pain and sorrow, one avoided the phone.

As Anna grew and matured, her head told her that there was nothing intrinsically wrong with the telephone. However, something even deeper inside her said otherwise. In her mind, the telephone remained a dark but necessary evil in modern society.

So when the phone rang at 6:23 PM on September 19, Anna was loathe to answer it. Normally, knowing and understanding (at least to a certain degree) her peculiar aversion, Tim would jump up and get the phone if he were home. If he was not around, she would usually let it ring and the machine would get it. On this night, though, she ran to the phone, hoping to see Tim's number and for him to be on the other end, telling her everything was alright. Instead, she did not recognize the number but she felt compelled to answer. With dread, she picked up the receiver.

"Mrs. Harrington?" a male voice asked over the line in a clearly urgent tone. The call was being made from a cell phone, probably from a car.

"Yes, this is Anna Harrington."

"This is Dr. Philip Mordecai, I've been working with your husband."

Anna knew in an instant that something was wrong. It was not just the tone in the doctor's voice. Tim liked that this doctor did not use his title when introducing himself. Invoking his title meant business.

Anna began to speak but nothing came out. The doctor then gave shape to her fears.

"Something has happened. Tim had a seizure or an attack."

Anna gasped.

"There doesn't seem to be anything life-threatening at the moment. His vital signs are good, but he's unconscious. I've tried to revive him, but he hasn't come to.

"I'm not totally sure what happened to him. An ambulance is taking him to Barton Medical Center. I'm on my way there now. Can you meet me in the emergency room?"

She threw down the receiver without answering, grabbed her car keys and ran out the door.

Ignoring two red lights, she made it to the hospital in seven minutes. She hurried through the emergency room entrance and surveyed the faces, looking for anyone who could be Dr. Mordecai. A dozen people were waiting for their turns. They ranged from a mother and her boy with Downs syndrome, both of whom appeared to have the flu, to a man in a torn shirt and blue jeans holding a cold pack over his eye, perhaps as the result of a fight. Everyone was ignoring the cable news channel droning from the television over in the corner.

She had expected to get a whiff of disinfectant when she arrived, but instead her nostrils detected the smell of freshly sawed wood due to ongoing renovations. The unexpected odor comforted her in several ways. First, although she worked in a clinic and breathed in the distinctive aroma of disinfectant all day, it was not a scent she wanted to associate with a place to which someone she loved had been taken. Second, Tim would often come home from a building site, the scent of the carpentry going on around him having permeated his clothes and hair. It was a reassuring odor. Third, and on this score she knew she was over-thinking the issue, she took it as a sign that this was a good hospital if they were spending money on renovations.

Not seeing anyone who could be Dr. Mordecai, she proceeded to the receptionist counter where an overweight and bored nurse sat doing some paperwork. Anna asked if her husband were there. The nurse kept writing but did acknowledge her enough to advise that the doctor was examining him now. He would come out when he was finished.

Anna asked if she could see her husband. This time, the nurse lifted her head and in an exasperated tone advised her a second time that the doctor would come out and see her when he was done.

"While you are waiting," the nurse intoned as she handed Anna a clipboard, "please fill out these forms and bring them back to me along with your insurance card."

Anna dutifully accepted the clipboard and sat down to start filling them out but then she got right back up and marched back to the nurse's station.

"Screw this."

She noisily dropped the clipboard, along with the unfinished forms, on the counter at the nurse's head.

"I'll fill those out later," she called back as she proceeded past the station through the double doors leading to the examination rooms.

"Mrs. Harrington," the nurse yelled out, "you can't go back there."

"Watch me!" Anna responded as she walked by each room, looking in to see if Tim were there.

"Mrs. Harrington, I'm going to have to call security!"

A short, balding middle-aged doctor emerged from the last room on the left.

"I don't think that will be necessary, Ginny. I know Mrs. Harrington. Your husband is in here."

The nurse glared at Anna but the word of the doctor was enough to make her retreat.

"Very well, Dr. Frazier," the nurse responded as she went back to her station.

Anna followed the doctor into the room. An intern who did not look to be over fifteen years old stood over in a corner.

Tim was in a semi-private examining room. Anna rushed to his side, kneeling down beside his bed. He appeared to be sleeping very deeply. No tubes or IVs were attached, just a heart monitor.

Anna, now with a tear streaming down each cheek, was almost afraid to touch him for fear that he might break. She noted how peaceful and serene he was. She gently took his hand into hers. She looked up at Dr. Frazier.

"What's wrong with him, doctor?"

Instead of Dr. Frazier responding, a voice came to her from behind.

"We don't know yet."

Anna turned around, startled there was another person in the small room that she had not noticed.

"And you are?"

"Mrs. Harrington," Dr. Frazier responded, "this is Dr. Philip Mordecai. He'll be consulting on your husband's case."

Dr. Mordecai extended his hand, which Anna shook. She noticed that he looked surprised for an instant, almost as if he recognized her, but she knew they had never met.

"Mrs. Harrington. I wish we were meeting under better circumstances."

Anna did not respond but turned her focus back to Tim. She looked back to Dr. Frazier.

"You told the nurse you know me. I'm sorry. You do look somewhat familiar but I can't place you."

"I play golf with Dr. Holt and have picked him up a few times at the children's clinic. Don't let him know that I told you this, but Dr. Holt raves about you. He always says how confident he is that things are being handled if you're there and he ducks out for a few hours."

Anna silently acknowledged the compliment.

"We've examined your husband. This is Dr. Baier, by the way,"

Dr. Frazier motioned to his youthful colleague who dutifully shook hands. They all soon went back to forgetting the intern was in the room.

"To be honest, I can't figure out his condition. He's not in any danger. All his vital signs are well in the normal range. His pupils react to light. He even seems to react to pain and other stimuli. There are times when I swear he reacts to verbal commands. But he remains in this deep, deep sleep. I'm going to run some other tests. I've ordered an EEG and I'd like to do a CAT Scan to see if they can offer us any clues. I've never seen anything like this before. Physically, he seems to be fine. What's been your take on this, Phil?"

"I'm as perplexed as you. One moment he was sitting there talking to me, the next he's like this."

Anna was hanging on the two doctors' every word.

"Mrs. Harrington," Dr. Frazier continued, "Do you know of any sleep disorders your husband has ever experienced?"

"He hasn't slept at all well over the past few months."

"As a result of recurring nightmares he was seeing me for," Dr. Mordecai interjected.

"Prior to that," Anna replied, "he'd always slept well, but he's a light sleeper and will wake with the slightest noise or prodding."

"Is there any family history of epilepsy or nervous disorders?" Dr. Frazier asked.

"Not that I know of."

"How about allergies?"

"Again, not that I know of."

"Any drugs or medication he's been taking?"

"Just the sedative Dr. Mordecai prescribed."

"We have that on his charts. Nothing else? How about alcohol?"

"He likes a glass of red wine or a beer on occasion but nothing more than that. I don't think he's had anything recently."

"Well, we're going to keep him here until he wakes up. If this continues much longer, we'll put an IV on him to make sure he doesn't dehydrate. If it goes on too long, a feeding tube may have to be inserted. I assure you, Mrs. Harrington, we will get to the bottom of this. You're welcome to stay around as long as you like."

Dr. Frazier gave Anna a warm smile.

"Thank you, doctor."

Dr. Frazier and Dr. Baier left, indicating they would be back soon. Dr. Mordecai remained behind, looking down on Anna and Tim.

Anna found something about the doctor's manner unsettling. Normally when men stared, her first though was that they were mentally undressing her but this seemed different. There was a type of fondness in his gaze that implied pleasant thoughts from previous encounters, but she was sure they had never previously met let alone had any interaction.

"Tim's in good hands. This is one of the best hospitals in the state. I did my residency here."

"Dr. Mordecai,"

"Please, call me Phil."

"Phil, please tell me what happened to Tim."

"Tim called me yesterday to see if I could fit him in for an appointment," Dr. Mordecai began, "I was out of town until this evening, so I asked him to come in at six. He seemed agitated and distraught."

"Yes, his dreams were more frightening last night than ever before. He'd been so full of hope after his first visit with you. He felt relief he hadn't felt in weeks. He filled the prescription and was confident he'd have his first uninterrupted night of sleep in months. The first night was great but after that it got worse. To tell you the truth, I'm guessing. He wouldn't talk with me at all. It was like we were strangers in the same room. He said he had to talk to you first."

"Well, we talked for a little while. He told me that instead of the drugs overtaking the dreams the exact opposite happened. The nightmare came, but a new frightening dimension was added. In addition to the usual pain and sorrow, another emotion was added: anger. I'm assuming I'm not violating any confidences here, that he kept you filled in on his dreams. Am I correct?"

Anna nodded her head.

"I thought so. As usual, they were carrying on in their respective languages that Tim couldn't understand. Initially, he couldn't figure out why they were so angry but then it occurred to him: they knew he was trying to eliminate them by using drugs. They just wouldn't have it!

"There was another difference between this particular dream and the past ones. Rather than being a detached observer, on this night he felt that he was the fifth character. In previous dreams he'd have his own thoughts that would go so far as his consciousness but no further. On this night, though, as the others drew closer and became increasingly hostile, he instinctively shouted, "Stop!" There was an immediate reaction: they stopped. Previously, it had never occurred to him to speak with his little group, so he never tried. When he communicated with them, everyone, Tim included, was so taken aback that no one knew what to do next.

"I must say I was intrigued with his narrative and expected him to go on. But when I looked over at him, his face was ashen and fixed in a catatonic stare. I asked him what was wrong, but I got no response. Then his eyes rolled back in his head as he slumped over and fell to the floor. Fearing he was having a heart attack, I prepared to perform CPR but when I checked, his pulse was a little fast but fine. His breathing was a little shallow but for the most part normal. I checked his eyes and his pupils reacted normally to light. Maybe he was having an epileptic seizure. I went to insert a depressor in his mouth to keep him from biting his tongue but there was no rigidity or signs of convulsions so I concluded that wasn't it. I tried to revive him but it was like he had fallen into a deep, deep sleep."

"Is he in a coma?"

"I can't characterize it as such just yet, but it is a possibility."

"Could he have had an adverse reaction to the sedative you prescribed?"

"I've never seen it happen with this particular drug. He wasn't taking any other medication was he? Maybe there was some form of interaction."

"Not that I know of."

"The sedative I prescribed is rather mild. If any allergic reaction were to happen, it would have happened within hours after that first dose. I wouldn't expect a delayed reaction like this, but of course we'll check it out."

Anna sensed the doctor's defensiveness so she interjected, "I'm familiar with the sedative. I've seen that particular one prescribed – at much lower doses, of course – to children by the doctors in the clinic.

Just want to check all angles."

"So do I, Mrs. Harrington. So do I."

A pretty blond nurse came in.

"Hello doctor, Mrs. Harrington. I'm Amy Philips. I'm the head nurse for the night."

Nurse Philips went about her duties. As she was leaving, she spoke to Anna

"We've put your husband's clothes in that closet there. You can take them if you'd like. I don't like to leave valuables lying around so here are his wallet, his watch and the medallion he was wearing around his neck. The medallion looks very old. Is there a story behind it, if you don't mind me asking?"

"No story that I know of. Tim's a coin collector and he bought this one when we were in Paris. It had a hole punched in it already so he thought he'd wear it on his neck. Kind of a good luck charm. He hasn't had a chance to look into its origin or value yet."

"It does look real old, like from Roman times or thereabouts."

Phil had not been listening to this conversation but at this, he looked up.

"Roman, as in Julius Caesar, Ben Hur times?"

"Yes, why?"

"Nothing. Tim described a character in nightmares he was having as being a Roman guard. Just seems funny that I've had two conversations about ancient Rome in one week."

The nurse just shrugged and departed.

Anna kept staring at her Tim, wondering what had happened to him. She also wondered about this "coincidence".

12

A week passed with no change in Tim's condition. He had been moved to a special unit that concentrated on head injuries and trauma. Anna was there every minute of every day. Periodically, a doctor or nurse would come in to stick a new tube or wire into him or take some blood or some other measurement. He needed tubes to feed him, to hydrate him, to carry wastes away. Wires measured more bodily functions than she knew existed.

Mostly, she sat and looked at him. She would talk to him, saying things that might get a reaction. None came.

The doctors convinced Anna she needed a night's sleep in her own bed. While she dreaded being there without Tim, she knew it was for the best. She decided to walk the two miles home, giving herself time to reflect and be alone with her thoughts.

The setting late summer sun highlighted the hints of gold and yellow in the trees that lined the boulevard. It was a pleasant evening and the street was still bustling as the shops were preparing to close and the restaurants and cafes were starting to fill up with dinner customers. Normally, Anna would enjoy her stroll as she watched the people in the crowd going about their daily routines. Tonight, her mind was too far away to notice much.

At one point her feet seemed to stop as if of their own accord. She looked up and stared at the beautiful hewn stone façade of Our Blessed Lady Catholic Church.

Anna's had attended masses at this church a few times, but she could by no means be termed a regular church-goer. However, she always had a need for a security blanket that she could come back to the Church regularly if she wanted to. That need, she was sure, was rooted in her mother.

Over the course of her life, Elana Dubcek's religious zeal had ebbed and flowed. Anna could not pinpoint when her mother's transformation into a religious zealot had occurred. Anna was not even sure whether it had been a gradual evolution or whether there was some epiphany, some event, that awakened her mother's fervor.

Elana Dubcek, nee Kolarova, was born in Prague while Czechoslovakia was under Soviet rule. Times were tough under the Communists, but Elana and her family always seemed to have enough to eat.

She met Georg Dubcek, an up and comer in the pharmaceutical industry, when she was nineteen. They married when she was twenty-one. Magda was born a year later; Anna three years after that. Georg was a member of the Czech Communist Party — in order to be an up and coming anything required membership in the Party. As the Soviets grip on the country waned, things became unsettled for everybody, including Party members who had thought they were safe and protected. Georg and Elana decided it wise to flee Czechoslovakia. Since Georg had connections in Canada, the family settled in Toronto. It did not take long for Georg to find work. He initially was employed as a mason but then was able to get a job with a Canadian pharmaceutical company.

After Elana and Georg divorced, Anna noticed her mother becoming disenchanted with the church in particular and religion in general. She would bring the girls to Mass and catechism, but Anna could tell her mother's heart was not in it. Anna often sensed that attending Mass was done more for the sake of the children than for anything else. When Anna reached adolescence and attendance was no longer required, she was glad to stop going. So was Elana, it appeared.

About five years ago, Anna called just to say hello and chat. It was around half past seven in the morning and Anna knew her mother's habits. On a normal day, she would be up at 6:30 to spend at least an hour doing housework. She would leave her apartment at precisely 8:30 to be at the bank by nine, where she worked as a secretary. On this day, however, there was no answer. Anna was concerned.

That evening, Anna found out the truth: Elana had gone to early morning Mass. Anna checked the calendar and confirmed it was a Tuesday, not Sunday. When asked why she was at Mass on a weekday, Elana very matter-of-factly replied that she had been going every day for the past few weeks.

Elana's daily attendance at Mass took on the air of not only something she wanted to do, but was something she needed to do. Religion became all the more important to her life after she was diagnosed as having multiple sclerosis three years ago.

Her strength and courage in the face of this debilitating illness were inspiring. She attributed her positive attitude to a renewed belief in God and the power of the Catholic Church. Unfortunately, there were other changes in her behaviors and attitudes, changes that Anna did not like. Elana was more judgmental and less tolerant of differences than she had been.

With this backdrop, Anna stood in front of this awe-inspiring edifice. Since Tim was not a Catholic—and not much of a practicing Methodist for that matter—she rarely went to Mass anymore. Today, however, she needed the solace of the faith of her youth, so she went up the front steps.

Finding the door open, she entered and called out. Hearing nothing, she went into the sanctuary, crossed herself and took a seat in a pew off the aisle about halfway down. She was not sure what she was doing there. Maybe she would just sit for a while or maybe say a silent prayer for Tim. She examined the stained-glass windows, hoping they could fill her with the spirit of the Lord. Each window depicted a station of the cross. She was moved by the rendering of Simon of Cyrene being forced to bear the cross, but she found most of the scenes a little too modern for her taste so she returned to her silent meditation. After a few minutes, a priest entered.

"I thought I heard someone come in. Can I help you? I'm Father Timothy."

Anna's heart soared. It was not the boring, humorless priest she had heard preach last time she was here. Maybe it was a sign: Father Timothy could help heal her Timothy.

"Hello, Father. I'm Anna Harrington. I needed to come in and sit for a few minutes. My husband's in the hospital and I wanted to reflect and say a prayer for him."

"Sit as long as you want. Is there anything I can do for you?"

"I don't think so, Father. I'd just like to sit for a bit."

"That's fine. What's wrong with your husband, if you don't mind me asking?"

Anna did not feel like talking about it but when one is asked a question by a priest it is proper to respond.

"He's in a coma."

It was the first time she had openly acknowledged Tim's condition to anyone. Instead of the spoken word being therapeutic, however, she felt worse. The helplessness she felt was magnified.

"God moves in mysterious ways, my dear. The trick is to look beyond our daily troubles to see things as part of a greater plan God has for each of us."

Standard priestly drivel. It was more rhetorical than anything and not needing a response. Father Timothy seemed to be waiting for an answer but, realizing that none was forthcoming, he pressed on.

"Would you like me to hear your confession?"

Even though she had not had her confession heard in months, she was not in the mood. It seemed obvious that he was not going to leave her be. She could not blame him; he was earnestly trying to help but if 'mysterious ways' was the best she was going to get, she might as well move on and look for refuge and comfort elsewhere.

"No, thank you."

"Are you sure, my dear?"

"No, I think I'll head home now. I just wanted to sit and reflect. I'm better now."

"Well, anytime you wish to come back, I'll be here for you."

"Thank you. Good bye, Father."

Anna exited the church. Instead of heading home as originally planned, she turned around and rushed back to the hospital to be with Tim. She could not possibly be alone in her empty home. She needed the consolation that only Tim could give her, regardless of the condition he was in.

•　　•　　•

On the twelfth day, Anna was dozing restlessly in the chair beside Tim's bed when Phil arrived. He gently awakened her.

"Anna, you should go home and get some proper sleep. You

should think about getting back to work. You're no help to Tim if you let yourself get worn down or if you drive yourself crazy."

She looked up with a weary expression.

"I tried heading home but couldn't bring myself to go to an empty house so I came back. But I guess you're right; I'm not doing Tim any good here." Her reply was a nearly inaudible monotone.

"I know I'm right. You need to force yourself to get some rest. Let me drive you home. Oh, where's your car parked?"

"On the deck, third floor."

"Why don't you give me your keys? I'll have someone drive it to your house later today."

"That would be great."

Anna reached into her purse. As she pulled her keys out, the coin on its chain came with them.

"Damn! I'm going to lose this thing yet! I need to get a purse with an inside pocket. Well, for lack of a better place..."

Anna slipped the chain over her head.

•   •   •

The drive was marked with a profound silence as Anna half dozed and half stared into space. As they approached the house, she spoke up first.

"Phil, I want to thank you for all the effort you're putting in here. I know this is way above and beyond the call. You have to be ignoring your other patients to focus on Tim."

"This whole affair has been so disconcerting professionally that I don't feel I can give it up. Plus, even though I met Tim the two times, I genuinely like him, and you as well."

"I have to admit that at first I held you responsible; I thought it must have been something you did. But I realize that you had nothing to do with this."

"Believe me, I wondered myself whether I played any role. I've rerun the whole sequence of events in my mind a number of times and I don't think so. It just seemed to happen. It was almost as if some outside force has taken over.

"Well, he did say you two met in church, after all."

Anna was incredulous as she burst out laughing. She was almost doubled over.

"I'm sorry. I'm so very punchy and exhausted but the concept of Tim anywhere near a church is so ludicrous. That's just our stock answer to people."

"I was somewhat doubtful, but I didn't pursue it."

Anna eyed Phil critically.

"I'll tell you how we really met, but I have to swear you to secrecy first."

"You have my word of honor."

"I first met Tim when I gave him a lap dance."

"You were a stripper?"

"We prefer exotic dancer, but yes, I was a stripper. Paid for nursing school. But you can't tell anyone. The lead doctor at the clinic and many parents do not feel the words 'stripper' and 'pediatric nurse' belong in the same sentence."

"I'll take your secret to my grave."

"Thanks again, Phil, for everything," she quietly stated as she climbed out the car and walked toward the house.

Phil gazed at her as she trod up the path.

13

Anna opened the front door of her brownstone and stood there for a few moments in absolute amazement. The place was spotless. The last time she had popped in to change her clothes and freshen up, the house was an unmitigated disaster area. She was never a great housekeeper to begin with; there was always something else she would rather be doing. If truth were ever told to the outside world, Tim did ninety percent of the cleaning and straightening. He never complained, which she appreciated immensely. He had mentioned in passing that if housekeeping was the price he had to pay to end up with a mate as terrific as Anna, it was a small price indeed.

When she was last there, the depths of the condition to which the house had descended were beneath even her low standards. Dirty dishes were haphazardly piled in and around the sink. Clothes, both those to be washed and those in want of a hanger, were strewn about the bedroom. Unread newspapers and unopened mail piled up on the kitchen table.

Now everything was clean and in its place. Who would do such a thing?

"Hey, little sister. 'Bout time you showed up." The voice came from the living room.

"Mags! When did you get here?" Anna cried out as she flew into her sister's arms.

"This morning. I was down in the Bahamas with Fred and flew back in yesterday." Anna did not bother reacting to the mention of the latest man in Magda's life. "I got home to about a dozen messages from you and about as many from Mom saying Tim was having trouble. I left a message on my boss's phone telling him my baby sister needed me and caught the first plane I could out of Logan. God knows if I have a job when I get back. I got here early this morning and saw what a dump the place was so I occupied myself until you got here. I called Mom, on your dime of course. She's worried as hell. She wishes she could be here with you, too."

This was a typical Mags statement: a string of sentences maybe related to each other, maybe not – all delivered in one breath. It was so good to have her older sister here. From a practical viewpoint, Magda would not contribute much. She was scattered and disorganized under the best of conditions. In an emergency she would be worthless but the moral uplift she gave to Anna was immeasurable.

Magda was not exaggerating when she said she arrived home to at least a dozen messages. Her style was not to let anyone know if she was leaving for extended periods. Anna had wanted to hear her sister's voice. If she had to settle for the ridiculous greeting Magda had on her voicemail, so be it. Anna knew that wherever Magda was, she would fly to her as soon as she got the messages. That is what had happened.

Anna had also phoned her mother many times. Unlike Magda, Elana Dubcek was home each time to take the call. Anna was heartsick over how her mother worried about Tim, especially since there was no good news to give her. Housekeeping deficiencies aside, Anna took more after her mother. Both were reasoned, practical and dependable. If they were going to be away from home for more than a day or two, calls were placed advising of this fact. One would never expect Elana or Anna to do anything on a whim or gut feeling.

Magda was more like her father, Georg. She was as good a person as you could find but a little shiftless and very carefree. Anna looked up to and idolized Magda, often wishing that she possessed more of those qualities instead of being the dull, practical one.

Her mother dearly wanted to be with Anna but since her multiple sclerosis diagnosis three years ago, she never traveled very far from Toronto. Some days she was just fine; others she could barely function. Both Anna and Magda had pleaded with her to come live with either of them but she resisted. Toronto was her home. Through Canada's health care system, she was able to get high quality assistance for which she would not be eligible in the States. She did not want to be a burden. Most importantly, her church, the center of her universe, was there. She assured both of them that she was getting along fine.

"So, how's Tim doing?"

Magda's question opened the floodgates. All Anna could manage was, "Not well," before she collapsed a sobbing heap into her sisters' arms. Magda held her and let her cry herself out.

"They'll get to the bottom of this, you'll see."

They sat in silence holding hands. Anna appreciated that her sister was there to offer positive reassurances and support; that's what was needed right now. Probing questions about Tim's condition could come later.

"What a mess you left this place in," Magda remarked.

"Yeah. I've hardly been here but when I was, I dumped things wherever I was."

"When did you start writing in code?"

"What on earth are you talking about?"

"You know I'm a snoop. When I was cleaning up the study, I leafed through some papers on the desk. There was a lot of junk there so I discarded most of it."

Anna shot her a look of horror, fearing things of importance may have been thrown out. Magda laughed.

"Don't worry, I just separated and didn't throw anything out. But after I removed a few layers, I noticed this red notebook."

Magda handed the notebook to Anna. Opening it, she saw Tim's handwriting, but nothing that she could decipher. She vaguely remembered him writing something in the middle of the night after waking up from his worst dream. Now she was wondering if these jottings were significant. Phil had asked her to call him if she recalled anything that may be pertinent to her husband's condition.

"I need to call the doctor."

"Go right ahead, girl."

Anna picked up the phone and dialed. "Phil, I found something that you should see."

He responded without hesitation.

"I'll be right over."

Phil arrived fifteen minutes later. Anna introduced him to Magda. Anna smiled and shook her head as she noted her sister's eyes go up and down as she performed her automatic appraisal that accompanied any single male she encountered.

Anna showed Phil the notebook and he started to leaf through it.

"Tim's dreams were vivid and detailed, so at the end of our first session I suggested he try to keep a journal of these dreams. This, I believe, is that journal."

"I saw him writing some things down the night before he, before he..." Anna did not know how to – or more accurately did not want to – verbalize the condition Tim was in.

"Before he lost consciousness," Phil completed her thought.

"At the time, I was thinking or maybe hoping, that his writing was work-related. Now I see that it wasn't. What does it all mean?"

"It's rather worthless at the moment. I find that a journal like this comes in handy, but the patient must be conscious. We talk about what's written and sometimes a door or two is opened. Without Tim's active participation, this is just indecipherable gibberish."

There was silence for a few seconds as Phil studied the pages more closely.

"I'm surprised at how much Tim wrote over the course of two nights. But it's all indecipherable."

"It may not be anything, but shouldn't we look into it? We need to do something, maybe seeing if we can translate it."

Phil and Magda shared a glance.

"Translate?"

"Yes, this is Tim's attempt to let us in on the conversations that have been occupying his brain. It may give us a key as to what's been going on up there for the past three months."

"Well, what I wanted him to do was to write down what he heard, and since these represent multiple languages that he doesn't know, these jottings are a phonetic conglomeration of all of these languages.

"I wish he'd put some sort of key down as to who said what. I guess he figured he'd walk me through this, not that we would have to be using it to piece a puzzle together. Are you okay?"

Anna, deep in her own thoughts, was startled at his voice.

"Yes, I'm all right. I'm so tired. I don't know why he didn't tell me about this or keep me clued in."

"Anna, before he lost consciousness, Tim was a very frightened man. He kept telling me how threatened he felt. The people in his dreams were getting more and more real to him. He feared he was losing his sanity but he was not just concerned about himself. I got the feeling that concern about himself was the least of his worries. He felt that if they could threaten him this much, they had the ability to threaten you. By not clueing you in, he was protecting you."

He allowed a moment for her to absorb his words.

"I know you want answers, we all do, and we want them now. But I don't think helpful to go grasping at straws. Like I said, this journal is a helpful tool but Tim must be an active participant. To look at it as a key into Tim's subconscious is a foolhardy endeavor. You might as well get on a plane to Haiti and consult with a voodoo practitioner or have a psychic give you a Tarot card reading. We'll find the answer, but it will be through medicine."

Anna gave Phil a quizzical, pained look.

"But I have to do something," she said in a tear-choked half-whisper.

"I'm sorry," Phil responded, "But I'm always so used to knowing everything, or at least convincing others that I know everything. There may be things in here that can help us. I have to keep pursuing the medical angle but if you'd like to take this on as a project, I don't see the harm."

Anna knew she was being placated, but she did not mind.

"The woman in his dream was the only one who spoke a language that he was fairly certain of. He was sure she was speaking French.

"Well, I don't speak French, but since I think we'll have better luck with French, why don't we go on the assumption that everything in here is French and see what we get. If any of the words make sense, we can piece them together. We can either get help from someone who speaks French or just start plowing through using a dictionary."

Anna knew she was grasping. She was over-tired and not thinking clearly but for some reason, she felt she had stumbled onto something that could help Tim. It was the most hopeful and enthusiastic she'd been since he had succumbed to this illness or whatever it was that plagued him.

"That sounds like as good a plan as any. I can't be much help since I have a conference call with Dr. Frazier and a physician in

California who is an expert in sleep disorders. That should last all morning as we go over Tim's condition and history."

"Okay, I'll start tonight."

"Why don't you get a good night's sleep and start fresh in the morning?"

"I'm okay."

"As you wish," Phil replied.

Once he had left, Magda made an observation.

"He's got a thing for you."

"Who, Dr. Mordecai?"

"Oh, yeah. He's got it bad."

"Mags. Once again your imagination is running away from you and, when it comes to men, that vivid imagination knows no bounds."

But Anna realized that Phil was interested in her. Ever since her dancing days, she vainly assumed that any man who met her wanted her. And she was correct in her assumption. She loved and wanted Tim, but she still held onto the belief that any man could be hers if she so desired. Tim would kid her as they walked down a crowded street asking if she had seen anybody of interest. She would blush a little and respond that there were about two dozen so far. They would laugh and hold each other that much tighter as they walked along. It always meant so much to her that Tim had confidence enough in their relationship that he could kid about other men. Anna wished they were strolling together right now.

"Aha, you see it, too! I'm glad to see that, despite all you're going through, you still have a little spunk in you."

"Mags, really. You know how much I love Tim. I'd never do anything to jeopardize what we have together."

"I'm not questioning you. It's him. There's something going on up in that head of his. I don't know what it is. Just keep an eye open. Okay?"

"Oh Mags. I wish we all had your imagination. What an exciting world it would be."

14

After Phil departed, Anna made a pot of strong coffee and she and Magda began leafing through the journal to see if there was something—anything—that might catch her eye as not being pure rubbish.

For the most part, Tim's jottings resembled a very poor attempt at Pig Latin. Anna and her sister despaired at anything making any sense whatsoever. Since neither of them spoke French, it was a bit foolhardy to hope that his phonetic approximations would lead anywhere. Magda suggested they pick it up in the morning. Anna said she would work on it a bit more and then go to bed. She kissed her sister good night.

She plowed on. About ready to call it a night, something jumped out at her. It was a name.

Tim had written: *Madam Fabian Delatoor, Countess Avignon.* Anna had never heard of this woman, but she seemed to be as good a place as any to start. She contemplated waking Magda to share in this discovery but then reconsidered. Although Magda had played along, Anna could see her sister yawn and roll her eyes. She would never have the patience for this type of research. It was also obvious that she thought the entire exercise to be downright silly.

Did this 'countess' hold the key that Anna was looking for? Tim described the woman in his dream as a nun, but here he writes of someone from the aristocracy. Was this yet another person? Were there other things that he never told her? She and Tim had the most open of marriages, one in which they knew as much about each other as any two people could. Now she was having her doubts, not about Tim or his love for her, but rather about how much one person can know about another.

How could she find this woman? It was definitely a French name.

Avignon, she recalled, was in the south of France. It was the once home of the popes and the children's song about dancing on a bridge. That was the extent of her knowledge of this city.

She decided to jump on the computer to see if there was anything she could find there about Madam Delatoor. A relative novice at exploring the Internet, she still knew enough basics to begin. She plugged 'Madam Delatoor' into a search engine and waited less than a second for the list to pop up. Over 200 screens of sites were referenced with everything from a site listing famous brothel madams to ones regarding the Tour de France bicycle race. She narrowed the search down somewhat. She remembered that quotation marks could help. Also, perhaps the 'madam' was sending her off in different directions. She would be better off using the name, Fabienne, this time spelling it correctly.

After she did this, she reviewed the first screen of website citations. As before, all she found was irrelevant garbage. The second and third screens were no different.

She was just about to refine her search and start again when an item on the fourth screen caught her eye. It was the Guyot Guide to Historical and Interesting Personages of France, 1500-1800. Mr. Guyot needs to get a life, she mused to herself. She vaguely remembered Tim describing the habit the nun in his dream was wearing as being old fashioned. This time period would definitely fit the bill. *It's worth a shot.* She clicked on the site.

After a few moments, a paragraph appeared on the screen:

Fabienne de la Tour, Comtesse d'Avignon (b. 1730(?), d. 1794(?)) —

Madame de la Tour was an aristocratic socialite who, along with her husband, Guillaume de la Tour, Comte d'Avignon, dictated who was in and who was out of favor throughout the South of France. Noted for hosting lavish balls and extravagant entertainments, the la Tours provided the elite and aristocracy of France and Europe with one diversion after another whenever they visited Provence. In 1778, after Guillaume was killed in a duel, Fabienne left the south of France and settled in Paris. There she renounced all her earthly

*possessions and started an order of nuns dedicated to meeting the
material and spiritual needs of the destitute and poor throughout
Paris. Using the proceeds from the sale of her possessions as well as
her former aristocratic connections, she was personally credited with
drastically increasing philanthropic donations during her tenure
with the order. In 1794, Madame de la Tour, who was now known as
Sister Catherine, suddenly disappeared, never to be heard from
again. Although it was never confirmed, many believed that, despite
her good works, her aristocratic background had caught up with her
and she went to the guillotine during this notorious revolutionary
period.*

What a remarkable woman. That would explain both the aristocratic
title and the nun's habit. Tim had a passion for history. He was
constantly reading books on the American Civil War and World War
II but she could not recall him toting around books on the French
Revolution or having any special interest in that era. How on earth
could someone who has been dead for over two centuries have any
connection with Tim?

Maybe he was referring to someone else who was alive right now.
That would make things somewhat easier... perhaps. She could track
this woman down and demand to know what she was doing to her
husband and why. Anna knew deep inside that she had already
tracked down the right person. She wished that there were some way
to determine if she was right. Then her duty would be clear: decipher
how this figure shrouded in history was reaching out to Tim.

Anna sat back and wondered what was happening. She had
always been a practical and straightforward person, depending on
reason and logic to guide her decisions and actions in life. When she
was in nursing school, it had always been Anna who had to push her
classmates to study instead of party. She had changed little since that
time; yet here she was, weaving the beginnings of a theory involving
a woman deceased for over two hundred years to explain Tim's
condition.

Phil had offered several medical explanations, each of them
rooted in science. He was working feverishly to test these theories in a
systematic manner. He was discussing Tim's case with colleagues all

over the country. He was narrowing down the possible explanations, discarding those that did not stand up to rigorous scientific methodology. Using this process, he was confident he would come up with the answer.

Something in her gut, though, said otherwise. She just had to follow any lead, no matter how ridiculous it may seem. She had worked with doctors long enough to know that they were not as infallible as they pretended to be. At the clinic, she had seen more than one misdiagnosis made or wrong prescription written. When she first started working there, she learned that there was a right way and a wrong way to point out these mistakes. It had to be done subtly, so that the doctor did not lose face. She played each doctor as an individual. At times, it had to be finessed to the extent that the doctors thought that they had changed the diagnosis or prescription themselves without any outside influence.

On occasion, she would go behind the back of the doctor. One time she gave unofficial advice to a mother whose daughter was being treated—with little success—for sinus problems. After several months of useless treatments, she took the mother aside and suggested an acupuncture clinic not far away. She worked with the woman and her insurance company so that the procedure was covered. All this was done unbeknownst to her doctor employers who would have been furious had they found out. Anna saw the mother and daughter six months later for the girl's annual check-up. Of course, when she looked in the girl's records, the doctor had noted that it was his treatment that had cleared up the sinus problems. Anna could only smile and shake her head.

She knew that if the doctors found out the truth, they would be livid. She had consistently seen physicians disparage any method for treating the ill that differed in the least bit from their medical school training. In other words, the prevailing philosophy was that most any ailment can be treated with pharmaceuticals, x-rays, expensive tests and other mainstays of modern medicine. Home remedies, acupuncture, ancient herbal treatments and the like had no place in a treatment regimen. They were discouraged in no uncertain terms. There was no attempt to understand them. Rather, they were relegated along with witchcraft and leeches to the medical dust-heap.

By and large, she agreed with the physicians. No one can argue with the results in terms of life expectancy and quality-of-life improvements over the years. She did have a problem, however, with their arrogance and complete disregard for new or different ideas they did not choose to understand.

Over the past week, she had spent a fair amount of time with Dr. Mordecai, or Phil as he liked to be called, and she did not lump him in with the more arrogant group of doctors. He seemed downright peculiar, but his heart and mind were in the right place. What set him apart was that he was open to other ideas. However, there was a line he would not cross. He had his standard medical school training and a predisposition to pursue his scientific methods. The idea that Anna was mulling—a long-deceased woman somehow influencing her husband—was just too outlandish to be taken seriously. If she were to suggest using acupuncture, the doctor might seriously consider it, but this was beyond any realm of credibility.

She could see it now. He would be nice to her, although in a patronizing way. He would be nice because he had a thing for her; Magda was correct on that score. He would gently suggest that the pressure was getting to her. He would prescribe a sedative to help her sleep. That was what doctors did. She ruefully thought to herself that maybe it was a sedative that got them where they were today, although she was fairly certain that Phil was not in any way to blame.

Anna was beginning to doubt her own sanity, but something kept telling her that she had to stay on this irrational course. Whether it was a gut feeling or a little voice in her head—maybe the voice of Madame de la Tour herself—or whether it was good old-fashioned exhaustion, she had a nagging suspicion that she was on to something. In any case, at least she could feel she was taking action instead of sitting around hoping and praying. She would do something to solve a piece of this puzzle that had made her life a living hell.

If she could get one bit of confirmation, it would be enough to get her going. For the life of her, she had no clue how to get this affirmation. Then it occurred to her. Normally, if she had a problem or a bad day at work there was one place for both advice and solace: Tim. She would go to him once again and ask for his counsel. She figured that, if she was going to act insane, she would take it to the limit and ask her unconscious husband for guidance. She had nothing left to lose.

With this plan of attack in her mind, she went to bed. As her head hit the pillow, she remembered she still had the coin hanging around her neck. She contemplated taking it off but even that minimal effort seemed too much for her. She could not recall ever being so exhausted.

A few hours later, around three in the morning, she woke, terrified by what she had just seen. She sat up. She could feel her sweating body quivering in fear. Where had she been? Then she remembered the description Tim had given of his dreams. That's where she was! The difference was that Tim was there, too. And he told her something.

He spoke it in almost a whisper.

"Go back to April; it all began there, with him."

And then a terrific wind came out of nowhere. Tim reached for Anna but the wind carried him away. His screams were the last things she heard as she awakened.

Getting her bearings once again in her bedroom, she put her head back down on the pillow.

"Go back to April? Go back to April? What does it mean?" she repeated to herself over and over again.

Afraid of going back to sleep but still desperately needing it, she closed her eyes and eventually drifted into a fitful slumber.

. . .

The next morning, Anna awoke early and went back to her computer. First she reviewed her calendar. Then she looked at Tim's. Nothing significant happened in April. She thought back to that month, but there was nothing momentous or meaningful that Tim would highlight.

I am going crazy.

She penned a note for Magda, who was still asleep, telling her she was heading to the hospital. In the note were directions to the hospital and an invitation for Magda to come there after she woke up and ingested some coffee.

Each time Anna walked into Tim's hospital room, she was shocked anew. Today, electrodes were attached all over his head. Parts of his scalp had been shaved away to allow for direct contact with the skin. Phil said they were going to measure brain activity over a period of time. As a result, Tim looked hideous.

What she did during her visits varied. Sometimes, she just sat there holding Tim's hand, looking at him and stroking his hair. Other times, she pretended he could hear her as she told him what was going on in the world or in her life. Since most of her waking hours were spent in this hospital room, there was not much to tell but that did not stop her. She would make things up just to keep the conversation, such as it was, flowing. At least this time she could tell him about Magda's arrival. Tim always got along well with Magda and maybe the sound of her name would elicit a response. Anna would convince herself that the flicker of an eyelid was a reaction to something she had said. It was not much, but it did offer her hope.

Today was going to be one of those days when she would look for a response, anything to let her know that she was going down the right path. On one level, she knew this was downright insane. The image of her grandmother back in the old country came to mind.

Anna was very young when she left Czechoslovakia with her parents to move to Canada, leaving her grandmother behind. In Anna's eyes, the old woman could do no wrong. She was perfection, an ideal to strive for.

However, both distance and Anna's maturation process clouded the enthralled view she had when she was young. She did not love her grandmother any less, but now she saw her somewhat differently. There were certain things about her grandmother that were not quite normal.

Some of her grandmother's behaviors, things that Anna had not previously noticed, or perhaps had chosen not to notice, now made her cringe. When they would talk on the telephone once a month and her grandmother would make an anti-Semitic remark, it set her teeth on edge. Things like that. Her grandmother was Old World. Anna was now viewing life through a modern, Western set of eyes.

She disapproved of her grandmother's comments, but she would never say anything. She had been brought up to respect her elders. As such, she always treated her grandmother, the matriarch of the family, with a great deal of love and esteem. The bond they had before, though, was altered. She sometimes regretted that she had 'wised up' on this and many other issues. All part of growing, she supposed.

Sitting at Tim's bedside, the particular idiosyncrasy of her grandmother's that popped into mind was that, since the death of Anna's grandfather over a decade ago, the old woman had become a professional griever. She and a group of similarly situated widows had gotten it into their heads that they had a mission to pray for the departed and to comfort those near to them.

Each morning after mass, the women would gather in one or the other's kitchen and peruse the obituary section of the local newspaper. Over coffee and pastries they would narrow the list down to a handful of those notices that they felt were worthy of their attention. Then they would debate about which of these souls would most benefit from their prayers and intercession. Having even the remotest acquaintance with the departed was not a prerequisite for making their final decision. The most important criteria included the person's profession and where they lived. A job that might potentially have had criminal connections was more in need of intercession than a simple clerk. Likewise, a person who had lived in a less reputable part of the city was given the benefit of the doubt that his or her life was also disreputable. A soul was therefore in danger of descending into hell unless the women made their services available without delay. Of course, it went without saying that the person had to have been a baptized Catholic. For all others, there was no need to bother; the women would just be wasting their time.

Once this arduous selection process was completed, the breakfast pastries consumed and the final decision made, her grandmother and friends would gather their belongings and head out to the wake. Once there, they would practically assault the deceased, often elbowing other mourners—people who were related or had some real connection to the departed person—aside as they surrounded the coffin.

They would then go into their mourning ritual. Citing qualities the lifeless body assuredly possessed when it was alive, they would plea to God to accept the soul into His bosom. This praying, wailing and lamentation would often last hours, to the astonishment of the onlookers. Knowing that their intentions were good, the family would not make a fuss. On those occasions when someone dared to lodge a protest with the pack of ladies, it was met with withering glances and reproaches. The person was advised that, if he or she cared that the soul of the deceased go straight to heaven, the women should be allowed to continue unabated. Scorned and chastised, the family member would return back to the true mourners for consolation and reassurance.

After the women made their opening prayers, a good part of the remaining caterwauling would be dedicated to asking God to send them a sign that He had indeed heard them and would intercede on the soul's behalf. The mourning would continue until a sign was received or the ladies tired themselves out. They most often received a sign, mainly because almost anything could be accepted. A gust of wind when a door was opened, a fly alighting on the nose of the corpse, a sneeze that was accompanied by a 'bless you', a shift in the sunlight through the blinds so that the deceased's face was illuminated: these all were accepted as valid indications God had heard their plea.

In those rare instances where nothing happened and therefore no sign could be discerned, the ladies accepted defeat with grace and equanimity. They were certain that, even if they were not successful in transmitting this particular soul to heaven, they kept it from the fiery clutches of hell. Their untiring efforts had at least bought purgatory for the poor wretch lying before them.

The one sign that Anna's grandmother talked about as her crowning achievement happened about three years ago. A 23-year old construction worker had died in a terrible accident, crushed to death by a heavy piece of machinery. His face and body were mangled, but the undertaker did an admirable job in making him presentable. Getting this fresh young soul to Heaven was to be a special challenge for the ladies. He was young and unmarried, so he had not had time to settle down and make a respectable life for himself. He was in the construction industry, which everyone knew to be rife with corruption and unsavory characters. He was working class and therefore lived in 'that' part of town. Their duty was clear.

They arrived at the home with their usual urgency and bluster, making their presence known to all. They began their routine and made their initial prayers. They had just begun their pleas for a sign when a wire that the undertaker had inserted to hold the young man's lower jaw in place came loose. The chin of the young man dropped and a rush of embalming fluid poured from the poor unfortunate's mouth. Instead of being repulsed, the elder gang practically danced. All the signs they had ever received or ever would receive taken together could not equal this one instance of God making Himself known.

Every time Anna heard the story, she was newly appalled by her grandmother's behavior. Here she was, though, doing the same thing, sitting by her unconscious husband's side awaiting a sign. A sign from whom, she was not sure, but she needed confirmation from someone or something that the lunatic path she was about to tread was the right thing to do. She was not sure if she would accept a fly on Tim's nose, but she figured she would recognize the sign when it came.

She did not know how to begin. She decided it was best to start talking.

"Tim...hon," she began hesitantly, "I was just thinking about when we first met. What I first remember about you was how quiet and serious you were. It took a while, but I got under that reserve and found the wonderful man underneath. You were intense, but never menacing. You also never were, and never are, judgmental. It's amazing that there were men who came into the club with such a superior attitude, like we girls were doing something wrong and they were pure and innocent. Here they were, there to get their jollies but looking down on me and the other girls for what we were doing. You didn't do that. I could see that you always treated everyone with respect and kindness. Believe me, it was appreciated.

"There were two things I remember about that first meeting. The first was that we were playing around during the lap dance. You kept looking at my face. Here I was sitting almost naked on top of you and you wanted to look into my eyes. You told me that every woman there has breasts and private parts and after a while they pretty much all look alike, but there was only one face like mine. That was what you were going to concentrate on. If nothing else, it was a great pick-up line.

"The second thing was that you thought I was too good for that place. You said that without even knowing me. You could tell it the first time you saw me, that I brought class to that dump. To tell the truth, I believed it myself but it was damn good money. I'm not ashamed of what I did; it was fun and didn't harm anybody. I am sometimes embarrassed that we have to make up a story of how we met. I can't tell my own mother or grandmother, for God's sake, about a period of my life. I know it's for the best. Not as many people are as open and kind as you are, but I still get a twinge of regret that I can't be totally honest whenever we meet somebody and they ask how we met.

"I don't know why I'm carrying on like this. I guess it's been playing on my mind. What I'm trying to say is that you are my love and my life. I knew it from day one and I am not going to let you go. I'm going to find the answer, whatever it takes. Dr. Mordecai is a good doctor. There's something a little strange and disconcerting about him but he's working so hard. I have a few ideas he'd classify as voodoo. Magda, I think, agrees with him. They're probably right. But if I believed that painting you with chicken blood and dancing naked around you in the middle of Grand Central Station would cure you, I'd do it in a heartbeat.

"I found the journal you were starting. I don't know why, but I have a feeling the key is in there somewhere. I need your help, Tim.

"I had a dream last night, your dream. I recognized the characters you described: the nun, the Roman, and the sailor guy. I saw the hundreds of almost transparent people, wandering aimlessly about. The one thing that didn't match your dream was that you were there, too. You told me I needed to go back to April. I don't know what you meant by that. What happened in April? I don't remember anything from then? What happened then? Please tell me.

"I always come to you when I need anything. That will never change. Please hear me, Tim. Let me know that I'm doing right. Who is Madame Fabienne de la Tour? Should I search her out? Tell me what to do. I need you, Tim. I need you so much. Don't leave me. Don't ignore me."

Anna's voice trailed off into nothing. Tears streamed from her eyes. There was no response. Nothing. Not a flicker of an eyelid. Even her grandmother would be hard pressed to come up with a sign.

Anna sighed. She leaned over to give Tim a kiss. As she did so, Tim's medallion, which still hung around her neck, clanged loudly on the metal railing on the bed.

"Damn this thing! Why the hell did you have to buy this fool coin?"

She took the chain off her neck. As she went to put it on the bureau beside the bed, it slipped out of her fingers and started to fall. The chain caught on Tim's IV tube. The medallion, the tarnished silver coin with a hole punched in it, was left dangling, swinging back and forth.

She started to reach for the coin but held back. Instead, she stared, her eyes transfixed. When the coin stopped swinging, the chain could no longer maintain its hold. The medallion dropped to the floor, releasing her from its spell, but her gaze still homed in on the blackened piece of metal.

"Wait, you said: 'Go back to April; it all began there, with *him*.' With him? You didn't say it began then. It began with *him*."

Anna's expression changed from doubt and anxiety to resolve.

She gazed at Tim, confident that she would not be deserting him. On the contrary, she would be helping him.

"Avril—French for April. You need me to track down the man who sold you this coin. It all began with the coin. Is that what you're telling me?"

Anna swore that from somewhere deep down in his subconscious, Tim gave her the most imperceptible of nods. She had received her sign.

"I will go back to Paris. I'll hunt down Madame de la Tour. I'll find out whoever or whatever it is that has its hold on you and make it let go by whatever means it takes. I won't let you down, my love."

15

Phil had been standing at the door this whole time. He turned away so that Anna would not see him. Tears were welling in his eyes. He gathered his composure and walked into the room to find Anna quietly holding Tim's hand.

"Hi, Jen, I mean hi Anna."

"Hi, Phil."

"Can we go somewhere and talk?"

"Yes, we should. There's something I need to tell you."

"Let's go get a cup of coffee."

On their way down to the cafeteria, not a word was spoken between the two. Anna had to figure how to phrase what she planned to do without sounding like she was a complete lunatic.

After they sat down, Phil started. "Anna, I have some disturbing news to tell you. We got some test results back on Tim and they are not good. I have to be honest. We're losing him. It's almost like a cancer is ravaging his body, but there are no tumors or other indications of a malignancy. His white blood cell counts are unaccountably way out of line, as if his body is mounting an all-out attack on this illness."

She looked straight into Phil's eyes without emotion. It was as if she was expecting this news.

"You still don't have any idea what this is, do you?" It was the first time she had used a tone that betrayed her impatience with the impotence of the doctors at Barton Medical Center. The tone was not lost on Phil.

"No, we don't," Phil responded, "I'd like to confidently tell you that we'll track this down, but we're no further along than when we started. Now, we're not sure how much time we have."

"Then I have to do what I can."

"Anna, I was listening and heard what you said when you were with Tim. You can't leave. Tim needs you to be here. I still have hope that he will come out of this and you have to be here for him."

Anna's eyes flashed. "How dare you think I would do anything that does not put Tim first and foremost?"

"I did not say that. But a jaunt to Paris? Now? I cannot understand what is going on in your head."

"Jaunt! You're way out of line, Dr. Mordecai. You act like you have all the answers, yet my husband lies lifeless in that room. Maybe you should come to France with me, for all the good you're doing here!"

"Think about what you're planning to do, Anna. I may not have the answers but I am not running around on some hare-brained mystical excursion. I admit that I do not know you that well, but I've seen enough to know that you are an intelligent woman who should know better than to run off half-cocked looking for some French woman when you are desperately needed right here."

She knew that this had the potential to spiral out of control, with things being said that neither of them meant. This man had been working night and day to find cause and cure. She needed him. In addition, her head told her that he was one hundred percent correct but her heart was irresistibly pushing her on. She had to defuse the situation. For one thing, time was of the essence. She had a lot to do, as did Phil. They could not waste time going back and forth.

She looked Phil in the eye and smiled.

"2004."

Phil slumped in his chair. The mere mention of the Red Sox' reversal of the curse, winning the World Series for the first time in eighty-six years and in the process humiliating his beloved Yankees, was enough to put any fan in his place.

"I'm sorry, Anna. I just don't want you to get hurt. You're so immersed in this you're losing the ability to think clearly. If you do not find any answers—and I cannot for the life of me see how you will—you're going to start feeling a responsibility that's not yours. If the outcome ends up being what none of us wants, I don't want you feeling a totally undeserved guilt for the rest of your life."

"You're talking as if Tim were already dead, as if you've given up on him."

"Not at all, and I hope you know better. It's just these new test results have thrown me. I have work to do here and I think your place is here with him as well. But I can't tell you what's in your heart. I'll just keep plugging here. I've called a couple more specialists, one bacteriologist and one neuro-chemist, to see if they can provide any insights."

"I do thank you for all that you've done. I can't explain what I'm about to do. Tim knows me, he'd understand. Besides, it'll get me out of your hair for a bit. Do you think I'm crazy?"

"Absolutely, but what a lovely world this would be if we could all be lunatics like Anna Harrington."

Anna smiled that smile that made dozens of men into putty and made children not only ready but willing to take their medicine.

"Thank you, Phil. You really are a darling."

"You're not escaping that easily."

Phil took his card from his wallet and wrote his home and cell phone numbers, his phone card number and the access code for his voice mail on the back.

He handed the card to her.

"You have no excuse not to call me every day. Give me the number where you're going to be. If you can't reach me, call my answering service. I'll leave messages for you there."

"You can count on it."

"Do you know what you're looking for?"

"I'll know it when I see it."

"I do believe you will."

•   •   •

"You're what? Going where? Now? Anya, we have to talk."

Anna was in for a sisterly lecture. Whenever her sister or mother used her given name, Anya, instead of Anna, she knew it was time for serious advice to be dispensed.

"This is not like you, going off irresponsible and half-cocked."

The words Magda used in her tirade were virtually identical to Phil's, but Anna did not react. She could and would give her sister leeway that she would not grant the doctor.

"You need to be here, Anya. I can't let you do this. I once talked you into doing something that wasn't you and I've felt guilty as hell about it ever since."

"I can't believe you still feel guilty about suggesting I strip. It may not have been me, but the dancing was a great experience. And, I never would have met Tim if it weren't for you."

"But Anya, flying to Paris when Tim needs you here? Please, think straight for a moment."

"Mags, believe me, I am thinking straight. It's something I have to do. I know you have my best interest at heart but I know what I'm doing; at least I hope I do."

"But Anya, you're acting like...like...me."

"Mags," Anna replied warmly, "I can't think of a better compliment you could ever give me. You'll just have to trust your little sister on this. I have no idea what I'm looking for but I feel it in my bones that this is something I have to do. Please support me, Mags."

Magda sighed. "You know I do. I'm always here for you. Since you feel you have to go, do you still need me here? I'm willing to do whatever you want but, to tell you the truth, I am a little worried about my job. I need to keep it. If this goes on much further, my boss's going to lose patience."

"Mags. You've already done so much for me. I can't tell you how much strength you gave me yesterday; the mere sight of you when I opened the door did wonders. Knowing that you'll drop everything at a moment's notice to be with me means the world. And to top it all off, you clean my house. You go back home to your job and Fred. That's his name, isn't it?"

"Oh yeah, Fred. That's his name, at least this week it is."

"I'll call you from Paris. Collect, of course."

"Make damn sure you do."

16

1148 A.D.

The waters were choppy. Although the sun shown bright in the azure sky, Atticus Tiompk knew a storm was approaching. It would be a rapid blustery affair that, in the end, blew itself out, inflicting little if any damage. His ship, a sturdy but unspectacular merchant vessel, The Bosphorus Maiden, had left port in this northernmost part of the Mediterranean Sea known as the Adriatic where she had taken on some unseasoned deck hands. He anticipated amusing himself watching them get in a panic over nothing.

Even if the storm turned out to be severe, Atticus would still be happier here on the water than on land. He had confidence in himself as a sailor and, although most of his mates were complete fools, a number of them were accomplished seamen as well. The vessel had a good chance of beating the sea even in the worst of conditions.

He also preferred the sea because he was totally ill-at-ease with other people. On a boat, he could do his duties and then separate himself from all human contact, spending hours at a time staring out to the vast expanse of the Mediterranean. On occasion, a new sailor would approach him while he was off on his own.

"You're Atticus, right?"

"What of it?"

"Nothing. Just wanted to introduce myself and pass the day."

"Well, you haven't yet, have you?"

"Haven't what?"

"Introduced yourself."

"No, I guess I haven't. I'm Ulysses."

"Charmed."

"Calm sea today, isn't it?"

"Seen calmer."

"You man the foremast, don't you?"

"Yup."

After a few more unproductive exchanges such as this, the sailor would retire and leave Atticus alone. The crew learned that it was better to let him sit and stare.

Whenever the Bosphorus Maiden made its way into port, Atticus usually stayed on board while most of the crew departed for rest, relaxation, and debauchery. He would help with restocking and outfitting the ship for its departure.

The ancient port city of Tyre, however, held a special allure for him. His first introduction to Tyre was when the Bosphorus Maiden transported knights of the Second Crusade into the city so they could launch a surprise attack on Aleppo, the heart of Muslim power.

The knights had commandeered the ship out of Greece in the name of Christendom. Atticus had no idea what was going on since the Crusaders spoke a strange language. His shipmates said that these Knights were on their way to defeat the infidels and reclaim the Holy Land for Christianity; it was an honor for their ship to be used in this way. Atticus did not feel honored, just put upon. Nor did he know what an infidel was. Once he got to Tyre, he went into the city to see for himself what the infidels were and why they deserved to be eliminated.

Walking through the streets of Tyre, he could not discern much difference between himself and these infidels. In fact, he found a great deal of similarity and kinship with these people. The merchants were ornery and brusque, like him. In his mind, there was nothing that demanded their extermination. They followed this relatively new religion, Islam, but, then again he was not fond of too many Christians.

He found that when he was in Tyre, it was the first time since he was a boy that he felt comfortable anywhere other than on the water. So, when the ship came into port, which was about once per year, he always headed into town.

He would go off alone, not telling his mates where he went or what he did. His fellow sailors made a sport of speculating as to his whereabouts. One theory was that he had a wife and kids somewhere in town. He would pop in just long enough to get her pregnant once again, give her the little money he had and be on his way. His shipmates thought that any wife of his would be more than glad to see him go after a day or two.

There was another widely held theory that Atticus was part owner of a white slavery ring. While he was in town, he would go to check on his holdings, making sure his partners were not cheating him. While they did not think Atticus bright or cunning enough for this line of work, it was more in keeping with his personality than him having a wife and kids.

They never did learn where Atticus went or what he did. They knew that, just as the ship was about to sail, he would rejoin them carrying a trinket or other decorative object that he bought to hang in his bleak quarters.

After returning from one such foray, a fellow sailor, Dimitri, wandered by and admired Atticus's latest purchases. He also noticed a bunch of coins strewn on Atticus' bunk.

"Win some money gambling?"

"Yeah, a little bit."

"What's that?" Dimitri was pointing to a coin that looked different from the rest.

Atticus picked it up to examine it and realized he had been cheated. This old, tarnished thing was worthless. "Why that bast," he started to blurt out but stopped himself short, "Some guy was short on cash. He gave me this as his IOU. I'll collect next time we're in port."

Dimitri laughed. "Yeah right, Atticus."

Atticus mumbled an expletive as Dimitri departed, laughing heartily.

Atticus was at least partially correct. When they returned to Tyre, he would look up that man to redeem this worthless piece of silver, with his fists. Until then, what the hell would he do with this thing? He came up with an idea: punch a hole in it and wear it like a charm. If he displayed it like a badge of honor, he could carry on with the pretense that it was what he said it was, an IOU. In addition, sailors were superstitious creatures. Many carried charms of some sort to ward off the evil spirits. He did not believe in spirits — either good or evil — but there was no harm, just in case he was wrong.

He pulled out an awl and drilled a hole just at the top of whoever's head it was on the coin. It took him awhile but he made it all the way through. He admired his craftsmanship as he noticed the hole went right through the eagle's eye on the back of the coin. He found a piece of twine, threaded it through the hole, and put it around his neck. Take that, Dimitri, you ass.

•   •   •

Over the next two months, Atticus slept fitfully and had disturbing dreams. He went about his duties and stared out to sea like usual, but he was unsettled by his nightmares. Nobody else seemed to notice that he was any more sullen than usual.

The choppiness of the water that Atticus had observed did not blow over. The new deckhands were correct to be frightened. Ten to twenty foot waves crashed into the side of the Bosphorus Maiden for three hours straight. The storm took her apart, board by board and mast by mast. She almost capsized on numerous occasions. Torrential rain and winds battered the poor craft. In the end, the experience of the crew was no match for the sea. It was arrogant to believe otherwise.

Atticus did what he could to keep himself alive and the ship afloat, but he was not going to get himself all in a dither like his shipmates. Maybe if he had realized that they had blown to within a mile of the eastern coast of Italy, he might have worked a little harder to keep the ship afloat. He resigned himself to his fate and settled down on the deck for the inevitable, but before he did so he grabbed a rope and secured himself to one of the few remaining barrels that had not yet been cast over the side.

In the ship's final minutes, Atticus Tiompk could not help but to burst out laughing. What struck him so funny was that two months earlier he had put a good luck charm around his neck, and now he was about to die.

On March 8, 1148, the Bosphorus Maiden succumbed, broke in two, and sunk to the bottom of the Adriatic Sea. Atticus was still laughing when he discovered that the barrel worked. For forty-five minutes the waves tossed him about like a rag doll, but he remained afloat. Then, as he bobbed down once again, filling his lungs with more seawater, his cheek was cut on a jagged rock. His arrogance re-emerged. He had indeed cheated the sea; he had made land.

He untied the barrel and started to stagger to shore when a huge wave hit him in the back, knocking him over. The undertow carried him back out and submerged him. He was too weak to resist.

In the coming calm and sunny days that follow a storm such as this, body after body of the Bosphorus Maiden crew washed up on shore. Each in turn was given a proper Christian burial by the local inhabitants of the region. The body of Atticus Tiompk was never found, nor did anyone think to look for it, not even the wife and two sons he left back in Tyre.

17

Anna heard the unmistakable tone of a European phone as it rang. She heard a click as the receiver was picked up.

"Allô?"

"Hello, René? This is Anna Harrington."

"Anna! This is surprise! How is Tim? You come to Paris again soon? There is much I have still to show you."

She melted when René spoke. The French accent of his excellent English was so charming. His kindness and generosity belied any stereotypes about the French people that she may previously have had.

"René, Tim's not well. He's doing very badly."

"What is wrong?"

"We don't know. I need your help."

"Anything, you tell me what you need."

"I'm flying to France tomorrow. I'll need you to help me track down the dealer that Tim bought a coin from, at a street fair."

"Yes, Tim did write to me about a coin he adds to his collection. This coin dealer has connection with Tim's illness?"

"I'm not sure. There are some things I need to find out."

"At what time will you arrive?"

"First thing Thursday morning, on Air France into Orly."

"The flight from Newark? I know it well. I will meet you. Where do you stay?"

"I still have to arrange that. I guess I'll call a couple hotels or go on the web."

"Nonsense, you stay with me, unless you are afraid of terrible scandal because you stay in apartment of single man."

"I don't want to impose. I'm asking a lot already and there may be a few other things I might need your help with."

"Do not be ridiculous! You stay at my place and that is that. For you and Tim, anything. I was to take two days to go and see my parents in Hyères. I will call them and say I go there later during the month. It is settled."

"Thank you, René. You're such a dear friend. I don't know how I'll ever repay you."

"I am sure to come to the States in next couple years. I will, how do you say it, impose on you then."

"It's a deal."

"You go now. You must pack and prepare, I think. I see you Thursday morning. Good bye."

"Good bye."

Anna did have a few things to take care of before she left. For one thing, there was her job. After missing the entire first week during Tim's illness, she had planned to go back on a part time basis. Two of the three doctors at the clinic understood. They told her that, as far as they were concerned, she could take whatever time she needed.

The other physician, Dr. Richardson, was in her opinion a son of a bitch. He was put out whenever she took a vacation. He let her know in no uncertain terms that the additional time she had just taken was uncalled for. Now that she was going to be gone yet again, she was sure he would hit the roof. Unfortunately, Dr. Richardson controlled the hiring and firing in the clinic. She was not sure how he would react but her attitude was that if he wanted to fire her, so be it. She was not blind to how good she was. If she were let go, a new job would come looking for her in an instant. She hoped they knew it, too.

To be on the safe side, she went into the office when Dr. Richardson would be out and asked to see Dr. Holt. He was a soft touch that Anna could finesse. She also knew that with him there was no need to provide a detailed explanation of where she would be going and what she would be doing.

Dr. Holt told her to take whatever time she needed. They would stumble along for a while longer without her. She hoped to be in the air by the time Dr. Richardson got word of it.

Now she found herself on a half-full plane heading to France. She was looking forward to seeing René again. The magnificent first impression he made on her in his full *Gendarmerie* uniform was still fresh in her mind.

When Tim had announced at the airport that they were to celebrate their anniversary in France, Anna was initially hesitant. She harbored all the stereotypes of the cold, aloof and rude French. René single-handedly erased these stereotypes in an instant. He greeted Tim as a long lost member of the family and then did the same with her, even though they had never met.

Deep in thought, she ate or drank nothing the whole flight. For one thing, she needed to figure out what to tell René and how to finesse what she presented to him. There were enough people who already believed she was daft; she did not need another.

First, they had to track down the coin dealer. She was able to find the receipt that the merchant had scratched out. It had a name, Gustave Avril, but nothing else. She suspected that he was not the most reputable businessman and did not want any detailed pieces of paper that could be traced to him if any tax or customs questions arose. Anna and René would have to locate him and then convince him that he was not in trouble. She was undecided whether it would be more effective to have René in or out of uniform when they located him. Maybe the uniform could scare the information out of him, if he proved reluctant to talk.

They had to act quickly. No matter how she tried to tell herself otherwise, Tim was slipping away. She could see it herself. Each day his eyes looked more hollow and withdrawn than the day before.

What in hell was she doing?

The plane skidded down the runway at Orly pretty much on schedule. René had promised to be there to greet her as she entered the terminal, but he was nowhere to be seen. She dutifully got in the line where her passport would be checked prior to entering the country. The line was about twenty people long, about a ten-minute wait. The entire time she looked around for René, but he still was nowhere to be seen. It was now time for her to walk up to the kiosk.

She was about ready to hand her passport and custom declaration document over to the officer to be scanned when a hand reached around her and took the passport from her hand. The other hand grabbed her arm. She was about to turn and protest.

"Excuse me madame, I'll take your passport. You'll have to come with me. Please, don't cause any trouble. Don't say a word."

It was René. She was about to greet him when she saw the serious, no-nonsense look on his face. He did not want her to say a word. She had no idea what was happening but it was best to comply. She let him lead her away through a side door to a passageway that would lead to the parking garage for the official staff.

Once on the other side of the door, René visibly relaxed and gave Anna a hug.

"What was that all about, René?"

"We talk in car."

He escorted her to his Citroën, not saying another word. Once they were out of the airport and on the highway, he spoke up again.

"Tim. How is he doing?" René started off.

"Not well. Not well at all. He has a disease that the doctors cannot diagnose. He is comatose."

"And you say you come to France to help him?"

"I know it sounds crazy, René. I think there may be some connection between Tim's illness and what we did in France."

René did not respond but was very deep in thought.

"René, what's going on? I feel we just acted out a scene from a Jason Bourne movie."

René weighed his words very carefully.

"I get to you just in time. If you did give your passport to the officer and he put it under the scanner, they will know you have entered France again and they detain and perhaps arrest you."

"Arrest! What on earth for?"

"You are wanted for questioning about the murder of Monsieur Etienne LaFleur."

"Murder! Who is Etienne LaFleur? René, I have no idea what you are talking about."

"This morning I see alert is, what is word, broadcast that there is evidence that ties you to the murder. It happen when you were in Paris three months ago."

"René, you have to believe me. I had nothing to do with this. Please believe me."

"I do believe you. But I call to get some information from the police. I know Inspector Archambaut, the officer in charge of the investigation. He is a very good police officer who will not stop until he solves crime. I speak with one of his assistants to get details. He say glass with your fingerprint found at the apartment of Mr. LaFleur on Rue de la Paix and he say witness identify you leaving apartment around time of murder. He also say witness hear loud argument about old coin."

"This is all preposterous. I have never met LeFleur or been to his apartment. I have no idea whatsoever how my fingerprints could be found there."

"Officer say they did get your fingerprints from FBI. Why would the FBI have your fingerprints?"

"It was a program many clinics and child care centers participated in with the State to help in cases of child abduction. The doctors and nurses volunteered to have ourselves fingerprinted so that if a child goes missing we will already be in the database so the police don't waste time if they find our fingerprints on something of the child's. I never imagined they could be used in something like this. Regarding the coin, Tim bought it from a Mr. Avril, not LeFleur. You've got to believe me."

"I do. Maybe we should go to the police station to straighten this all out."

"René, you're an officer of the law. I know you're obliged to turn me in, even if you do believe me, but I'm begging you not to. I think Tim is dying and if I waste even a day trying to fight this, we may lose him. Don't ask me why I believe this, because I don't know myself. But I can't ask you to do more than you've done already. You can get into serious trouble here."

René dismissed Anna's concern with a wave of his hand.

"We will handle that when it happens. Someone is going to much trouble to, what is word, is it implicate, you. We must find out why but first things first. You must find the coin dealer?"

"Yes, there was a market or exposition that Tim went to. I have a skimpy receipt with his name, but no address."

"He should not be hard to find."

"I also need to find out about a woman who died two hundred years ago."

"She does not have anything to do with Tim, I am assuming."

Anna found it so endearing when the Frenchman mixed up his tenses. "Yes, I think it may."

René cast a quizzical glance over at her while at the same time trying to concentrate on the cutthroat traffic of the *périphérique*, Paris's beltway.

"I am not going to ask how she connect to Tim. I trust you completely. Since I fell in love with you the first time I saw you, I am under your magic. I must say yes to everything you want."

"René, you are so French but I think you have some Irish in you, too."

He looked puzzled but pressed on.

"Let me take you to my place so you get some rest."

"Only if you're sure. I can stay at a hotel."

"No, they may work with FBI to track your credit cards. You stay with me. Nobody knows that way."

"Okay, but I can sleep later. There's not much time to do what I have to do."

"I know good place for a café and croissant. We can sit and plan what we need to do."

"Thank you so much, René."

"*De rien, ma petite.*"

Driving through the streets of Paris, Anna made a conscious effort to pull her mind away from her current troubles as she noted yet again how beautiful, in fact how perfect, this city was. This was her third trip to Paris. Her first was when she was six and her parents were going through their messy divorce. Her mother, attempting to squeeze as much as she could into a week and a half to escape, or at least forestall, reality for awhile, packed up Anna and Magda for a whirlwind trip through Europe. In addition to Paris, they barreled through Vienna and Amsterdam, ending up in Prague where they visited with their grandmother. Because of the rushed nature of the trip and her age, she remembered little.

The second time, a few short weeks ago with Tim, was far different. She'd felt like she had found a second home. It was special because she was there with the love of her life. He was so enthralled with the city. They both were. Tim continually noted how the buildings of Paris, many of them well over a century old, were not only beautiful and but were still in full use. They were built to complement each other, the street they were on and the city as a whole. In New York, certain neighborhoods will have a distinct look and character. In Paris, the look was spread across the entire city. To an architect with any sense of perspective or appreciation of urban design, not to mention one who had an interest in history, this was a dream come true.

Anna could still hear Tim rhapsodizing about Paris as René darted and crisscrossed the city's side streets. Normally, she was a fidgety passenger, preferring to be at the wheel even when the best of drivers was beside her. Today, she was so lost in her reveries about Paris and Tim that she was startled when the car stopped and René opened the door to get out.

A few minutes later, they were seated in a dark booth at the bustling Brasserie Louis Philippe on Avenue Victor Hugo, not far from René's office. It was clear from the greeting he received from the restaurant owner that he was a preferred regular. It was clear from the greeting she received that she was in France.

She felt pangs of guilt at being excited to be back in Paris without Tim. She was on a mission, not a vacation. Still, the sights and sounds of the city enticed her. She took in the waiters in their black pants, white shirts, black bow ties, black vests and white aprons as they bustled about with arrogant efficiency. She marveled at the man behind the counter as he simultaneously dispensed four deep, rich espressos at a time while keeping up running conversations with waiters and customers alike. She gazed at her fellow patrons, lazily sipping those espressos and reading *Le Figaro* or *Paris Match* with a disinterested ennui invented and perfected by the French. She was amazed at how well put together even the most casually clad person was. She was convinced that the French person's ability to tie a scarf was genetic. Of course, since this was a hangout for locals, not tourists, there was not a sneaker or running shoe to be found.

Anna ordered a *café au lait* and a *pain au chocolat* while René went with a straight *café noir*. Then they got right down to business.

"I need to locate the coin dealer. His name is Gustauve Avril. I have no idea where he is located, whether it's in Paris or somewhere else."

"I do not think that Archambaut has found him yet, which may be good for us. I have a friend who works for the Paris Office of Licenses and Permits. I am certain the market must obtain permissions from that office. Anyone with booth will be registered. Isabelle will give me a list."

Anna smiled. "How would I have guessed that your 'friend' was a woman, René?"

He blushed a little bit. "I would not want that you are disappointed."

"Do you think she can get the roster to us today?"

"Yes, she is special friend." He blushed a bit more and they both burst out laughing.

After regaining his composure, he continued. "Now, who is this two-hundred-year old woman?"

"Actually, she died over two hundred years ago. She'd be closer to two hundred seventy now."

"*Bonne anniversaire!*" he joked, "Tell me of her."

Anna went into an abridged discussion of Tim's dreams and the mention in his journal of Madame de la Tour. She revealed her "theory" that somehow this dead woman had a hold on her husband. While in Paris, Anna would get as much information on this woman as she could. The whole time she was talking, she kept a close eye on René's face to look for any facial gestures of disbelief. She was shocked when she finished and handed him the Internet description of Madame de la Tour that his expressions were unchanged throughout the story telling. She paused and waited for the skeptical remarks or the patronizing attitude about "the pressure that poor Anna was under." When this was not forthcoming, she was the one who questioned her own credulity.

"You seem to believe what I'm saying. You don't think I'm stark raving mad or a bad person for leaving my husband to run off on a fool's errand?"

"I am not familiar with the American expressions you use, but yes I believe you. And even if you are mad, I help."

"Why?"

"I owe Tim my life. He save me."

"He did? He told me you were very supportive of him when his father died. He never said anything about saving your life."

"It was on lake. I am with Tim and his father. A violent storm did begin and boat, what is word?"

"Capsized?"

"Yes, capsized. Tim's father knocked out and carried away from boat. I start to drown when Tim grabs my shirt and pull me to boat. Tim swim for father but winds too strong. We cling there for hour, maybe more until another boat come our way."

"I never knew."

"But even if Tim not save my life, I help you. You want know why?"

"Absolutely."

"First, I am a member of the *Gendarmerie*. I hear many stories. There is no person who tells a better story than someone who does not want to go to jail."

"Gee, thanks. You're equating me with criminals trying to save their skins."

"I think that lose something in translation. What I mean to say is that I recognize the people who believe what they tell to me. You are a person like this, Anna. Also, when I say I fall in love with you from the first time I see you, I half joke. I am, how do you Americans say, 'party in your hands'."

"Putty. The phrase is 'putty in your hands' unless you mean party, in which case I have to remind you that I'm a married woman."

René smiled.

"I like my translation better," he said with as much mock sincerity he could muster. "You I trust. What you ask me to do, I do."

"Why? In all honesty, you barely know me. The first time we met was when I came to France on vacation."

"*Au contraire*. I know you very, very well. Remember, I am a police officer. I make quick judgments about people. Hundreds of people might hurt if I am not correct in my judgment. I make, what is word, assessment of you when we first meet. You are genuine, kind person. You are loved and you love. The French, they appreciate this. You have a, I do not in English, a *joie de vivre*."

"It's the same thing in English."

"Ah, *très bien*! Remember, I correspond with Tim for long time. It is difficult for him to write a letter that he does not talk about you."

"I don't know what to say, René."

"Say nothing, then."

"Do you think I'm crazy, running to Paris when Tim is so ill?"

"*Peut-être*. Maybe if you are, then I say *viva l'insanité!* Now, about Madame de la Tour, there is one person to see."

"Who's that?"

"Oncle Pierre, of course. I call him this afternoon."

"Your uncle?"

"*Bien sûr!* He is family expert on *la Révolution*. He is national expert. He works at research in the *Bureau d'Histoire*. He has an office at the *Conciergerie*. That is where they the people were found guilty and put in prison before they went to the *Place de la Concorde* to remove their heads. If anyone will learn anything about this aristocratic nun, it will be Pierre Bouvil."

"You can talk to him today?"

"Yes, my father talk to him day before yesterday. He is to stay in Paris for a week to finish a project. I will talk to him now. You realize that when I tell him I need information for a pretty lady, he will demand to have dinner with you. I warn you, when he begins to talk about *la Révolution*, he will not stop."

Anna laughed. "I trust you will be along to protect me from your dreaded uncle."

"Oh yes, I will be there, but my powers are not of use around Oncle Pierre. If I say three words during the evening that interrupts his conversation on the revolution, he will consider it a big triumph for Louis XVI and Marie Antoinette. No, no. That must not happen. Now, you are looking exhausted. I will drive you to my apartment and then I get to work."

"I am tired. Can I use your phone? I need to check on Tim. I'll reimburse you, of course."

"You insult me, *madame*. My home is your home. No more such talk. Anyway, I cannot think of French translation for reimburse. Use what you like. I let you sleep. I come back in the afternoon to let you know the information I have found."

"Thank you, René. I cannot tell you how much this means. Just during this time we've been sitting here, you've been able to make me forget for a little bit the hell I've been living. Thank you."

"*De rien*. We French are famous for our warm hospitality to Americans, *n'est-ce pas*?"

Anna noted the twinkle in René's eye as he mocked himself and the stereotypical French snobbery. Thinking of the wonderful friend René was and how at home she felt with the French, she responded without a trace of irony, "Yes. Yes, you are."

18

René dropped Anna in front of his apartment building and proceeded on to his office.

Her first impression upon entering his third floor apartment was that it was a typical three-room bachelor pad. The furnishings and artwork had a dorm-room feel to it. Anna was relieved that there were no paintings on black velvet hanging anywhere; Tim had remarked how big an Elvis fan René had been in high school. The kitchen was stocked with the basic pots, pans, and utensils, but not much more. She appreciated his partially successful attempt at straightening and cleaning the place.

She was dog-tired and needed to get some sleep. She was to sleep in his bed while he used the fold-away sofa. On this, René would accept no argument. As she entered the bedroom, her eyes opened wide. Whereas the other areas of the apartment had dreary fake-wood paneling on the walls, these walls were painted a beautiful powder blue. The bed was queen size with a modern European teakwood design with matching bureau and end table. Several geometrically-shaped vases and statues were placed throughout. On the walls were a variety of Paris street scenes. The real work of art, though, was the large picture window through which was an unobstructed view of the *Tour Eiffel*. The bed was located so that René and (fill in the blank) could lie in bed and gaze at the tower. It must be quite some sight at night when the city is all lit up.

Anna went over to the phone. Before falling asleep, she needed to check in with Phil. René had given her instructions on how to dial the United States. She was hesitant to pick up the receiver, partially from her hatred of the telephone, partly from fear of the news she might receive, and partly from the shame she could not shake that she had deserted her husband when he needed her most.

"Hello?"

"Hi, Phil."

"Hi, Anna. How's the research going?"

Anna was offended by the way Phil said "research" but she was too tired to make a fuss; so she let it pass. René had put her in a positive mood for the first time in days and she was not going to let Dr. Philip Mordecai's superior attitude diminish it.

"Okay. How's Tim?"

"No change. The latest tests aren't any worse than the last, but they're no better, either. When do you think you'll be coming back?"

She knew what he felt like asking was when she would end this foolishness and come back to reality.

"I'll know better by this evening, but it should be only the matter of a day or two."

"Good. Did you hook up with your friend?"

"Yes, I'm calling from his place. I gave you his number before I left. He's going to be a big help. He has many contacts."

"I contacted a couple more specialists. After I described the case to a Doctor Tierney, he said that he was involved in a similar case three years ago. He was not the primary physician but he worked closely with a doctor out in San Francisco who used some experimental drugs that seemed to work. It might be a promising lead. Dr. Tierney was a little fuzzy on the details and would look at his notes and talk with the doctor in San Fran. He also wanted to follow-up to see if there were any long term effects of the drugs."

"That all sounds very positive, Phil."

"I hope so. How are you holding up? You seemed at the end of your rope before you left."

"I'm exhausted. But if I keep getting little snatches of hope here and there, I can keep trudging on."

"Well, even if you don't find anything, maybe getting away is what you needed."

Again, Anna was offended by his tone, but she didn't think that Phil meant anything by it, at least not consciously. Anyway, it was tough to argue with his position.

"Well, I'm going to get some rest now."

"You take care and remember. Call me anytime, anywhere."

"I will. Good-bye."

She hung up and got ready to go to bed. Her head hit the pillow but sleep did not come right away. Her mind was racing from Tim to LaFleur to René to Phil to Madame de la Tour to Oncle Pierre. She had so many questions and no time to answer them. Finally, exhaustion overtook her.

After what seemed to be a few minutes but was actually two hours, René was shaking her awake. He was excited.

"Anna. Wake up! I find the coin dealer."

She groggily opened her eyes and for a few seconds had no comprehension where she was or who was shaking her out of her sleep. Gradually the whole situation came back. France, René, Tim, coin dealer!

"That was fast. Where is he?"

"In the city. In Montmartre. My friend locate him and I telephone to him."

René paused to regain his breath. Anna could tell how excited he was by the extent his English had slipped.

"I do not identify myself as police officer or tell him what I want. I not want to scare him. If he maybe think something wrong with sale, he might run. He appear friendly but he say he to leave the city in two hours. He goes to the south for a month. We need to leave now if you will talk to him."

"Give me two minutes to throw some clothes on."

A few moments later they were back in the Citroën racing along the streets of Paris. Montmartre was about two and a half miles away. René took out a blue emergency light and placed it on the dashboard to help get through traffic. Normally, he was reluctant to use these devices unless there was a real emergency but he could not let her down. They made the distance in less than fifteen minutes.

Driving up to the address René had written down, they saw a properly dressed, rail thin tall man with gray hair and razor-thin mustache closing up a shop and starting to walk away. René shouted after him.

"Monsieur Avril!"

The man turned around, but kept walking. René walked after the man and yelled to him in French.

"Je m'appele René Bouvil. J'ai vous parlé plus tôt." ("My name is René Bouvil. I spoke to you earlier.")

"Je suis desolé. Je ne peux pas rester à la conversation. J'ai un train à la prise." ("I am sorry. I cannot stay to chat. I have a train to catch.") He yelled back as he kept on walking.

"Ceci devrait prendre un moment." ("This should only take a moment.")

"Je suis desolé. Au revoir, monsieur." ("I am sorry. Good day sir.")

René, who was practically running by now, pulled up next to Mr. Avril and showed him his official identification.

"Non, monsieur. C'est moi qui est desolé. Il y a quelques mois, vous avez vendu cette femme une vieille pièce. Il peut y avoir eu quelques irrégularités avec la vente. Il faut que nous parlons. Nous pouvons aller au station ou nous pouvons parler ici dans la magasin comme des gens normals." ("No sir, I am the one who is sorry. A few months ago, you sold this lady an old coin and there may have been some irregularities about the sale. I need to talk to you. We can all go down to the station or we can just go back in your shop and talk like normal, civilized people.")

Mr. Avril, who was ashen, balked slightly.

"Irregular? Il n'y a rien irregular! Et je doit faire un train pour aller à Lyon ce soir." ("Irregular? There is nothing irregular! And I have a train to catch to be in Lyon this evening.")

"Si nous parlons ici, je vous conduirai personnallement à la station de train. Si nous devons aller à mon bureau, il y a une belle station de métro deux blocs loin. Vous devriez pouvoir attraper demain pour entrainer." ("If we talk here, I will personally drive you to the train station. If we have to go down to my office, there is a very fine Metro station two blocks away. You should be able to catch tomorrow's train.")

Mr. Avril sighed and reopened his shop. They went in.

"First, I understand that you speak perfect English so, for the sake of Madame Harrington, I request that we speak in that language."

"Of course. I apologize for my abruptness before. You mentioned irregularities?"

"Yes, there is reason to believe that a coin that you sold to Mrs. Harrington and her husband may have been stolen."

"Stolen! I never..."

"No one is accusing you, sir. We need some background on where you did receive the piece and any information you may have. Mrs. Harrington, you have the coin, do you not?"

"Yes, here is it." Anna pulled the coin and its chain out of her purse and gave it to René who in turn handed it to Mr. Avril.

"Ah yes, I remember this piece. A Shekel of Tyre; the tetradrachm; very old and quite rare. The image of the god Melqart on one side and the standing eagle on the other. It is coming back. I sold it at the exposition." Mr. Avril was looking very pleased with himself.

"Yes, well, do you have the records of where this coin came from?"

"As I mentioned, it's the Shekel of Tyre and comes from the area that is now Lebanon. It dates from the time of Christ."

"I mean," René interrupted, "you personally, where did you get it?

"I am sorry. Coins are my life and once I begin to speak about a rarity such as this; it is hard for me to control my enthusiasm. I do not need my records since I remember perfectly well from whom I did receive the coin. I had it a very short time. Even though I am familiar with this particular coin, I did not have the time to research the piece. I am sure that I did not get anywhere near its worth. But I was too busy preparing for the exposition and I gather things together to sell there, including this coin. It is quite rare and I might not have done as well as I could have. The hole in it has unfortunately reduced its value. If it is more valuable than the price I sold it to you, *c'est la vie*, as we say here in France."

Anna and René exchanged a glance. They both sized up Mr. Avril as a shrewd businessman who was aware of the value of anything he bought or sold, but it was not in their interest to contradict the Frenchman.

René attempted to speed up this process.

"Monsieur Avril, your train?"

"Oh, yes, yes. I purchased the coin from an old friend, Etienne LaFleur. He specialized in purchasing estates and then reselling the various pieces of those estates to specialty dealers such as myself. His goal was to buy the estates and then parcel them out as quickly as he can. Otherwise he was paying for storage and insurance. He did not do a lot of research but I can assure you that Monsieur LaFleur was a scrupulously honest man."

"You talk about him in the past tense."

"Yes, unfortunately Etienne was killed a few months ago. It was a couple of days after he sold the coin to me. I miss him very much."

"LaFleur was the man who was killed and then made to look like a suicide, correct?"

"Yes, his killer has still not been arrested."

"Do you know where Mr. LaFleur obtained the coin that he sold to you?"

"In many cases, I do not know precisely where Etienne obtained a certain coin he is selling me, but he did tell me on this occasion because he was very happy to help out a convent in St. Denis, just north of Paris."

"My parents did move to St. Denis when I was twelve, so I know the city well, but I do not know a convent. Do you have an address of the nuns?"

"I think they are not too far from the *basilique*. Remember, they are a secretive, withdrawn order, so they do not have sign out front. They are known as the *Ordre de la Tour*."

Anna and René sat forward in unison with the mention of this name.

"One more thing, did you happen to contact Mr. LaFleur before his death and tell him you had sold the coin?"

"As a matter of fact, I did."

"And did you mention who you had sold the coin to?"

"You know, I did. I knew that Etienne relished such information. He liked to know where rare items ended up; they were like family to him. If I remember correctly, I gave him Mr. Harrington's name and that he was American. I think your husband had told me you were staying on *Île de la Cité*. I passed this information on to Etienne. Did I do something wrong?"

"No, monsieur. We are just trying to put together a puzzle. Thank you, Monsieur Avril. You have been most helpful. Now, let me get you to your train."

"I am afraid it is too late. I unfortunately left no time to spare. The train leaves in ten minutes and we are at least as many minutes away. As I said before, *c'est la vie*. Can I make us some tea?"

"Wait one minute."

With that, René stepped outside the shop. Anna could see him talking on his cell phone. A few minutes later he returned.

"Shall we go? Your train is waiting."

"But it is to leave as we speak. We are too late."

"I have a friend who works for the SNCF." René winked at Anna, knowing that she realized it was a female friend. "Your train is being unavoidably delayed a half hour. You should have plenty of time."

"You can do that?"

"Who knows? But we will not find out if we stay here."

After they dropped Mr. Avril at the station, Anna mentioned the obvious.

"You heard the name of the order. You don't think it can just be a coincidence, do you?"

"I never believe in the coincidences. And now we know how whoever killed Mr. LaFleur found you. LaFleur must not have divulged the name of his friend, Avril. Otherwise I think he may have been visited as well."

"What would you have done if Mr. Avril had not been as cooperative and called your bluff about bringing him down to your office?"

"I think of something, but I do not think that would be necessary. He is a respectable person who wants to cooperate. He is also businessman. He knows an officer can always find something—an omission of the collection of taxes, for example—that can get him in trouble. Better to, as you Americans say, "play ball" and maybe these slight "problems" will not be noticed. He does not know that I have no interest in his business operations."

"This is all coming together."

"Yes, our luck is good; let me call Oncle Pierre and see if he has anything."

During the sixty-second conversation, René's entire contribution to the conversation was: one *'Allô, Oncle,'* five *'d'accords,'* and one *'au revoir'*. He ended the call.

"As I predict, we will not escape. He did find out something about our favorite Sister but would not give information over the phone. Oncle Pierre wants dinner with us tonight. He wants dinner with you but he say he would allow me to come as well. He wants that we should meet him at eight thirty at his favorite restaurant, a little Basque place in the Marais. Okay?"

Feigning annoyance, Anna responded, "I do have to eat, I suppose. But I'll go on the condition that you are there to chaperone."

"Believe me, this you will need."

19

1778

It was a perfect cloudless late morning in the tiny fishing village of San Paolo, a collection of small wooden shacks with a dirt street running through the center, located on the eastern coast of Italy. Many of the boats were out, attempting to land their catches in the Adriatic Sea.

Two women walked along; one carrying a child on her hip, the other a basketful of produce. A two-wheeled sturdy wagon, filled to overflowing with various vegetables, pulled by an ancient draft horse slowly trundled its way along. The wagon's driver was Vito Callucci, a white-haired mustachioed stooped man with weathered skin and permanent squint lines from being out in the sun much of his life.

"Hello there, Vito! You're a bit late to be running to market, aren't you?"

Vito looked up to see a much younger man, Pietro Fratelli, calling to him. Pietro was tending his small garden plot on the edge of town. Vito stopped the wagon.

"Good morning, Pietro. This is my second run today! I've never seen the market this busy. You have anything you'd like me to sell for you?"

"No, not today. I've got another week before these radishes are ready. I'll have some carrots for Friday."

"Where's Guido?"

"He's diving, with his friends."

Vito gave Pietro a disapproving look, tsking a few times.

"Diving? He should be here helping you. That's where he should be! You can't manage all by yourself. A son's place is by his father's side, especially if the mother is no more! How old is Guido?"

"Twelve."

"Twelve is almost a man. He should be here, living up to his

responsibilities, not idling his days away doing childish things."

"But he enjoys it so."

"You coddle that boy way too much. He needs a firm hand at that age."

"But his diving has helped. You remember the pearl he found just last year?"

"Of inferior quality, wasn't it?"

"But a pearl nonetheless. My mistake was not taking it to Bari to sell it. You can always get much more in the city."

"And another thing about his diving. You've heard that Father Dominic is telling people he believes the boy is possessed. Nobody can stay under water that long without assistance, divine or the other. Since Guido doesn't seem to be blessed, Father Dominic is convinced it must be the work of the devil that allows him to go so deep and stay under for so long."

"Father Dominic is an old fool who has nothing better to do with his time than to gossip like a woman about everyone in town. All I know is that Guido has been a blessing to me since the day he was born, even though it took the life of my dear Sophia."

"If you won't make Guido do his part, maybe it's time you got yourself another wife who can produce you some more sons who will help. You're young now, Pietro, but someday you'll be old like me and you'll appreciate having the help around. That widow, Teresa, she has her eye on you. I can tell. You two would make a good match."

"Thanks Vito. I'll keep your advice in mind. In the meantime, your lettuce is beginning to wilt in this sun. And who knows? Perhaps Guido will find some treasure on one of his dives."

Vito smiled and shook his head.

"Perhaps, Pietro, perhaps. I will see you later."

Pietro waved as the wagon departed as slowly as it had arrived.

* * *

Guido and his friends were in the small skiff about a thousand feet from shore as Guido went over the side. His sole objective — as it was on all his dives — would be to retrieve something from the bottom. It could be a rock, a clamshell, anything to prove to his friends that he had indeed made it all the way down and back.

He would dive in and start straight for the bottom. This was his idea of heaven. He would look around and marvel at the schools of fish swimming in perfect formation. Often, he would complete his dive and come back up to the surface with air to spare. He would emerge to victorious cheers.

On this particular warm August day, Guido's dive was taking longer than usual. On the surface, the boys worried. Ernesto, the titular head of this little band, was concerned as there was no sight of his young friend.

Guido grabbed a stone from the bottom and began his ascent. Seeing the bottom of the skiff, he headed for the stern of the boat. He popped up through the surface.

Ernesto was the first to see him as he breathed again in relief. Guido held up the stone, his trophy proving he had made it all the way down. He climbed back on board, somewhat winded but otherwise fine.

The boys headed back to shore. Stefano and Arturo were rowing while Guido and Ernesto chatted.

"I don't know how you do it, Guido, staying under for so long."

"I don't know either, Ernesto."

"Ah, it's nothing special that he does. It's a calm sea. Hell, I could do it here," Arturo piped in.

"Right, Arturo. Seems to me you can barely stick your head under water without gasping for air."

Arturo ignored the barb. "Now, if Guido were to dive to the bottom of Shipbottom Cove, then I'd be impressed."

The skiff was about fifty yards away from Shipbottom Cove. Even from that distance, they could see the water churning about. The cove was at most thirty feet deep, but there was a strong current that eddied around, creating violent riptides. At the bottom were razor sharp crags. Boats had trouble navigating there, hence the name; a swimmer would definitely be overmatched.

"No, I forbid it," Ernesto countered. "The currents there are way too strong. Not even Guido could handle it."

"Of course if he's too scared..." Arturo challenged.

"I could do it, Ernesto. Let's go there right now," Guido replied defiantly.

"No, this foolishness has gone on too long. It's too dangerous. This is my father's boat and I say no!"

Guido loved Ernesto like an older brother but he could be such an infuriating mother hen. Guido brooded for a few seconds and then, without warning, he jumped over the side and swam towards the cove.

"Guido, get back in this boat. Now," Ernesto commanded. Guido kept on swimming.

They turned the skiff about and headed toward the Cove. As Ernesto had predicted, the current was too strong, making rowing impossible. The boys aborted the detour and aimed once again toward the shore.

After swimming less than a hundred feet, Guido made the frightening realization that Ernesto had been correct. The current was strong but even worse, it was unpredictable. One moment, it was propelling him toward the rocky shoreline, the next dramatically away. He felt powerless and was tiring by the second.

He shouted out, "Ernesto, help." But they were already too far away.

Guido's best chance was to do what he did best: dive. Perhaps by getting far below the surface, he could swim under the currents. Then he could feel his way along the rocky sea floor and work back toward shore. He hoped he could keep his orientation.

He filled his lungs and submerged, diving to the bottom. He felt his confidence increase as he started to grab onto the rocks. He was still buffeted by the current, but it was manageable. Within minutes, his hands started to bleed but he did not care. He was making progress. However, his entire concentration was on his hand over hand crawl; he did not notice that it was steadily getting darker as he moved along. He happened to look up and realized that he was in an underwater cave. He had been below the surface for many minutes and his gift was starting to fail him. No one will ever find me down here. I want to see sunlight again. Papa. Ernesto.

He mustered his last bit of strength and swam as frantically as he could. He had no idea which direction he was heading. He struggled for his life. At the precise moment he was sure he was going to die, his head broke through the water's surface and his lungs drew in glorious, but stale and musty, air.

Panting like a hound, Guido looked around, but everything was in total darkness. He was in an underground cavern. It took him a moment before he realized that he could stand, the water coming up to his neck. The panic of the moment was now replaced with a young boy's curiosity and feeling of triumph. Guido had conquered the cove! His gift had not failed him.

He developed a simple plan for getting out. Instead of following along the bottom, he would swim until the roof of the cavern met the water and then follow the top out to the open cove. Then he could climb up the shore and nobody would be the wiser. There were three things that kept him from venturing out. First, he was exhausted. He had nearly died and he knew it. He needed some rest. Second, he had to wait until the tide ebbed a bit. Third, he wanted to explore his new cave.

As he started to walk, the water grew shallow. He reached dry land and he sat on a narrow bank. He was disappointed to learn that there was not much to explore. What seemed like a huge underground cave turned out to be thirty feet in diameter with an underground lake in the middle. It was by no means spacious, but big enough for a small boy to walk around and not feel cramped. He wished he had a little light to help him in his search, but his curiosity would not be deterred.

After resting a bit, he began to feel his way around. He walked no more than six steps when he kicked something in the darkness. It sounded hollow as it rolled away from him. It was not a rock or stone, nor did it seem to be a shell. Getting down on his haunches, he felt around until he found the object he had booted. As his hands worked over the rounded smooth surfaces and his fingers found their way into various holes and indentations, he realized he was holding a skull.

Initially, Guido was a trifle downhearted thinking that someone had previously discovered his secret place. Then it occurred to him that this person had found his way in but could not get out. Whoever this was had died here on the banks of this underground lake. Instead of the first person to discover this cave, Guido would be the first to go in – and come out.

He rubbed his hand along the top of the skull, wondering who this could have been. Story after possible story swirled around in his imagination. Maybe it was a shipwrecked sailor. Maybe this mysterious underground visitor was a pirate on the run. If he was a pirate, maybe there was a hidden treasure. Guido's excitement swelled as he felt around the bank. His hands were already so cut and beat up he could scarcely feel anything at all. It was a sound of metal clanking across the stones that drew his attention.

He located the sound's source and picked up a coin. He could not control himself. There was indeed a treasure! He was sharing a cave with a pirate!

Guido stayed in the cavern for another hour or so, fingering and fondling the coin the whole time. He could feel the raised features of someone's face. The coin had a hole punched into it. Finding no additional treasure, it was time to return back to the world of light.

This time, his simple plan worked to perfection. With the coin securely stuffed in his trousers, he began his methodical swim out of the cave. The waters were calmer than they had been. He was soon out in the sunlight, swimming toward shore.

Ernesto was the first to see him. He jumped up and down waving and yelling for Guido's father. When Guido walked out of the water, Pietro fell to his knees and held his boy close.

"Guido, Guido, I thought I lost you. The whole village is looking for you. I ought to tan your hide, but I'm so happy you're alive!"

Guido said nothing as his father hugged him tightly.

"I'm sorry, Papa."

He looked over and saw Ernesto standing off to the side.

"Hi Ernesto!"

Ernesto came over to join in the happiness.

"Ernesto, Papa! I found a cave, an underwater cave! I found this in it!"

Guido pulled the coin out of his trousers and handed it over to Pietro while Ernesto looked upon his young friend with awe. Pietro examined the coin.

"This is silver; it could be worth a lot of money," Pietro noted.

"I don't want to give it up, papa. I found it in a secret place."

Guido could not look his father in the eye.

"I know, son. But this coin could buy us an a lot."

Guido looked up at his papa. A tear streamed down his cheek, but his papa was right. Papa was always right.

"Yes, Papa."

Pietro suggested that they take a ride into the city of Bari to see about selling it. They could not get much for it in the village, he explained. In the city there were always people willing to buy anything, and pay good money, too. Pietro also knew such a trip would be a reward for his son.

Guido's eyes lit up. He had never ventured out of the village. Going to Bari over five miles away would be an adventure. As far as he knew, Ernesto had been the only one of his friends to ever make a trip to Bari.

That night, Guido could hardly fall asleep he was so excited. He held the coin tightly in his hand as he drifted off. As he was sleeping, he brought his hand up to his chest, placing the coin over his heart.

The next thing he knew, Pietro was holding him, rocking him back and forth. Guido, disoriented and terrified, looked up at his father's face illuminated by candlelight.

"There, there, Guido," Pietro soothingly intoned, "you were just having a bad dream. Everything's going to be okay."

Guido, somewhat comforted, snuggled close to his father. He fell asleep in his father's arms.

.   .   .

Pietro and Guido wandered around the bustling market in the city of Bari, looking very out of place. Pietro asked several people where he might sell Guido's coin but they rebuffed him, too busy to answer his questions.

A pair of men, Philippe and Antoine, were standing off to the side, as the father and son worked their way through the market. Philippe walked over to Pietro.

"Excuse me, but you look lost. Maybe I can help you."

"That would be most kind of you," replied Pietro. "I am looking to sell this old coin. Would you know anyone interested in buying it?"

"You are correct, the City is the best place for that type of business. I may know someone who would be willing to buy this coin from you, and for a very good price."

"Then it is most opportune that I ran into you! Is this person close by?"

"Oh yes indeed. My associate and I would be most pleased to escort you to him right away."

"That is very kind of you. My son and I would like to head back home so we are not traveling the roads after dark."

"Then let's go. There's no time to lose."

The two men led Pietro and Guido around a corner into an alley. Convinced no one else was around, Antoine slipped behind Pietro, pulled out a small length of pipe and hit him over the head. He reached down and pulled the coin out of Pietro's pocket. Philippe grabbed Guido.

"Papa! Help!"

Clamping his hand over Guido's mouth, the two men hurried from the alley with Guido, leaving Pietro lying in a heap.

.   .   .

Philippe knocked on the door. After getting a response, he walked into an ornate dressing room where Guillaume de la Tour, the Count of Avignon, was sitting at his dressing table. A fashionably dressed man with a powdered wig, the count eyed Philippe expectantly. Philippe made a slight bow.

"My Lord. I have some wonderful news for you. I know how you revere antiquities and I was able to obtain this coin for you."

He handed the coin over to the Count.

"It has a hole in it."

"Yes, in which case it would make a wonderful medallion for you to wear."

The Count's eyes brightened.

"Or better yet, it would make a magnificent present for my wife. You know how she loves it when I give her things when I return from my trips. A fitting trinket for the Countess of Avignon to wear, don't you think?"

Philippe realized it was a rhetorical question. Guillaume de la Tour looked down and spoke without looking back up.

"And were you able to obtain anything else for me?"

"Yes, my Lord. He's in the bedroom. Antoine is keeping an eye on him. He's young and handsome, as you like them."

"Excellent!"

The door to the bedroom opened with a bang. Antoine staggered in, blood seeping through his fingers from a wound on his forehead.

"Antoine, what happened?"

"The little bastard, he hit me with a candlestick when I wasn't looking."

The count was fuming.

"And the boy?"

"He escaped, my lord."

"Out of my sight, both of you. I'll deal with you when we get back to Avignon."

20

Anna wanted to get another hour of sleep, shower and change clothes before their rendezvous with Oncle Pierre. René had some business to take care of so he dropped her off at the apartment and went on his way.

She was tempted to call Phil with an update, but his "research" comment still played in her mind. He was so dismissive of what she was doing. Not that she could rightfully counter his arguments. Facts and logic were definitely on his side. She would wait until tomorrow, after they had gone to the convent, to call him. Hopefully, at that time she would have a better idea when she could leave Paris. She wanted to be back home, with Tim.

At around half past seven René returned. Anna noticed something different about him. He seemed more reserved than he had just a few hours earlier. Anna guessed that something happened at work that preoccupied him.

René cleaned up a bit himself and they set off to meet Oncle Pierre. On the ride over, René didn't say a word. Parking was somewhat limited so René did a classic Parisian maneuver, with the car at an impossible angle substantially on the sidewalk.

"René, is something wrong?"

"We can talk about it later."

They walked into the restaurant, precisely on time. As they entered, they heard a bellow from the far corner as Oncle Pierre rose to greet them.

"Oncle, may I present my friend, Anna Harrington. Anna, this is Pierre Bouvil."

"Madame Harrington, it is indeed a pleasure. My nephew, I am afraid, did not do justice in describing how lovely you are. From his description, I was almost afraid of meeting you for fear that you might have some hideous deformity. I am greatly relieved"

"The pleasure is mine, monsieur. René is indeed a master of understatement. He also did not adequately prepare me to meet you."

"I think he may have wanted to keep you for himself, and you a married woman. That has never stopped my dear nephew before, I am afraid."

"Or his uncle?"

Pierre burst out laughing loud and long. "Ah, somebody who can give it out as well as take it. This shall be a splendid evening indeed. I have a tendency to—what is the word in English—intimidate many people. Look at my poor nephew here, I doubt that he will say a word the entire evening."

"Yes, Oncle, I am overwhelmed in your presence. Your light shines too bright for my eyes."

"See, again he misspeaks. When a lovely lady like Madame Harrington is in the room, that is the light that is shining. I do have to take this boy aside and teach him a thing or two about how to treat a woman, *n'est-ce pas*?"

"Oh, I have a feeling he does just fine, but it is always good to learn things from a master."

"Yes it is. Let us sit down and eat, drink and talk things over. I have taken the liberty of starting a bottle of wine. I like a full-bodied wine so I ordered a Cahors. Some people say that Cahors is too heavy for them. I once heard that back in the 1600's, when the Bordeaux region was just starting to produce wine, the wine there was rather thin and watery. They used to mix in Cahors to make it stronger. Now, Cahors is sort of a forgotten region of France, which is fine by me. This keeps the price from getting out of control. If you would like something a bit more refined, I am sure that can be accommodated."

"This shall be fine, monsieur. I like a nice hearty wine myself."

"I knew I would like this woman! Married or not, René, hold onto her!"

Anna was in for an evening in which every subject that seeped into the conversation generated a full-scale dissertation by Pierre Bouvil. She did not mind in the least. For one thing, she knew this was a French meal. One does not hurry through it like an American. Also, Oncle Pierre was fascinating, an expert on everything he talked about. She had sat through tedious dinners with blowhards who claimed to know a lot but, in actuality, they knew how to be a pompous ass but not much else. Pierre knew his stuff and was entertaining to boot. It was a nice way to spend the evening.

She glanced over at René. Pierre assessment of his nephew was right on the mark. René seemed overwhelmed by the older man. He was in awe of his uncle, but there was something else that Anna could not put her finger on. His mind was definitely elsewhere.

They ate their meals, which were delicious. Pierre made sure she tasted everything each of them had. She made a mental note to see if there were any Basque restaurants in New York when she got back.

When the waiter discovered that Anna was American, he practiced his shaky English on her, adding another positive note to the evening. Through the appetizers, main course, several bottles of wine, cheese and dessert, Oncle Pierre held court on a host of subjects. Anna was beginning to fret that they would never get around to the reason for meeting: Madame Fabienne de la Tour.

As if he was reading her mind, Pierre said, "So, you want to know about Fabienne de la Tour, also known as Sister Catherine."

Anna's worry was unwarranted. Pierre was not one to disappoint a pretty lady and soon he began to talk about Madame de la Tour. Of course, the conversation took frequent entertaining detours and side trips.

"François Guyot did his usual fine job in summarizing the life of Madame de la Tour. Did you know that I went to university with François? Of course you did not know. François is a brilliant man, but he is never one to go into depth on any one subject. The encyclopedia entry that you found on the Internet is a perfect example of what he does best. He finds out the main pertinent facts on a subject, writes about it very clearly for the layman to understand and then he moves on to the next subject. I do hope the English translation that you saw on the Internet did justice to his work; he is so exacting that he would be very upset if it is not.

"What he wrote about Fabienne de la Tour is entirely correct except there is more. That is why you come to me."

Pierre took a sip of his coffee and ordered another round for the three of them.

"You were saying there was more, oncle?" Except for the wine steadily disappearing faster than if two people were drinking it, Anna and Pierre could easily have forgotten that another person was also at the table. René had been that quiet.

"Ah yes, my nephew, never one to let the suspense build to an appropriate crescendo. Monsieur Guyot is correct about the rumors that Madame went to the guillotine. However, in his usual manner my friend does not go far enough. It is confirmed that she did in fact lose her head. It was October 3, 1794, a full year after she was arrested. That was quite unusual in those days. Justice was most often dispensed without hesitation. A trial of the people's court would render its guilty verdict usually within weeks."

"Why did it take so long?"

After asking this question, René returned to brooding.

Anna also noticed that he kept glancing over at a gaunt, dark man who was eating by himself at a table across the room. The man, it seemed, had a special interest in them as well.

"It does not say. Perhaps they were nervous about executing a nun. Perhaps all the good she was doing weighed on them. Even during those dark times, there were still a few men of conscience. It was a brutal era for the very poor people. She relieved suffering and did much good. I think maybe there was some argument for sparing her but, in the end, I do not think they wanted to set a precedent. For the greater good of the people, she was to be put to death, or something like that."

Anna was puzzled. "I understand that once they arrested her they had to go through with the sentence but why arrest her in the first place? If they had just looked the other way, she would have been able to continue her good works and they would not have been in that situation. Also, where was the church in all this? She was a nun. Wouldn't they have protested her arrest and execution?"

"I think you are correct. The authorities would have preferred to overlook her. Whatever wrong she had done as an aristocrat, she had more than made up for since then. However, it appears that she was turned in and from the evidence, it appears that she may have been turned in by someone from within the convent."

"Why?"

"That is not clear. The letters that are on file seem to point to, as you Americans say, 'an inside job'. As to the church, there is no evidence of any protest whatsoever. We can speculate why they did not do anything. It could have been that the church leaders were afraid to speak out. Not just the aristocracy was imperiled. It was a time of extreme enlightenment, which to many people meant it was a time to be against anything traditional. Nothing is more bound to tradition than the church. Maybe it was wise to, how do you say it, lay low.

"Another theory could be that Madame de la Tour, in her role as Sister Catherine, was not very popular with the church hierarchy. She did extraordinary things in improving the lot of the Parisian poor in a relatively short time. She made the church look bad, doing the work that they should have been doing all along. Or maybe she had some views that they did not agree with. They could not very well tell her that her work was too excellent, please go away. But when the State took her away, the church may not have been upset. Whether the church turned her in or whether it was someone else, we will never know. Perhaps another nun was jealous of her power and popularity. Politics are everywhere, even in a convent."

"Oncle, we are going to a convent in St. Denis tomorrow morning. The nuns there belong to what they call the Ordre de la Tour. Do you think this is the same convent?"

"I would not doubt it. They without doubt fled Paris to get away from the spotlight. It was a crazy time. Who knew when the knock on the door might come again? Maybe they would want to hunt down Sister Catherine's accomplices. People lived in fear during those days."

A question about the convent popped into Anna's mind. "Monsieur, the order started by Madame de la Tour concentrated on helping the poor, giving to those in need. The present convent is shut off from the world, devoted to contemplation. If it is indeed the same order, doesn't it seem a bit strange that they would change like that?"

"Not really. While a convent is a type of institution and you would expect institutional continuity over the years, it still is a function of who is in charge. A new mother superior may have come in at any time. Perhaps she believed that feeding the souls of her nuns, not feeding the mouths of the poor, is where they should put their efforts. Perhaps it was safer to be insulated rather than being out and about. Given what I was saying before about the church, it would not surprise me if the church authorities put a person in charge specifically to change the mission of the convent. Again, this is speculation but I would say yes, it could very well be the same convent."

"Thank you, monsieur. You have been most helpful. You mentioned that René understated my qualities. Well, he did the same to you. You are even more gracious and kind than he led me to believe."

"What will we do with this boy? His father and I have long given up on him finding a nice wife and settling down to raise a family. Now, if he met someone like you who was not already taken, I do not see how he could resist."

"You are most kind."

"Not at all. René told me something about why you are looking for information about Madame de la Tour. He advises me that you are on a quest to save your husband. I can see that you will not stop until you find the answers you are looking for. I wish you luck in your quest. I just have one small request."

"Anything, monsieur."

"If you find out any information on this remarkable woman, please let me know. This is what we old historians live for. Also, if there is anything more I can do for you, do not hesitate to call me."

"*Oui, monsieur. Merci.*"

21

As René walked Anna to the car, Anna grabbed him by the arm, stopping him.

"René, something is definitely wrong. Please tell me what it is."

René paused for a moment, as if trying to figure out how to phrase what he had to say.

"René, please tell me what's wrong," Anna persisted.

"I received a call from Avril. Archambaut track him down as the coin merchant LaFleur sold the coin. The Inspector call him in Lyon."

"What did Avril tell him?"

"The truth, or most of it anyway. He told him that you are in France and that he met with you. Mr. Avril appreciate that I stop the trains just for him so he did not mention to Archambaut that I am with you. At least that is what he said."

"So Archambaut knows that I am here," Anna stated the obvious.

"Yes, and like I say, the Inspector is a pit bull who will not let go. But he still has to find you."

"René, you've been such a dear but I can't let you risk yourself anymore. You could lose your career and possibly go to prison because of me. I'll go the rest of the way on my own."

"That is out of the question! I will help you get the information you need and I will get you out of the country before Archambaut finds you. I give you my word on that."

René said this with such conviction that Anna had no choice but to believe him.

.　　.　　.

At nine thirty the next morning, René and Anna were in front of the *Basilique St. Denis*. Nestled in a blue-collar community that had increasingly become home to a steady stream of Arabs from former French colonies, this was not a cathedral frequented by many tourists. She noted that it was indeed an impressive Gothic structure dedicated to Saint Denis, the first bishop of Paris who was martyred in the third century AD.

The convent, located on a small side street behind the *basilique*, was indeed a hidden secret. From the street all one saw was an ivy covered brick wall with a solid wooden door. There was no sign, no street number or anything else that would betray what lay behind the wall. René pounded on the door; there was no bell or ringer visibly available. After a period of time that made it seem like nobody was home, the bolt could be heard sliding over and the door opened a sliver. A matronly face surrounded by the white and black of a very traditional nun's habit poked through the crack. Not recognizing either visitor, she was reluctant to open the door. René flashed her his badge and told her that they needed to speak with the Mother Superior regarding the death of Mr. LaFleur. Only then did the nun agree to let them enter. She motioned for them to enter into the courtyard.

Without saying a word, she bolted the door behind them and started walking toward the main part of the convent. It was an unimpressive two-story stone building that looked as if the last work that had been done to it was when it was constructed at the end of the eighteenth century. While it was a bright, sunny day, in this courtyard the world had taken on a permanent dreariness. It seemed the nuns pulled themselves away from their contemplation long enough to keep the place clean, but that was about it.

Anna imagined the convent in Paris as it must have been when Sister Catherine was in charge. Her very presence filled it with life and joy. Anna could not understand how anyone could stand cutting themselves off from the world like this. Maybe there was a role in the world for this type of reflection, but is this what God wanted out of people who devoted themselves to his service? Wouldn't he prefer the nuns to be out using their talents to the fullest, doing good works that improve the lives of other people? Anna would never comprehend it.

Anna and René entered the main building. The dreariness continued as Anna noted the cracked plaster on the walls and ceiling of the entryway. A carved wood crucifix was the solitary adornment. There was not a single chair or even a bench in this part of the building. She imagined that they received very few visitors, so there was no need for amenities. Again, at least it was clean.

They were led to the room that Archambaut had occupied just a few days before. Anna rather liked the painting of Jesus delivering the Sermon on the Mount but had a feeling the eyes on the statue of the Virgin Mother were following her, judging her. As with Archambaut, the escorting nun motioned for them to take seats in the straight back wooden chairs around the large oaken table. She then departed, all the while not saying a word.

For five minutes they sat there, not knowing what to say or do, so they said or did nothing. At last, the door opened and the Mother Superior, accompanied by an attending novice came in. The Mother Superior wore a full starched black habit. The only exposed flesh were her hands and a dour, stern-looking face, encircled by a white headpiece, which had black draped over it. She was so enrobed that Anna could not for the life of her even venture a guess as to the color of her hair — or whether she even had hair at all. Who knew? Perhaps this order was so strict that they yanked their hair out once a year as a sign of their devotion. The Mother Superior's outfit and age were such that, if it were not for a downcast expression etched on her face, Anna half expected her to belt out "Climb Every Mountain" at any moment.

The novice, on the other hand, was lovely, although it was difficult to get a full view of her face. Her gaze remained permanently transfixed on the floor. She was in a novice's uniform so one could see her long dark hair, and what luxurious jet black tresses they were. They framed an oval, perfect face befitting a Raphael painting. Her skin had an unusual amount of coloring, given that it received limited amounts of sunlight.

Anna felt a pang of jealousy course through her veins. Ever since her days as a dancer she had compared her looks with other women. Back then, it was believed that coming out ahead in the beauty competition resulted in a bigger share of the money that men were willing to dole out over the course of an evening. Much later it dawned on her that men spent money on a particular girl not only because they enjoyed her looks but her personality and attitude as well. In the meantime, a primal competitive instinct took over and made her dislike dancers whom she thought to be better looking than she, not that there were many who fell into that category.

Anna believed she had matured a great deal since her dancing days, but on occasion she found herself reverting to her former self, comparing her beauty with another woman's. Sometimes she made light of her egocentrism, playing a game that she often shared with Tim as they walked through the mall or down the streets of New York. Almost always, Tim's (and her own) appraisal had her coming out ahead. This appraisal was inevitably seconded by other less biased opinions, gleaned from the looks other men gave her. Since she often fared well in this rivalry, it was a fun game that constantly stoked her ego. The one thing that was different from her dancing days was that, on the rare occasion that another woman was found to be superior, she gave the winners their due when she was beaten fair and square.

Now, for a moment, here in a convent, no less, she found herself regressing. She instantly sensed that this beautiful novice had bested her, and she was greatly bothered by it. In another time, another place, instead of training to become a nun, this beautiful woman would be a highly paid fashion model. It was a bitter pill for Anna's vanity to swallow. For a fleeing instant she felt herself back in the ludicrous beauty competitions she used to hold in her mind.

The two guests arose as Mother Superior Angelique introduced herself to Anna and René.

The novice was introduced as Marie. She raised her head briefly. In the few seconds that Marie's eyes were lifted, Anna's initial feelings were replaced by great warmth and sympathy for this young woman. Anna had been beaten soundly but, to her surprise, she did not care. Marie was even more striking than she originally thought, having the most piercing set of hazel eyes one could ever hope for, but there was more. Anna noticed a profound sadness and a haunted, haunting quality that made Marie even lovelier. She displayed a vulnerability that most men, and many women as well, would find irresistible.

Unfortunately, she looked back to the floor after the introduction. It was almost as if she was afraid of being stricken for insubordination if she dared look anyone in the eye for too long. Anna hoped that, once Marie became a full nun, she would gain some self-assurance.

Mother Angelique invited the two of them to sit down at the table. She occupied the chair at the head. Marie remained standing off to the side. Anna was amazed as she witnessed this caste system. She was tempted to show her solidarity and stand beside this untouchable, but she knew this would be inappropriate. In addition, standing alongside Marie would invite comparisons of beauty and Anna, not Marie, would come out wanting.

René had warned Anna that this whole meeting would most be conducted in French. He had no idea if the nuns spoke English, but he imagined not. In any case, he did not feel it appropriate to request that English be used. He would converse with the Mother and then translate for Anna.

"Thank you, Mother Angelique, for seeing us."

"You are welcome, but I already told everything I know to the other officer, Inspector Archambaut."

René and Anna looked at each other at the mention of the Inspector's name.

"Unless you are here to return the coin to us."

"No, we are here to discuss the coin and see if you have information on its origins or background, not to return it."

"It is our coin that never should have been included in the items to be sold. Sister Marguerite, who catalogued the contents of the chest to be sold and Sister Genevieve, who was put in charge of making the arrangements for the sale, made a dreadful mistake. The coin never should have been sold by Monsieur LaFleur, God rest his soul."

"I am sorry, but Mrs. Harrington bought it legally and is not willing to sell it at this time. It is her husband's coin and he is very sick right now. She would have to wait until he got better in order to obtain his permission."

"It is extremely important that it be returned to its rightful place, back with us, with the church."

Mother Angelique's voice trailed off and she lowered her eyes. She had been getting increasingly distressed; now she fell silent. Anna, who had been sitting on the opposite side got up and went around the table to sit in a chair beside the Mother. Anna took her hand.

"Mother Angelique, you know something about this coin that you're not telling us, don't you?"

The Mother looked to René, who translated. She nodded.

"Yes, but that is all I can say. Please, I must have it back before... before..."

After René translated, Anna responded.

"Before what, Mother Angelique?"

Without waiting for the translation, the Mother answered.

"I have said too much already. I have sinned greatly."

With that, Mother Angelique got up and hurried out of the room. Anna could see tears streaming down her cheek. Novice Marie stood in her place, uncertain what to do. Anna turned to René.

"René, I can't give it up. I need to learn everything I can about that coin. Don't ask me why, I don't know. Tim is..." Anna stopped before completing this thought. She was practically sobbing. "Tim's life may depend on me holding tight onto this coin. Don't ask me why because I don't know. Until I know what, if any, significance the coin has, it is staying with me."

"I know. I guess we should leave. I wish we could ask her about Sister Catherine. I believe she's connects somehow."

"So do I, but I don't think we can get anything more here. Let's go."

At that point, René, followed closely by Anna, got up from their seats and headed for the door.

They were halfway across the courtyard when Anna heard Marie call out, in English.

"Madame Arrington. Please stop."

René kept walking. "Anna, do not stop. Archambaut has been here. He might suspect you to contact the Mother as well. It's not safe to stay here."

Against his advice and her own better judgment, she stopped and walked over to Marie.

"Just one second, René, please."

"Madame Arrington," Marie said, "please let me know where you stay. I need talk to you. Alone."

Anna hesitated. René had already unbolted the door in the wall and was beckoning her to follow him.

"Please, Madame Arrington. Mother Angelique return soon. Trust me."

Anna gave her René's address and then headed out the door. As she was leaving, she glanced back but Marie was no longer anywhere to be seen. When they got to his car, they sat there for a moment and looked at each other.

"Well, what do we do now?" Anna asked as they climbed into René's car.

"This I do not know. We go back to my apartment to talk."

As René started to drive he pulled out his cell phone, hit a speed dial number and waited.

"*Allô Isabelle, je regrette*"

Anna put her hand on René's arm.

"René?"

He spoke into the phone, "*Pardon Isabelle. Un moment, s'il vous plait,*" then to Anna, "Yes, Anna."

"René, I don't speak much French but I know you're talking to Isabelle, who you mentioned was a "special friend" and I know that "je regrette" means "I'm sorry." Did you have plans with her this evening?"

"Yes, but we can do another time."

"No, I will not hear of it. I've imposed so much on you already to the point where you might go to jail because of me. I will not allow you to cancel your date."

"But Anna."

"No buts. You yourself said Archambaut is not aware of your connection with me. I will be safe in your apartment. At most, I may go out to the pizza place around the corner for something to eat. I doubt that there are posters up yet announcing to the pizzeria patrons that I'm a fugitive on the run. You will go out with Isabelle and that is that!"

This time it was Anna's tone that dictated there was to be no argument. René smiled and put the phone back to his ear.

"Isabelle, à sept heures? C'est bon. Au revoir."

They arrived back at René's apartment. He had several hours before he had to get ready for his date so pulled a bottle of rosé out of the refrigerator and poured a couple glasses for them to sip while they talked.

"You think this coin is very valuable?"

"I think it may be worth a lot of money, but I think there is something else that makes it very, very valuable to the nuns."

"How?"

"I don't know but there is something I haven't told you. I didn't because you'd believe I was crazy."

"You are crazy, so what?"

They both laughed.

"Since that's the case, I'll just tell you. When I put the coin around my neck, I had the same nightmare Tim was having: the same wasteland, the same people in costume, the same spirits of hundreds of other people floating around aimlessly. The difference was that Tim was in it, too. He tried to warn me. He's the one that told me to look for Avril. There's something with this coin. I don't know if it's a curse or something more scientific but I have to keep hunting.

"The key has to be Sister Catherine. From what we can gather she couldn't destroy it but she hid it away so nobody would find it. But somebody did."

"The novice, she speak to you when we did leave. What she say?"

"Nothing much. She wanted to tell me something but she couldn't there. Maybe we'll hear from her again. I don't know."

"She seem nice. And beautiful, too."

Anna laughed. "René, keep your focus on Isabelle."

"Ah yes! I should get ready."

As René prepared himself for his date, Anna tried to call Phil. All she got was his voicemail so she left a message. René emerged from the bedroom in black pants and a light gray pullover sweater.

"Very handsome," Anna cooed. "I doubt that Isabelle will keep her hands off of you."

"Let us hope. Are you sure you will be okay?"

"Yes, go. I'll be fine with some pizza in me."

"Yes, it is quite good but I warn you, you will have to suffer with Italian wine instead of French."

"Oh, the things we have to do. I guess I'll just have to grin and bear it."

22

Anna had no idea if the novice Marie would contact her that evening, the next day, the day after or ever. She sat in the apartment well into the evening, hoping Marie would show up. When it got to be nine, Anna realized she was starving and started for the restaurant. As she reached the downstairs vestibule, she found Marie standing on the sidewalk looking uncomfortable and out of place. Her eyes were in their customary position, locked on the ground in front of her. Anna noticed that she was wearing civilian, totally out-of-style, clothes rather than her novice uniform. She was also carrying a large purse that seemed very passé.

Anna opened the door and acknowledged Marie who nervously nodded in return. Anna wondered if she could get anything of much worth from the novice.

"Hello, Marie. I'm very glad you came. Are you hungry? I was about to get some pizza. Would you like to join me?"

"I will be in many trouble if someone see me."

"We are miles away from the convent so I doubt anyone would see you. If you would feel more comfortable just going upstairs, we can do that."

She could see Marie wavering but did not want to pressure her in any way.

"I have hunger. I so nervous to come here that I not eat all day. If you are sure no one recognize me, I have not eat a pizza in many years."

"Okay, let's go."

The restaurant was a small, dark establishment with the requisite checkered tablecloths, candles in wax-encrusted Chianti bottles, a wood-burning oven and a basic pizza and pasta menu. Anna looked at Marie reviewing the menu and deciding what to order. She was as excited as a little girl in a toy store after receiving her allowance. Marie was even more beautiful than Anna remembered. She had Italian or Greek features and skin color. All she needed was a peasant skirt and she would fit in perfectly in this restaurant.

Four other tables were occupied when they walked in. Anna had to admit that she was not used to, nor did she like, men looking past her to stare at another woman, but she had gotten over her grudge and told her vanity to go to hell. She conceded that she had met her match. She wanted to get to know Marie; she was sure they could become friends. She chuckled as she wondered how these men would feel if they knew that the object of their admiration was a nun in training.

They each ordered a pizza and agreed to share a *pichet* of Chianti. Anna found it interesting that the pizza Marie ordered came with an egg on top. Try asking for that at an Original Ray's in New York and see what kind of a look you will get, she mused.

After ordering, both women awkwardly waited for the other to break the silence.

"You're nervous about being here?"

"Oh yes, they ask me to leave convent if they know I here."

"I do not want to offend you but it seems to me that you are not very happy. I can see it in your eyes. I do not think you would mind leaving the convent."

"I not happy, is true, but I know in my heart that I born to be nun. I suffer now to be good nun later."

"I do not understand why you think that. There is so much good that you can be doing here and now. Did you know that your convent was originally created to help others? It was devoted to feeding and clothing the poor. The nuns went out into the community to minister to the sick and destitute."

"I like that but I must obey my orders and do as told."

"It is so unfortunate when a person is as unhappy as you are. I am sure that God does not want you to be unhappy. Aren't you disobeying your orders right now being here?"

"Yes, I am shamed." Marie looked away. Anna could see that her young friend's eyes were beginning to well up.

"Marie, why don't you tell me why you are here? Take your

time."

Marie hesitated but then she pulled a manila envelope out of the purse she was carrying and handed it to Anna. All the while, Marie's eyes were darting around the room to see if anyone noticed. Not a person cared.

"What is this?"

"You say name Sister Catherine. These are pages I think she write in prison. It may answer your questions."

"How did you get this?"

"It was in chest. Mother does not know it there. I sinned by take from chest but I have too much fear to return them. I am much guilty. I confess to priest that I have papers, but he is new and does not tell me what to do. I was in Mother's chamber when you come because I speak some English to maybe help Mother. Then you say Sister Catherine's name and how sick your husband is. Maybe I can help."

"Tell me about the chest."

"No one ever go to attic. It is place the sisters never go. Then roof leak and Mother Angelique tell Sister Marguerite to see where leak. Attic is dark and Sister Marguerite falls. She find chest, it hide way in corner, in the dark. Four Sisters take heavy chest from attic. They see many old things in chest. There are tapestries and old Bibles. Mother very worried about convent. She say that God help to find chest. Mother knows about outside world. Old things are valuable. We sell chest and everything to fix convent.

"It is so exciting for nuns as they look through chest. I am novice so I have no right to look into chest. But I be curious like everyone. That night all nuns in bed, I look in chest. Under tapestries and Bibles and everything there is a drawer that hides. In drawer are papers that no one look at. I start to read papers but I hear Sister Marguerite come near so I put papers under my blouse. I disobey and will be punished. A few days more late, Sister Genevieve call to Monsieur LaFleur. He come and take chest away.

"Monsieur LaFleur then sell chest. Monsieur LaFleur send to Mother list of things in chest and how much he sell it and money the convent will receive. When she read about coin, Mother Superior is very upset. She want it return but Monsieur LaFleur does not have it anymore. We not know what to do.

"When police call Mother, she hope that they have found coin, but they did not. They tell her that Mr. LaFleur is dead. Then, when you come, Mother has hope again, but it is not to be. I want to tell Mother truth, but I am afraid. I have nowhere to go. I think maybe if I give papers to you, things will be okay again. I do not know."

"You speak English very well, by the way."

"Thank you. I hear what you say. You have much pain."

"Do you know anything about the coin? Why is it so important that the convent get the coin back?"

"I say more than I allowed already. Please do not ask more. The pages explain much, I hope."

"You are a good person, Marie. You will make an excellent nun but I think maybe you are not right for this particular convent. You have too much to offer the world that will get lost if you are shut away like this."

"Perhaps you right, but not for me to say. I must go back. I hope your husband be better and you find happiness. Thank you for pizza. It is delicious."

"Thank you. And may you find happiness, too."

Anna watched Marie as she headed out the door. She had courage. Too much, perhaps. On the one hand, she wanted—and even needed—to be a nun. On the other hand, she followed her heart too often and did one thing after another that will get her expelled from the convent. The poor dear did not know what she wants. No matter what happens, Anna knew she would forever be indebted to Marie.

Anna hurried back to the apartment, the manila envelope tucked tightly under her arm. She still had no answers but she felt the questions were coming into focus.

Before she attempted to decipher the diary, she tried calling once again Phil to see if there were any developments. She dialed but again got his voicemail. After leaving a message, she returned her attention to the diary.

There were seven tattered, yellowed loose pages. The first page seemed undamaged and was totally legible. After that, it was hit or miss. Some pages were torn while others were water damaged or looked as if they had been chewed by rodents.

On the whole, if Sister Catherine had indeed written this in prison, considering the austere conditions to which she was subjected, her handwriting was exquisite. Anna could imagine Sister Catherine starving and cold, sitting hunched over in the corner of a dimly lit stone cell with no heat. Only the faintest bit of light would be available to her while she scratched out these words. She penned these words when no one was looking. It was doubtful that prisoners were allowed many privileges.

When she was small, Anna, like many young girls, wrote her innermost thoughts in a diary, one with a small lock on it. At the time it was a fun thing to do. It was difficult to imagine writing something like this under the conditions Sister Catherine experienced. She could not fathom how terrifying it must have been, knowing that at any moment the word you were writing could be your last. One of these days when she was feeling blue, Anna would go up in the attic at her mother's house to try and locate her old diary. All those things that she once found to be so important would now seem trivial in comparison to Sister Catherine writings.

If what Pierre Bouvil said was true, Sister Catherine was not just writing a diary, she was penning her last will and testament.

That explained why the diary was so short. Over the course of a whole year, one would expect a lot more than these seven pages. It could be that there were certain days she could not write. Perhaps being in a cold and damp prison with inadequate nutrition for that long had caused her health to fail. Perhaps there had been more but the guards discovered the pages before she could give them to one of her nuns. Perhaps the rest of the diary, if there was a rest, had been lost or destroyed over time.

For the life of her, Anna could not imagine why she was expending so much mental energy trying to recreate the life of Sister Catherine. There was something about this aristocratic nun that fascinated her. Anna was feeling good old-fashioned empathy for this woman, like she had with Marie. *Enough, I have to get to work. Leave the psychobabble to Phil.*

She fired up her computer and connected to René's Wi-Fi.

Her plan for translating the diary was simple. There were numerous websites on the Internet that offered free translation services. She would type in one paragraph—or whatever was left of a paragraph—into the space provided, hit "translate." Her main hope was that the French language had not changed significantly over two centuries. For those words that stumped the translator, she would leave blank, guess or ask René.

She began to type. Except for an occasional word here and there, she had no clue what she was entering onto her keyboard. After what seemed an eternity, the first translated paragraph emerged:

Four officers of the national police arrived at the convent three days ago and took me away from the place that I love and have called home for these past fifteen years. Although I have not had much to eat or drink, my captors have been kind. I forgive those officers who came to get me and those who guard me now. I know that, although what they do now is wrong, they are devoted to their cause and have good souls. I have not yet been advised officially of the charges under which I am being held but a guard told me that I am arrested for crimes against the people I committed as Fabienne de la Tour. Someone had informed the secretariat about me. I also forgive whoever that person is.

The first paragraph did not offer any great insights. The words 'national police' jumped out at her. She imagined René in that situation. Somehow, she had a feeling he would have done whatever was right and proper, not what others told him his "duty" was. Then again, it is difficult to know how anyone would react in similar situations. Everyone likes to think that they would act in the noblest of ways but it would have been so easy to get caught up in the fervor of the day. Sister Catherine, of course, had a forgiving soul but, as she wrote, the police officers felt that they were serving a cause to which they were devoting their lives. So, who knows?

Nothing else of note here, except maybe confirmation of Oncle Pierre's contention that she was betrayed (as if there was ever any doubt that Oncle Pierre knew what he was talking about). Other than that, it started off just as one would expect a diary written by a nun, full of good will and forgiveness. Anna moved on.

I am writing this journal so that the quest for truth and redemption does not stop with my death. Yes, I do realize that I am going to be put to death. No one leaves this building except those who are heading for the guillotine. I expect this to happen and I accept it as my fate. I hope that the good work I have started will continue. There is so much suffering in Paris, so many people who need comfort and assistance; it cannot cease with my death. I will go to my God knowing that I have tried to do my best. Although I know that I may be succumbing to the mortal sin of pride, I also know that I have succeeded where others have failed.

A chill passed through Anna. Again, she found herself feeling profound sympathy for Sister Catherine and what she was going through, had gone through. It must be terrifying knowing that you are going to die and not just a normal death but you are to be beheaded. Sister Catherine's words displayed, however, not terror but an inner peace. She had knowledge that her soul would survive and endure whatever cruelty man could dole out.

Anna wondered how Sister Catherine would feel about what had since happened to her convent in the two centuries since her death. Given the words written here, she would feel great remorse over the fact that the sisters were now totally withdrawn from the world. Those who followed had not carried on her good works. They no longer ministered to the poor and destitute. There were enough places out there where one could meditate; not enough that provide assistance to those in need. Anna got angrier and angrier the more she thought about it, so she continued on in her translating.

The details of my life before I became Sister Catherine, as Madame Fabienne de la Tour, shall soon be public knowledge. It shall be discussed, scrutinized and distorted in short order so I will not waste my time recounting the events of that period of my life. While not an exemplary life, it was not one that deserves the ultimate punishment I am about to receive. However, I am not going to write about that period except to note those occasions and events that relate to the present. To focus on the past, a past of which I am neither proud nor shamed, would be as if I were trying to mount a defense to save my life. This I will leave to God and to others. Should He determine that my sins during that period warrant that punishment, His will be done. Let me, therefore, describe how I came to be Sister Catherine.

If nothing else, this was a life devoted to something higher. Ninety nine point nine percent of people who found themselves under these conditions would be thinking up schemes and defenses they could use to save their lives. What was it René had said? The most creative people he had ever met were those who were in danger of losing their freedom. If only that creativity could be channeled for a common good like Sister Catherine had done.

Sister Catherine's line about being neither proud nor ashamed of her life as Madame de la Tour struck a chord with Anna. The period of time she was a stripper came to mind. It was a wild time. It was a time during which she met Tim. It is also a time that she could not talk about with certain people. Her mother, for example, had gotten increasingly conservative and religious in recent years. It would be difficult if not impossible to ever tell her about what she had done during this time of her life.

Damn, I cannot wax philosophical about each paragraph. Keep moving! Tim has so little time.

I owe my life as Sister Catherine to my late husband, Guillaume de la Tour, Count of Avignon. The gift he gave me opened my eyes. It forced me to look upon my life and how sinful it had been leading up to that point. His gift started me on a new road, the true road.

Anna could not help but speculate as to what his gift had been. Could it have been the love between a man and a woman? Maybe she did not realize how great his love for her had been until he died. Then, when he was gone and it was too late to offer as fine a gift back, she found she could not bear to offer her love to another man. Instead, she gave herself up to God. Nothing could be nobler. The love he gave her through the years was such a gift and she came to appreciate it. After he died, she turned this into love for others. Anna was finding it difficult to keep her eyes dry. Enough speculation, though. She must continue onward in the translation.

The Count and I were such good friends, such fine companions. It is such a shame that we did not love each other as husbands and wives are supposed.

So much for my glorious romantic theories, Anna sighed.

It was at this point that the quality of the pages became poor. She could decipher a few words or a line or two at a time.

We were perfect [gap] *I pray for Guillaume's soul every day.* [gap] *God did not favorably look on his fondness for young boys.* [gap] *Guillaume is at peace now.*

Anna exclaimed out loud, wondering whether she could be reading this correctly or whether she had mistyped some of the information. The plot was surely thickening. Could the founder of *l'Ordre de la Tour* be tainted by association with her late pedophile husband? It must be too painful a memory for the nuns to bear, even these two hundred years later. Anna knew that abiding love, at least not the type of physical love enjoyed by married couples, was not the gift that Fabienne de la Tour received, but the question was still out there: What was this special gift?

It all started the day Guillaume [gap] Guillaume was always so sweet when he gave me gifts, and I was normally ecstatic when he brought me home something from one of his trips. He was in Bari, a city on the southeast coast of Italy, walking by a merchants' shop and stopped in his tracks when he saw it. He had to get it for me. I must admit that I was spoiled and was accustomed to the finer things. I therefore was not particularly impressed when I first saw this gift. [gap] Guillaume was quite downcast [gap] it is pure silver. It is also very, very unusual.

Could she be referring to the medallion, the one hidden away in Anna's bag? Was that the special gift that meant so much? How did it lead her to a life as a nun? How did it get her in trouble? So many burning questions remained and so few pages were left to provide the answers Anna desperately needed.

[gap] I slipped the chain over my neck where it remained until three months ago when I was taken away. I did not want these people to get it. My sisters will hide it and protect its secrets.

Anna reached into her bag and took out the medallion. She examined it closely. She felt the smooth edges between her fingers. She held it by the chain, hoping that maybe its magic would become obvious as it dangled in front of her eyes. Nothing profound came. She put it back down.

"What secrets do you hold? Please let me know. Please," she pleaded with the coin.

She typed on.

The very night Guillaume gave it to me, the [gap] I was so lost and confused. When he died the next week, confusion gave way to clarity. It all became clear. I must devote myself to God and helping the poor. I had thought of myself my entire life. [gap] My dreams started [gap] aware of what I must do.

Dreams! This present catastrophe started with Tim's dreams, dreams that may have included Sister Catherine. What was the connection? Was there a connection? What or who was behind all of this? Again, Anna's focus returned to the coin in her purse. She pulled it out and stared at it once again hoping that its secret would jump out and become evident to her. Nothing jumped.

The final few pages were a complete mess. The ink, a different color than that of the rest of the diary, had faded. There was not much that was decipherable, an occasional word. Of what she could read, the handwriting seemed different, too. It was still definitely Sister Catherine's but it was tentative and illegible. It was almost as if she had broken her hand and was trying to write through the pain. Anna theorized that Sister Catherine must have been sick or beaten or both. Maybe her captors had found out about her diary and were punishing her. It would not be a surprise that the authorities would be reluctant to let accounts of what went on behind those walls out into the world. It was ironic that Sister Catherine would have been punished for the words she wrote when all her thoughts about her captors were full of love and forgiveness. Truth is anathema to those types of people, no matter what the truth is.

The partial sentences that Anna could discern included:

Blessed be the Lord and may the Lord at last look favorable on the Master of my dreams.[gap] *my arrest is because* [gap] *redemption for he who cannot be redeemed.* [gap] *Forgive the unforgiven and unforgivable* [gap] *Release him from Aceldama*

After that, two whole paragraphs were basically obliterated. The last sentence, however, was intact and shown out like a beacon at the bottom of the page:

I am facing death because of my quest to say the heretical Kaddish for him who was and still is the most reviled man on earth, but who came to me in my dreams and led my soul to salvation.

Then there was nothing. Novice Marie had told Anna that this diary would provide the answers. Instead, Anna was faced with riddle after riddle. It was almost as if parts were purposely wiped out to test her. It was like in Greek mythology when the gods, after looking down on earth and finding everybody a little too complacent, would throw down some mischief to stir things up a bit.

While everything contained in the seven pages was of interest, it was these last two legible passages that intrigued her. The unforgiven and unforgivable...most reviled man on earth... Aceldama...Kaddish.

She had never heard of Aceldama but she had heard the term Kaddish before. It was a Jewish ritual.

She went back to her search engine and typed the word Kaddish. The definition read:

Kaddish Judaism, 1. a liturgical prayer, recited during each of the three daily services and on certain other occasions. 2. the five-verse form of this prayer that is recited by mourners.

Why would a Catholic nun be looking to recite a Jewish liturgical prayer? Who was she mourning? Catholics have plenty of incantations and prayers to say when someone dies. *Just ask Grandma.* Why look to another religion, to Judaism? While not having the worst record of historic relations with the Jews, the French have not always been sterling in how they treated these people. The Dreyfus Affair and the record of Vichy during World War II were perfect examples. Sister Catherine must have known that she was putting herself at grave risk. It was extraordinarily important to her.

Anna was about to type in *Aceldama* when her phone rang, startling her in the late night. It was Phil.

"You have to get back here immediately. Tim has taken a turn. He went into convulsions and stopped breathing. We have him stabilized and put him on a ventilator that is doing his breathing for him. We've detected a great deal of cranial pressure and have inserted a tube to drain fluid from around his brain. He's stable now but it does not look good, Anna. He's not in imminent danger at the moment but he is slipping. How soon can you get here?"

Anna was able to reserve a seat on an Air France flight into Newark leaving at 7:00 the next morning. She dialed Phil. He would be at the airport to pick her up.

As she was packing her things, her phone rang again. This time it was René.

"René, I was just writing you a note. I have to run back to the States. Tim's not doing well."

"Anna, they're coming for you! They're going to arrest you! Archambaut believes he has enough to charge you with LaFleur's murder. You have to get out. Now!"

"Go where?"

"Grab a pen and write this down. Get on the *Métro*. The *Trocadéro* station is two blocks away. Take the Number 6 line towards *Nation*. Switch at *Place d'Italie* for the Number 5 toward *La Courneuve*. Get off at *Porte de la Villette*. I will meet you there and drive you to the airport. Do you have all that?"

"Yes, René, but I can't ask this of you. You'll get into deep trouble."

"It is certain I am in trouble but there is no time to argue! Go! Take what you need. I'll send the rest back to you."

Anna did as she was instructed. Every step she took she imagined she was being followed. Around every corner was a policeman ready to cuff her and throw her in a dark cell.

She arrived at the *Métro* station. She gazed at the big board. A train was to arrive in six minutes, the longest six minutes of her life. She had been on the Paris subway before, but never on her own late at night. Every cough and every rustling of a paper made her jump. She examined each person on the platform, thinking they could be her adversary, but no one cared.

The train came and she got on. She sat near the door and counted the stations. Fifteen stations to *Place d'Italie*. And then twenty-three more stations after the transfer to get to *Porte de la Villette*. It seemed like she could have taken a more direct route or even a taxi to get to this station on the outskirts of Paris. René must have a reason for this route so she followed it to the letter.

She kept examining the few people as they got on and off her car at this late hour. Everyone seemed to be going about his or her own business, not paying her any attention. When she switched trains at *Place d'Italie* she noticed a young dark-haired man in a beige raincoat. He had been on her previous train car, switching trains when she did. *She was being followed.* She was paralyzed with fear. Her phone would not get signal down here. She had no place to go.

She remembered the defensive training Tim made her take when she was dancing. She should be able to protect herself if she was ever attacked. She reached into her bag for her keys, slipping the individual keys between her fingers, making an effective weapon.

The ride took an eternity. Station by station it progressed. The number of passengers dwindled with each stop the further the train moved from the center of Paris. After the Stalingrad station, Anna and this man were the only ones left on the car. She still had four stops to go. She acted as nonchalant as she could while still keeping an eye on him.

The train slowed as it eased into *Porte de la Villette*. Anna got up and stood by a door. The man also got up, but stood in the middle of the car. The train stopped and Anna opened her door and started running. She looked back and the man was following her. She picked up her pace as she arrived at the turnstile. She barged through and then ran up the closest set of steps she could find.

She reached street level and there was René, waiting in his tiny Citroën. She rushed into the car.

"René, I'm being followed! There he is!"

Emerging from the *Métro*, the man stopped, looked over at Anna and René, and then nodded. René nodded back. The man disappeared back down into the *Métro*.

"Anna, that was Sergeant Pasquale. He's my best man. I had him accompany you to make sure you were not followed by anyone else. I did not have time to give him special instructions or introduce himself. His English is not good. He might confuse you if he try. I am sorry to frighten you."

Anna could feel the tension ease from her body as she slumped in her seat. As she did so, she glanced in the side view mirror and noticed a man sitting in a car under a street light about a half a block away. It was after eleven at night and, except for René, her, and this person, the street was totally deserted. She knew why they were there; she could speculate that he was there because of them.

She turned around to get a better look.

"René, there's a man in a car under that street light. I can't get a good look at him but I think he may be the guy who was in the restaurant that you seemed to be watching."

René adjusted his rearview mirror to see if he could get a look at him, but he could not.

"Well, there's only one way to see if he is interested in us."

René started the car, put it into gear and raced out of the spot. He looked back; the other car had also pulled out and was now in pursuit.

He turned right onto *Avenue Corentin Cariou*, a major thoroughfare, which soon broadened into the *Avenue de Flandre*. Despite the late hour, traffic was relatively heavy. René gradually accelerated, constantly checking his rearview to find the car keeping pace as they both weaved in and out between the cars, trucks, and occasional scooters.

Although they were on the very outskirts of Paris in an area totally unfamiliar to Anna, her innate sense of direction told her they were heading southwest, back into Paris. She was about to question why they would do this when they needed to get to Charles DeGaulle Airport, which was to the northeast, when René told her to make sure her seatbelt was buckled and to hold on.

He suddenly hit the brake and sent the car into a spin. Three other cars in the vicinity swerved, two of them crashing into each other. He straightened out his vehicle and crossed through a break in the median whereupon he headed in the opposite direction. He cut off a car going in that direction that was subsequently rear-ended. Horns were blaring everywhere as the drivers of the four cars all jumped out to curse at René and to survey the danger to their respective vehicles.

As they drove on, René and Anna looked over and their suspicions were confirmed. It was the man in the restaurant who was angrily banging on his horn as his car was suddenly moving nowhere because of the accidents.

"How could he have followed me?" Anna asked. "Your *Métro* directions should have lost anybody."

"I think perhaps he was following me, not you. I maybe have not been as careful as I think. But I do not believe he is with Archambaut."

"Do you think it was LaFleur's killer?"

"Perhaps. But you are safe for now."

From there, René steered his way onto the *Périphérique*, the beltway around the city. Anna expected him to exit the belt and head northeast. Instead, he kept going, making the loop.

"René, my flight's out of Charles DeGaulle. Shouldn't we be there by now?"

"No, you are flying out of Orly. The best I could do is JFK. Sorry.

But you will be back in the States two hours earlier than the other flight."

"I don't understand."

"Archambaut knows you are in France. He is watching all the airports and train stations. When you make your reservation, he receive an alert. There are men there now, waiting for you. I am certain."

"Won't they know if I'm travelling from Orly as well?"

"Not if you travel as Mathilde Fontaine."

"Mathilde Fontaine? How am I traveling as Mathilde Fontaine?"

"I have friend at Air France. Nathalie is special friend. Your ticket waits for you."

"But my passport won't match my ticket."

"That is of no concern, not if you are with captain who headed security at Orly for two years."

"René, I can't let you do this. You can get in trouble. And so can your friend."

"Tim saved my life. He needs you. No more discussion."

With that, René concentrated on his driving. Twenty minutes later, they arrived at the airport. He pulled the car into a special parking lot near the main terminal. He reached back and grabbed a beat-up Yankee baseball cap and a rain jacket with a hood. He handed the jacket to Anna and he put the cap on.

"Put this on, with the hood up," he ordered.

"But it's not raining."

"Yes, but there are many security cameras. I don't want that Archambault review the images to see me help you. Oh, this hat, Tim gave to me many years ago."

They proceeded into the terminal. René knew where each camera was located. He deposited Anna in a secure room. Before going off he handed her a phone.

"If you want to call someone to pick you up at JFK, call from this phone, not yours. Just in case. I will be right back."

René departed and Anna called Phil to tell him of her change in plans. She would take a cab back to Hoboken. But as she expected, he would have none of it. He would make the drive out to JFK to pick her up.

Ten minutes later, René returned with her boarding pass. The plane was not scheduled to depart for two hours so they sat and waited. One of them would throw out small talk, but for the most part they were quiet.

The time came for the plane to board. René escorted her through a passageway around security, using a keycard to open locked doors. At one point, they passed a checkpoint but all he had to do was to flash his badge and they were permitted to pass. They arrived at an entrance to the gates.

"Your gate is through that door. All you need is your boarding pass. There are no more security checks but there are many cameras in the waiting area, so I better not go farther. Archambaut will need to file for extradition for anything to happen at the other end."

"René, I don't know how to thank you."

"One of your smiles and a big hug will be enough."

She gave him both—and tear-filled eyes as well—and then went into the waiting area.

•　　•　　•

As Anna settled into her first class seat, the adrenalin rush she had been experiencing for the past few hours wore off. But she could not sleep. She was now focused on Tim. Phil had made it sound like Tim's condition was dire.

For all she knew, she had just wasted precious time that she could have spent with Tim. *He could be in his final hours or even minutes.* Phil was correct: *a jaunt to Paris while Tim rots away!*

Anna burst into uncontrollable sobbing. A torrent of tears streamed from her eyes. A flight attendant came over to see what was wrong. The people around Anna each offered looks of concerns and in some cases, tissues. She ignored them all until she cried herself out.

Although anxious and worried about Tim during the whole way back, she could not help drifting into memories of Paris and the people she had encountered. Oncle Pierre, Mother Angelique, Novice Marie, Monsieur Avril, and of course René. Each had in their way gotten her closer to finding the truth about Madame de la Tour and the coin. But did it get her any closer to curing Tim?

It was a trip she would never forget. If only Tim had been there to share it with her.

For the thousandth time, she reached into her purse and felt the smoothed surfaces of the coin. She examined it closely. Then, knowing and fearing what the result would be, she slipped the chain back over her neck. The medallion hung down between her breasts, over her heart.

She put her head back and drifted into sleep.

23

"Hon, you don't belong here. Leave. Leave now!"

"Tim, I'm not going anywhere without you. I need you back where you belong: with me."

"I can't leave. I can't ever leave. Go and forget about me. I doubt my body can last too much longer. You go and have a good life. Perhaps Dr. Mordecai would make a good companion. Just go."

Anna could not let on to Tim how distraught she was over his remarks. She maintained the appearance of strength. Regardless of how upset she was, there was one thing that heartened her. She recognized that Tim was not totally unconscious of what was going on around him. He still had a connection. Hopefully, it was something to build on.

Anna looked around. It was as Tim had described it and she had remembered it in her brief foray here: nothing but arid wasteland. Other than the four images that stood before her and the sepia images of people that walked aimlessly around, there was nothing that could remotely be termed as having any life.

"You don't belong here, Tim. You belong with me. Don't you remember how we used to talk for hours on end without ever getting bored; how we had so much in common; how we both recognized that we were soul mates practically from the beginning? How can you think of letting that go?"

Tears were visible in his eyes now. "I know it's tough but I just can't. You must understand and go."

"Tim, I need you more than anything. I am nothing without you. I will never understand. And I don't believe that you don't need me. Why don't you just leave with me?"

"I must stay. It is my destiny."

Anna looked at Tim. This was not her husband. It was almost as if hypnosis or drugs had transformed him. Still, there was something she saw that gave her hope. While he was saying he needed to stay, his eyes told her otherwise; they were practically pleading with her. She tried a different approach to pry him loose from whatever had its grip on him.

"I'll go, my love, but why don't you introduce me to your friends first."

Tim did not expect this. He looked confused but he walked her over to the group.

"This is Marcus Carolis. He was a Roman sentry. He marched all over the Roman Empire as part of Caesar Augustus' legions. He was stationed at the Temple in Jerusalem before it was destroyed in 70 A.D. He heard Jesus speak once. Isn't that something? You know how much of a sucker for history I am; we have had much to talk about. It's amazing how I can understand Greek now. I always assumed that all Romans spoke Latin, but the soldiers generally spoke Greek. It was the lingua franca of the time. Wait, that's Latin, isn't it?"

When Tim gave a self-deprecating laugh, Anna saw a flicker of the man she knew and loved, but just for a brief instant.

"Next we have Atticus Tiompk. He was a sailor who was born in Anatolia. That's Turkey now." Tim whispered an aside to Anna, "Frankly, we don't have much to talk about so I don't know all that much about him."

Anna shook the sailor's rough hand. "It's a pleasure to meet you." Atticus nodded his head in acknowledgment.

"And this is Sister Catherine. She's from Paris."

"As a matter of fact, I've gotten to know you quite well, Sister Catherine," Anna interjected. "It's truly an honor to meet you. You lived most of your life in Avignon as Madame Fabienne de la Tour, Comtesse d'Avignon. You went to Paris shortly after your husband's death and headed a convent for approximately fifteen years where you helped the poor and downtrodden. This is until someone turned you in and sent you to the guillotine. It is sincerely my pleasure to meet you, Sister. You are, or were, a remarkable woman."

The Sister appeared quite embarrassed. Anna moved to appease her.

"I apologize if I spoke out of turn. I do find you to be a remarkable woman. You gave a lot to the world and to its poor and needy. You have nothing to be ashamed of."

Sister Catherine acknowledged the compliment.

"I do have some questions to ask you. I have the diary you wrote while in prison. There are some words that jumped out at me. The first is Kaddish. That's the Jewish prayer for the dead, isn't it? Why would a Catholic nun be interested in Kaddish?"

A look of utter dread shot across the Sister's face at the mere mention of the word.

Sister Catherine spoke. Tim translated.

"You must never say that word while you are here. It is a large part of his anguish that no one, not one person, ever stood up to say Kaddish to mourn his death!"

When Sister Catherine mouthed the word herself, she looked all around as if a bolt of lightning would strike her out of the blue. Anna persisted, it was necessary to get at the truth.

"I am perplexed as to why anyone would condemn you to the guillotine. Your good works speak for themselves. Was it because you wanted to say Kaddish for someone? I doubt you even knew what it was when you first heard the word and you had to hunt it down. However, you lived in a time and place when Jews were not well regarded. A nun making inquiries about a Jewish ritual would raise more than one eyebrow. There may have been some, including your fellow sisters, who believed you were dabbling in witchcraft or other heresies. Rather than disgrace the convent, they could conveniently capitalize on your aristocratic background and turn you in. Who knows? They may have thought they were helping you. By doing this, even if it involved you going to the guillotine, your soul would be saved from eternal damnation. Your continued association with Jews would condemn your soul. Is any of this correct?"

If Anna hoped she would elicit a response, she was mistaken. After getting over her initial terror, the blank expression returned to Sister Catherine's face. She made a slight bow and started to walk away. Anna was not going to give up.

"Sister Catherine, you wrote a word in your diary. *Aceldama*. What is *Aceldama*?"

When the Sister did not turn around or respond, Tim replied.

"My dear, we are in *Aceldama*. It is my home now, home for all of us. Forever. Even you. If the coin remains on your chest, you will be like us. If not, you will be like them."

His arm did a sweeping motion to indicate the hundreds of translucent ethereal spirits wandering around them.

"Their advantage is they don't feel his pain, day in and day out. We do. In any case, *Aceldama* will be your home, as it is mine."

"Tim, who is this 'he' you talk about?"

"No, there's nobody. Just us four."

"I could have sworn you mentioned somebody or something else, a presence."

"No, he's not here right now. I mean, there's nobody else." Tim responded as his eyes darted furtively around.

Anna knew Tim well enough to see that, even in this state, he was trying to tell her something. She just had to be patient and coax it out of him.

"I see. So, what do you do all day?"

"We talk. We recite the Bible a lot. The sister knows it pretty much by heart. I never knew it could be so fascinating."

"Anything in particular that you find fascinating?" Anna was fishing, hoping that a hint would be provided so long as they kept on talking.

"The stories of Jonah and Daniel, the Psalms, the parables of Jesus. Some verses fill me with awe: James 1:17, Proverbs 21:31, I Corinthians 16:57, II Thessalonians 3:16, Matthew 27:5. There is just so much there. I recommend it highly."

"I'll pick it up as soon as I get back." Anna repeated the verses to herself over and over, hoping Tim had given her a clue somewhere in there. He had sent her to Avril; perhaps he was directing her towards a different piece of the puzzle.

"I better go now my love. Is there anything I can tell anybody? Your mother? Your sister? Your friends?"

"No, just tell them I miss them but that I have everything I need."

"Everything except one. You don't have me."

Tim smiled sadly as he turned away and walked back to his little group.

Anna woke up. Looking around the cabin of the plane, everything was normal. She took the chain off her neck and slipped the coin into her bag. All the while, she repeated the Biblical citations Tim had recited.

She grabbed a pen but did not have any paper so she pulled the air-sickness bag out of the pocket in front of her and jotted down the chapters and verses. Hopefully, she remembered them correctly.

24

René hoped he had covered his tracks.

As much as he loved Anna and Tim, he did not want to either spend years in prison or have his career destroyed. As he sat in his office, he reviewed in his head the number of laws he had broken over the past couple of days. Hindering a criminal investigation; assisting in the flight of a criminal suspect; falsification of travel documents — these were just a few of the charges that could be filed.

There was plenty of evidence that could conceivably be gathered against him, but nothing hard. Then again, convictions have been attained on far less.

He had met but did not know Archambaut personally. He was aware of the inspector's reputation, however. The man was a bulldog who was tough but fair. He also would not be too thrilled about losing a conviction. How he found out that Anna was at René's apartment was a mystery; but the fact was that he had information that this suspect was in the country but now was gone would drive him to investigate how she got away.

The best way René figured to stop this investigation from going very far was to prove Anna's innocence. And René was certain she was innocent; that he never doubted.

He had to figure how he could conduct his own investigation without arousing suspicions. Jurisdictionally, his branch of law enforcement, the *gendarmerie*, was not involved in criminal matters, at least not in Paris. Within the city and its environs, the *gendarmerie* would handle security at airports and government buildings but criminal investigations would be under the purview of the National Police, Archambaut's branch.

Traditionally, there had always been friction between the two agencies. There was talk of merging the two, but René knew that would never happen, at least not in his lifetime. At the moment, relations were fairly good.

He was aware of a witness who had positively identified Anna. He had to find out the identity of this witness and determine whether the person was mistaken or whether he or she had lied. If the latter, why lie?

There was also a question of the physical evidence. Anna's fingerprints were definitely at LeFleur's apartment. How did they get there? Who put them there? Was this witness involved? These were all questions he had to answer.

René had gone to school with someone who was now an officer in the National Police, Charles Boril. Because students in the classrooms were seated alphabetically, the two boys were side by side for six years and had gotten close over that time. They went their separate ways after university but still kept in contact. René picked up the phone and dialed.

"Charles, it's René. How are you? That's good to hear. I was wondering if you could help me. The National Police are conducting a murder investigation. The victim's name was Etienne LaFleur. What I need is the name of the witness who came forward. I know. Just some side research I'm doing on a similar case. I just want to see if there's any connection. Don't worry, I won't interfere with the inquiry. You know me well enough, I trust. Thanks. I'll wait."

René doodled while Charles looked into the case's database. A minute later, Charles came back on the line.

"René, this is kind of strange. The woman identified herself as Sophie Alain. 3145 Rue Pouchet, Apartment 4B but when Archambaut's guys tried to follow-up with her, she did not exist. That address does not even exist.

"It says here that they went back to the original statement given by this mystery woman to see if she left any fingerprints when she signed the statement. There were and they got a hit on Interpol's database. Her real name is Alexa Fontaine. She's had some arrests for drug possession and distribution. She lives in Brussels at 221 rue de la Louvain. Because she lives in Belgium, Archambaut is going through official channels to get permission to interrogate her, but you know how that can go. That's about it."

"Got it. Thanks a million, Charles. Let's get together for drinks soon."

René typed her name and address into his database. Within seconds, a file came up with information on Ms. Fontaine. Her record displayed half a dozen arrests, mostly petty drug-related stuff. He was surprised she had never done any jail time. He clicked on each arrest in turn and soon he noticed a pattern. On five of the six arrests, bail had been posted by a William Canford.

He forwarded all this information to his phone and then hopped in his car for a three-and-a-half-hour drive to Brussels. Archambaut may have to go through channels to get approval to speak with her; he would need to go through the formalities in order to build a case that would stand up in court. René was not so constrained. He would talk with her directly. He was going to get to the bottom of Etienne LaFleur's murder and why someone is going to such lengths to frame Anna.

25

Phil was waiting at JFK Airport's International Arrivals as Anna emerged from Customs. He was nestled in between a rather dapper limousine driver holding a sign for "Moscowitz" and a boisterous Hispanic family, each of whom was craning his or her neck hoping to be the first to catch of glimpse of incoming kin.

Anna noted the broad smile on Phil's face followed by the big hug he gave her as she emerged through the doors. She was sure the Hispanic traveler would receive a comparable greeting. She doubted that poor Mr. Moscowitz would be so welcomed.

Anna could never be sure about Phil. He had an intense way of looking at her that was affectionate but at the same time disconcerting. It was as if he was excited to see her but disappointed she was not someone else. Maybe it was her imagination but, each time they met, that expression seemed to be more pronounced than the last.

"Did you find out anything on your trip?"

"I did get a lot of information. I still have to sift through it to see what is or is not useful."

Anna appreciated that Phil did not make any snide remarks or disparaging looks about her trip and the information she gathered. They swapped small talk while waiting for her luggage. She was postponing asking about Tim's condition as long as she could, figuring that if anything had changed, he would have volunteered it instantly without her prodding.

On the ride to the hospital, Phil briefed her on Tim. He was unresponsive. Many of his test results were steadily getting worse. His breathing slowed down to nothing and a ventilator was necessary to keep him alive. The pressure on his brain was a continual concern, although they had it under control at the moment. There had not been any more convulsions. His heart, though, was beating strong and regular.

When they walked into Tim's room, Dr. Frazier greeted them. Another doctor was bent over Tim, examining him. His back was to the door, not that Anna would have recognized the gray-haired man anyway. She just assumed it was another in the parade of specialists who had poked and prodded her husband over the course of the past few weeks.

Phil, however, stopped short.

"You? What are you doing here?"

Phil turned to Dr. Frazier, ignoring the other doctor.

"Steve, how dare you let him near my patient. I made it crystal clear he was not to be consulted!"

"In theory he is your patient, but I am responsible and will bring in anyone I think will help in a case."

The two doctors stared at each other. Phil looked at Anna, almost as if he expected her to agree with his assessment that this interloper was not welcome. When Anna did not provide support, he turned on his heels and stormed out. Dr. Frazier turned to Anna.

"I'm sorry about that little scene, Mrs. Harrington. Not the most professional of us, I'm afraid."

The other doctor stood up and turned around. As soon as he saw Anna he did a double-take, as though he recognized her, but he quickly recovered.

"No need to apologize for my son or me, Steve. Mrs. Harrington, I'm Dr. Alexander Mordecai. Dr. Frazier asked me to consult on your husband's case. My son, I'm afraid, hasn't had use for me in the past ten years."

Anna vaguely recalled Tim recounting that Phil, in attempting to gain Tim's trust, confided about his sister's suicide for which he blamed his father and that they had not spoken in a decade. But Phil had never mentioned his father to her, not even in passing. Now she recognized him.

She thought back to some years ago when she was working in the pediatric ward at Toronto's Saint Vincent's Hospital. A young boy came in with a severe head trauma resulting from an automobile accident. The hospital had the capability to stabilize the boy but could do no more. The chief surgeon knew of one surgeon who had the skill to undertake the type of surgery necessary to save him. He called his medical school colleague and asked that he fly in from Boston to perform the emergency surgery. The doctor agreed without hesitation.

She was a very junior nurse at the time and therefore did not assist in the operation or the recovery. But she remembered the surgeon arriving at the hospital. She had never seen anybody who exuded so much confidence as he took charge of everything.

Anna checked days later and found out that the boy was doing fine. The surgery had been a complete success. It did not mean anything at the time, but the surgeon's name was Dr. Alexander Mordecai. With an unusual name like that, she should have made the connection when Phil came on the scene, but many years had passed.

Anna did not care about any father-son feuds, her sole concentration was on her husband. The ventilator—its tube extending into Tim's mouth and its constant hum—were vivid reminders that he was totally dependent on a machine to stay alive. He was so ashen and lifeless. She would be horrified to see anyone in this condition, let alone the man she loved.

She was also horrified at herself. How could she have left him, realizing that there may be so few minutes left for them to be together? What kind of a wife was she? She grasped her bag and felt Sister Catherine's diary and her opinion of herself as a totally unfeeling monster dissipated somewhat.

The doctors excused themselves, allowing Anna to be alone with her husband.

She was exhausted. Her last full night's sleep had been two nights ago. On top of that, she had a severe case of jetlag. If she was to be of any use to anyone, she needed to get some rest. She took a taxi home.

She walked through the front door, hoping that Magda had come back, but the house was empty. Before she could think about going to bed, she had one more thing to do.

She searched the bookcases for a Bible. They had one somewhere. She could have sat at the computer and typed in the passages Tim had given her, but that did not feel right. She needed the book in her hands. It was just a matter of finding it. Then it occurred to her that it was stored with a bunch of other books boxed up in the basement. She was somewhat embarrassed, imagining her mother's horrified reaction if she knew how her daughter treated the Holy Book.

She hated the basement in this 100-year old brownstone. It was dank and dark. Crawly things ruled this domain. She detested going down there, even when Tim was with her, but she had no choice but to recover the dusty old Bible. The dustier it was, the better. She had followed her instincts and superstitions thus far and she was not about to betray them for modern technology.

She flicked on the light and descended down the creaky cellar steps. Although she was repulsed being down here, oddly enough she felt a sense of comfort. Perhaps she was able to picture the type of environment in which Sister Catherine lived for over a year. She realized this was a gross exaggeration; she could never know the level of privation that the Sister endured, but her little fantasy helped her to carry on.

Since Tim was the one who regularly came down here, she didn't have a clue where to begin. She began prying open box after box. After the tenth box she wondered aloud how in hell they had amassed so much junk. As she opened the fifteenth box she saw the Bible lying right on top.

Emblazoned in gold was The Holy Bible. Down in the lower right hand corner, also in gold but in much smaller type, was Anya Katerina Dubcek. It was the Bible presented to her on her First Communion. She had been going by the name Anna for so long that she sometimes forgot that her actual name was Anya. Somehow, the name Anna seemed more grown up when she first started using it as a pre-adolescent. She was not sure where she got that notion. *The things we do as kids.* She laughed to herself. She grabbed the Bible and headed back up the stairs. She was not going to spend a second longer in this dungeon than required.

She sat down at the desk in the study and caressed the Bible for a few seconds. Fond memories, and a couple not so fond ones, came flooding in. She remembered her First Communion when her parents were barely on speaking terms. They both were there for her but a thick tension hung in the air. It was the first time they had occupied the same room in several years. Each acknowledged the other's existence, but that was as far as it went.

By the time of her Confirmation, her parents were on speaking terms; they had become friends again. Anna was not sure who was prouder, them of her as she marched in the procession or her of them as they sat together smiling broadly.

On both occasions, she remembered having to get on the dreaded telephone to talk to her grandmother. Of course, in both instances the calls were as perfunctory as possible and then she ran upstairs to her room to write long letters providing details of the day. *Will I ever get over that phobia?*

She opened the Bible and started to track down the passages Tim had recited.

The first verse, James 1:17—"Every good and perfect gift is from above, coming down from the Father"— seemed innocuous enough. Likewise, the second, Proverbs 19:23—a "The fear of the Lord tendeth to life: and he that hath it shall abide satisfied; he shall not be visited with evil."—was, as far as she could determine, nothing of note. She read the third verse, I Corinthians 16:57—"But thanks be to God, which giveth us the victory through our Lord Jesus Christ"—and nothing jumped off the page, a dread came over her that maybe Tim was not providing the answers she was seeking. Maybe he had just been involved in delusional rambling.

The fourth verse, II Thessalonians 3:16—"Now the Lord of peace himself give you peace always by all means. The Lord be with you all."—made her worry. This had the sound of a benediction, a blessing given at the closing of church services to send the people on their way, bathed in the love of God. She fervently prayed that this was not Tim saying good-bye, sending her on her way with a blessing.

Maybe she had misread Tim. Maybe he was not sending her a message. There was also a distinct possibility that she may not precisely remember something revealed to her in a dream. If she were off by just one number, say for example if Tim said: I Corinthians 16:57 but Anna remembered it: I Corinthians 16:67, it could mean the difference between life and death.

Another possibility popped into her mind. Perhaps Tim was not giving her one obvious clue but was being coy and had inserted pieces of the code into each verse. She would then have to put it all together like a puzzle. She was never any good at these types of parlor games. She hated mystery novels. If Tim was counting on her to play Sam Spade, he would be sorely disappointed. Anna had to trust that, while Tim had many positive qualities, being clever in this way was not one of them. Hopefully, this aspect of his personality would continue to hold true and any clues he was trying to give would be obvious. Then again, this was not the same Tim. He had never been a linguist and now he was conversing in four different languages.

She finished the five verses, writing them all down on a piece of paper. The first four were lofty expressions of God's love and power. Nice thoughts. About what one would expect from a group of people sitting around reading and discussing the Bible, striving to be filled with the majesty of the Almighty.

The fifth verse stood out from the rest. Matthew 27:5 was a simple sentence that expressed an event. There were no lofty expressions of faith and devotion. What an odd verse to quote. Maybe she remembered this one incorrectly. Maybe Tim got his verses mixed up. Maybe...

It couldn't be. This would be beyond her comprehension, beyond anyone's comprehension. She could not bring herself to believe it until she had one more fact to verify her worst fears.

Anna went back to her hi-tech tool and fired up the computer to access the web. Using the search engine that had served her so well previously, she typed in one word: *Aceldama.*

She went no further than the very first sentence on the very first site on the list. She read: *Previously called "the potter's field," the word means "field of blood" and was appropriated as the burial-place for strangers.*

It all came crashing down on her. Going back to her Bible, she read and re-read the verse from Matthew: "And he cast down the pieces of silver in the temple, and departed, and went and hanged himself."

She reached into her bag and pulled out the piece of silver that, along with twenty-nine others, sealed the fate of Jesus Christ. And the unseen presence—the one nobody dared talk about—who could he be other than Judas Iscariot himself? She literally had to battle the devil to reclaim the soul of her husband.

Anna Harrington carefully placed the coin on the end table. She had never been so terrified in all her life.

26

Dr. Philip Mordecai and the entire medical staff at Barton Medical Center were no closer to finding out what ailed Tim Harrington than when he was admitted. They had run every test they could think of. Every possible idea had been discussed and dissected and then tried out, many in a variety of ways. Numerous head injury and coma therapies, including one where constant stimuli were presented to every sense, were employed. Tim's head and much of his body had been scanned from every conceivable angle using the best equipment that modern medicine had to offer. Everything they did had no effect. The latest setback even made them wonder if something they had done made the condition worse. They were scouring the literature and contacting the Centers for Disease Control to research experimental procedures that they could try or antidotes for rare viruses that they could give him.

Phil had contacted every brain and head injury specialist he could find but no additional clues were forthcoming. That is, every specialist had been contacted except one. And Phil would never call the doctor who was one of the best neurosurgeons in the world, the one doctor who could provide the answers: his father, Dr. Alexander Mordecai.

Never.

. . .

Six year-old Phil walked through the back door of his house in Newton, an upscale suburb of Boston. His left eye was sporting a fresh shiner and his pants were ripped at the knee. It was obvious he had been crying.

He hoped to escape detection as he darted through the kitchen heading for the stairs up to the safe confines of his room, but luck was not with him.

"Phil, what happened?" his mother asked as he passed her in the kitchen.

"Nothing," he lied.

"Come here," she commanded. He complied and she looked him over.

"It's that same boy, Sam Wallace, isn't it?"

"No, Mom, it's nothing. Honest."

"I spoke to his mother before and I'm going to call her right now."

"No, Mom! I fell. Don't call her. It was nothing."

Phil ran out of the room, fresh tears emerging.

Unnoticed by both Phil and his mother, Phil's sister, Jennifer, was sitting in the next room. She listened in on the entire exchange.

Jennifer was older than Phil by three years. At this stage in her life, she was a gawky tomboy, an ugly duckling waiting for the beautiful swan that would emerge a few years later.

The next day after the final bell sent the elementary students streaming out to the warm spring weather, Jennifer waited until Sam Wallace and his two friends emerged. The two friends lived close to the school and Jen knew they would peel off first, leaving Sam to walk alone four more blocks on his own.

Jen followed at a discreet distance until the friends were well out of sight. She then ran up to Sam. At this point in their lives, she towered over him by at least three inches. She grabbed his shoulder, twirled him around and delivered a perfect right hook to the younger boy's nose and then a left jab to his eye. Sam went down to the ground, his butt making a thud as it landed.

"You ever touch my brother again, you'll get worse," she vowed.

She turned and strode away as a rivulet of blood emerged from his left nostril. She was confident of two things. First, Sam Wallace would not pick on Phil ever again. Second, Sam would never tell on her. He'd be too embarrassed to admit a girl beat him up.

And so it was throughout their young lives. Jennifer would look after her bookish younger brother. In return, Phil would idolize and adore his sister. They got closer as the years progressed, especially after their mother died in a car crash when Phil was fifteen.

Phil had just completed his freshman year at Harvard when he arrived at Tercentenary Theater for Jennifer's graduation from the same school. Jen was all smiles when she saw him walking towards her prior to the commencement ceremony, but the smile faded when she noticed he was alone.

"He's not coming, is he?"

"I'm sorry, Jen. He wanted to be here; he really did. There was a big accident on 278. They called him in to operate. There were several kids with head trauma involved. He'll be here this evening."

"Maybe I should get into an accident. You think he'd notice me then?"

"Jen, Please."

"Stop defending him!" she yelled at him before she stormed away to get in line for the procession.

Eight years later, Phil had just completed his residency at Barton Medical Center when he phoned Jen, who was now living in Manhattan, and got no answer. He called a couple of times more, each with the same result.

Phil and Jen would normally talk on a daily basis, so he got concerned when he could not reach her and she did not return his calls. He took the PATH into the City. Getting no answer when he rang the bell, he pulled out his key to her place and walked in. Her purse was on the counter.

"Jen? You here?"

He checked the various rooms in the apartment and then stopped dead in his tracks as he approached the bathroom. Dropping to his knees by the tub, he wailed inconsolably.

"Jen, what did you do? Oh, my God no! Jen, please speak to me. Say something, anything."

Phil held tightly on to her, sobbing uncontrollably. At one point, he looked up to the heavens.

"I'll never forgive you. You were her father. You caused this. You were never here for her. You should have been here for her. I'll never forgive you."

Following that, Phil contacted the Barton Medical Center and announced he was taking an extended leave of absence. He abandoned surgery, enrolled in NYU's doctoral program in psychology and charted a new course for his life.

The last time he had any contact whatsoever with his father was at Jen's funeral.

27

René sat in his car across the street from 221 rue de la Louvain, in Brussels. He had been waiting for an hour and a half, holding a mug shot photo of Alexa Fontaine. He had contemplated going up to her third floor apartment but he decided against it. He would rather catch her on neutral ground, not somewhere where he may be forced to break the door down to speak with her.

He had to remain as anonymous as he could. To the end he purchased a pair of thick-rimmed reading glasses and a tourist baseball cap with Brussels emblazoned on the front. In his apartment he had a fake mustache and beard that were available for such occasions but he was never any good at putting these on himself.

He let her get about thirty feet away before he got out of his car to follow her. She walked on, oblivious that anyone was tailing her. René gradually closed the gap until they reached the gate entrance to a small park at which point he drew up beside her, grabbed her arm and with him other hand pushed the gun that was in his jacket into her ribs.

"Scream out, you're dead," he threatened. If she did scream René would run away, he had no intention of hurting her, but she did not know that. The threat worked and she was compliant as he led her into a wooded area of the park. He indicated for her to sit on a bench as he sat beside her.

"Please don't hurt me," she whimpered. "I don't have much money. If it's sex you're after, let's go back to my place where we can be comfortable. Just don't hurt me."

"I have no intention of hurting you, Ms. Fontaine, or should I say Ms. Alain."

Alexa Fontaine's eyes grew wide at the use of her alias.

"What do you want then?"

"Information. I want to know what you were doing at Mr. LeFleur's apartment, who you are working for and why you are trying so hard to pin Mr. LaFleur's death on Anna Harrington."

"I don't know what you are talking about. I told everything I know to the police."

"You lied then and you're lying now. You don't want to get hurt and I don't want to hurt you but if you keep lying…"

René did not need to finish the sentence, the implication had its effect as Alexa burst out in tears.

"I was there because of my uncle. He killed Mr. LaFleur but it was an accident. He made it look like a suicide but then he realized that the police would see through that and he asked me to help him. I owe him. I could not say no.

"He gave me the address he had gotten from Mr. LeFleur's files. It was on Ile de la Cité. I was to break into apartment to look for a very old coin. If I could not find it, I was to grab something that I was sure would have fingerprints on it and bring it to him without smudging them or putting my fingerprints on them. I brought it to the apartment that night and then I went back to LaFleur's apartment the next day and tell my story to police."

"Your uncle, is his name William Canford?"

"Why yes, yes it is. How did you know?"

"That doesn't matter. Is he French?"

"No, English."

"Do you happen to have a picture of your uncle?"

"Yes I do. He doesn't like having his picture taken but I took this one without him knowing it."

She pulled out her phone and, after a few taps on the screen, showed him the picture. This confirmed what René had suspected; it was the man in the restaurant, the one who tried following them on the streets of Paris.

"Thank you very much, Mademoiselle Fontaine. You can go now."

"I can?" she responded. She seemed almost disappointed it was over. It was as if she enjoyed the attention.

"Yes, you've been most helpful. I would suggest you change your ways. Also, I'm not sure your uncle has your best interests at heart."

Alexa Fontaine said nothing in response.

"One last thing. The French police know who you are and will be paying you a visit very shortly. I would suggest you be honest with them this time."

"I will. Thank you."

28

Early the next morning, Phil arrived at the hospital to examine Tim. When he walked into the hospital room, Anna was there, sitting beside her husband.

"Hi Anna. How's he doing today?"

"Same."

"I'm sorry about yesterday. My father and I don't get along."

"That was pretty obvious."

"I...I don't know if I can continue on with this case if my father is involved."

"But Phil, we need you. I need you to stay on. Please."

Phil was about to respond when the door opened and Dr. Alexander Mordecai walked in.

"Hello, Mrs. Harrington. Hello, son. You're looking well; it's good seeing you after all these years."

Phil stood there, saying nothing. He looked at Anna, then at his father, and then back at Anna before racing out of the room.

Alexander stared at the door. "That went well, didn't it?"

"Dr. Mordecai?"

"Alexander, please."

"And you can call me Anna."

"After going over your husband's records and after my cursory examination, I am leaning towards surgery to relieve cranial pressure. The main thing that concerns me is that we don't know what we're looking for. In the past, I've done surgery where I am basically on a fishing expedition, dealing with symptoms, not causes. You open the patient up and start looking around. Usually, the answer presents itself to you but there are times where it doesn't. I've done it, but I don't like it one bit. However, reducing and stabilizing the pressure is our first priority."

Alexander pulled no punches, describing the miserable choices facing Anna. First, the doctors had to address the immediate life-threatening problem: the elevated pressure on Tim's brain. There was already a thin tube penetrating his skull that removed excess fluid but this was a temporary, makeshift measure. A long-term remedy was required. Medication could possibly achieve the desired result but surgery was a more likely solution. Alexander believed that stabilizing his pressure might in fact be the key. He theorized that a blood vessel had ballooned in an as yet undetectable spot. They should be seeing it on the MRIs, but the fact that it did not appear was not too unusual. This ballooning, and there may have been some leakage also, was pressing on the brain, inducing unconsciousness. Finding and repairing that vessel may lead to total recovery but Alexander told her she should not get her hopes up.

If Tim did not regain consciousness once the pressure was stabilized, another course of action would be required. Alexander described an untested and experimental procedure he had heard about at a conference. It was a fascinating process that depended on proper sequencing of steps and split second timing. After he returned from the conference, he made some follow-up inquiries and was astonished at the high rate of success it enjoyed in treating patients like Tim. He recommended flying the physiciancwho had pioneered it, Dr. Manesh Pritak, in from Chicago.

Alexander laid out the stark reality. He could not make an educated guess of this procedure's probability of success but he had to warn Anna that there was a high failure rate. The consequences of failure could mean death or total paralysis. He was not even sure that the hospital would allow it to be performed. It would take all of his prestige and persuasive powers to pull it off, but perhaps he could convince the hospital officials that it was necessary. Given how much Tim had slipped over the past few days, the probability was steadily increasing that the consequence of doing nothing was death. Anna understood the consequences but acknowledged there were no alternatives.

"Doctor," Anna began to ask.

"Alexander... please."

"Okay, Alexander. I appreciate all you're doing, all that both of you are doing. I realize you'll have to return to your practice in Boston before too long. I hope that you will perform the surgery when and if it is necessary."

"I've told Steve that I'd be available for as long as he — or Phil — needed me."

"Thank you, doctor."

"I hadn't had contact with my son in over ten years. He holds me responsible for his sister's death and I can't say I entirely blame him. I was not there for her when she needed me. I loved her dearly, but that wasn't enough. It wasn't enough for Phil.

"I hope you don't see me as being callous about your husband's condition, but I see it as a golden opportunity. It's my last chance to get my son back. I have to see this through, for myself as much as anybody."

"Were you and Phil close?"

"When he was very young, incredibly so. He looked up to me as if I were a god; and I let him. He wanted to follow in my footsteps as a surgeon and he was on his way to being a good one. His symbolic slap in my face after Jen's death was to leave the field and become a psychologist. From what I understand, he's damn good at that, too.

"Phil had always been a little neurotic and very eccentric. His fascination for baseball, for example, when he had never played the game, always puzzled me. He didn't get that from me. This and his other idiosyncrasies, I've always passed off as being personality quirks, but now I wonder.

"There's one other thing. You may have noticed how I did a double take the first time we met. I can imagine that Phil had the same reaction when he met you."

"Now that you mention it, he did."

"Let me show you something."

Alexander pulled out his wallet from which he extracted a worn, wrinkled photograph. He handed the photo to Anna. Her eyes widened with astonishment.

"Oh my God! It's me! The hair's different but this could be me ten, fifteen years ago."

She handed the photo back.

"That was Jen, my Jen," Alexander replied as his eyes welled and his voice choked up. After a moment, he recovered.

"Getting back to your husband, you don't have to decide this minute. You may want to get a second opinion."

"I've gotten enough second opinions to last a lifetime," Anna responded. "I have the best opinions I can hope for right here. We have to do it. There is no need to think it over. I want Tim back."

"I've placed a call to Dr. Pritak. As I mentioned, he's from Chicago. I spoke with him briefly and he would be willing to fly in. All he is waiting for is word from me and he is on his way."

"Call him."

"Your husband's pretty stable at the moment so we can wait a couple of days to operate. I'd like to have Dr. Pritak present from the beginning. There is a lot we need to do even before he arrives. As I mentioned, I will have to do a fair amount of arm-twisting to convince the hospital and the FDA to let us proceed. I'm sure they are afraid they'll be threatened with lawsuits."

"I'll sign anything you want me to."

"It will get done."

"Thank you, doctor."

Like Alexander, Anna had found Phil's behavior to be odd, and had gotten increasingly so over the short time she had known him. His stare, which could be intense, was disconcerting. She had no idea if Phil would remain on the case, leave entirely, or do something in between, such as only work when Alexander was not around. The best course of action, at least for the time being, was to do and say nothing.

Anna had work to do, too. Her ultimate faith in the physicians did not displace a persistent feeling that it would take more than medicine to revive Tim. She got in her car and drove to the Childcare Clinic, not to work but instead to have a personal conversation with Doctor Cohn.

29

When Anna entered the clinic, Dr. Richardson was standing at the reception desk going over a file.

"Are we working today or just visiting?"

What a prick. He did not even have the decency to ask how Tim is doing. She had no time or energy for confrontation and said hello but nothing else. She then addressed Beverly, the office receptionist.

"Is Dr. Cohn in, Beverly?"

"Yes, he just finished with a patient so he should be in his office completing the paperwork."

"Thanks."

Anna walked back and knocked on Dr. Cohn's door.

"Come in."

When the doctor saw Anna he rose from his desk and gave her an affectionate hug and a smile.

"How are you holding up, my dear? How's Tim?"

Dr. Howard Cohn, who was approaching seventy, was the oldest physician in the group. He was also the kindest man one could ever hope to meet, a consummate gentleman. She loved working with him best of any of the doctors.

"Doctor, I have a strange question to ask you."

"Have a seat and fire away."

"What is Kaddish?"

The question took Dr. Cohn off guard, but he recovered quickly.

"Ah, you come to me as the resident Jew, not as the eminent physician I am. I'm sorry that I do not have a yarmulke in my drawer but I shall do my best. Kaddish is a prayer. There are different variations but the one most everyone thinks of is the mourner's prayer, the Jewish prayer for the dead. It is said daily for a year after the death of a departed loved one that you want remembered to God.

After that, one recites Kaddish at certain times during the year like the anniversary of the departed's death.

"The ritual for saying Kaddish has been well-established over the centuries. In general, the mourner stands and the congregation responds in unison at certain intervals. At every service an opportunity is provided for congregants to say Kaddish for those they had lost. It can often be quite moving."

"Can anyone say Kaddish?"

"I don't see why not."

"Even a non-Jew?"

"It depends on who you ask. An Orthodox rabbi would say definitely not. Some would even prefer that only men say it, and it has to be said in the presence of a minyan. That's basically a quorum, a minimum number of ten men, for a service to be conducted. Conservative rabbis would say that it depends on the circumstances. I'm sure if you searched the literature you would find hundreds of pages of discussion on the topic. Reformed rabbis would say, 'Why not? The more the merrier.' I would assume that any rabbi would find it highly unusual."

"Is it always for a specific person?"

"Not necessarily. Every Jew likes to think that there will be someone saying Kaddish for them after they die. It can be reassuring. There are cases when there is no one left to remember. Ever since the Holocaust, a Kaddish is often said for the six million en masse. You can be sure that many of them did not have anybody left to pray for them individually.

"Keep in mind that I'm not the most knowledgeable Jew in the world. You may be asking the wrong person. May I ask as to your sudden interest in Jewish ritual?"

Anna already had way too many people thinking she had totally lost her mind; someone as dear to her as Dr. Cohn should not believe it, too. Also, she was not sure that any Jew — at least not one who was as observant as he appeared to be — would countenance someone toying with a sacred prayer, regardless of the motive. So, she had a white lie already made up.

"I have an elderly neighbor that I've gotten to know recently. She's alone and her mind is going. She should be in a nursing home but so far she's been able to cope in her apartment. I drop in to see her every couple of days. She keeps telling me that she's all alone. She's distraught that she has no one to say Kaddish for her when she dies. I've tried asking her what Kaddish is but her mind is going and I can't get a straight answer. All she keeps saying is that she has no one to say Kaddish for her. I want to tell her that I would do it for her to put her mind at rest. Before I tell her, I wanted to find out what it is and what I'm getting myself in for. That's why I came to you, our resident Jew, as you put it."

Dr. Cohn smiled his warmest smile.

"It is a good thing, a *mitzvah*, what you are doing. Knowing you as I do, it does not come as a surprise that you would do such a thing. Even with your husband lying in the hospital, you would think of being this kind to an elderly neighbor."

Anna felt a flush of guilt for lying to this gentle man, but it was unavoidable.

"Tell the dear lady that you will say Kaddish for her. Let her mind be at rest in her final years. I stand ready to help you in any way I can. When the time comes, I will escort you to temple and help you get through it. It is always my pleasure to be of service to you."

"Thank you for agreeing to help me."

"The least I can do. Don't worry about things around here. Since you're the person who knows what's going on, it has been tough without you but you take care of your business first. We'll muddle through."

"I wish everyone felt that way."

"Richardson, eh? He's not so bad once you get to know him. Trouble is, he's never let anyone get to know him. Don't repeat this, but I hear it wasn't until his third year of medical school that he discovered the difference between his ass and his elbow."

Anna could not help herself from bursting out laughing.

"He's just a blowhard. Don't let him get to you. Any problems, you come to me or Dr. Holt. Okay?"

.   .   .

Anna was at the same time enlightened and hopelessly lost. She was losing Tim. One just had to look at his face to know he did not have long.

There was a distinct possibility that the surgery and procedures Alexander Mordecai and this Dr. Pritak were to perform could solve everything and bring Tim back. To hear it described, though, there was just as much of a possibility that he could die.

She figured she had about forty-eight, maybe seventy-two, hours to do everything she could to revive Tim. Once the doctors said they were going to proceed, there was no way she possibly could—or should—postpone the surgery. She realized that she was very well losing her sanity. How could she possibly tell the doctors to hold off performing essential surgery while she mixed her potions and recited her incantations? But she had started down a path from which she could not turn back. She must speed up whatever it was she needed to do.

30

Inspector Archambaut received his approval to cross the border into Belgium and interrogate Alexa Fontaine.

"Damn bureaucrats," he mumbled as he drove out of Paris with Officer Dubois. "I should have been able to do this two days ago."

Dubois knew better than to respond where his boss was in a mood like this. Even agreement would stoke his fires more.

They arrived in Brussels and pulled up in front of her building, a day after René had spoken to Ms. Fontaine. Not seeing any place to park, Archambaut pulled into a loading zone and stuck his "Official Police Business" placard on his dashboard.

"It would be my luck that they don't recognize the placard here in Belgium and the car gets towed," he muttered. Again, Dubois thought better than saying anything.

They buzzed her apartment and received no response. When a tenant exited through the front door, the two officers flashed their badges and let themselves in. They then climbed the three floors to her apartment and banged on the door, announcing they were police and wanted to talk with her. Hearing nothing, they banged again. An elderly woman two doors down stuck her head out into the hallway to see what the commotion was all about.

"Are you looking for Ms. Fontaine?"

"Yes we are," Archambaut responded, "do you know where we can find her?"

"I saw her leave early this morning. She seemed in an awful hurry."

"Do you know if she's planning on returning anytime soon?"

"We weren't that close so I don't know her whereabouts or her intentions but she had two large suitcases with her. It can be safely assumed she's not planning on returning anytime soon."

"Was anybody with her when she left?"

"No, she was alone, but yesterday when I was returning from the market I saw her in the park not far from here yesterday. She was sitting on a bench talking with a man I've never seen before."

"Could you describe the man for us?"

"I'm afraid not. He was wearing a hat and my eyes aren't what they used to be."

"Okay, thank you. You've been very helpful."

The old lady closed the door as Archambaut and Dubois started back down the steps.

"Damn," Archambaut snapped as he got back in the car. "She was our one witness. Without her we don't have a case never mind getting an extradition order. Let's check the rail and air lines to see if they have any record of her traveling but my guess is she's in the wind. Let's get back to Paris. I want to have a chat with Captain Bouvil. It was in his apartment that our source reported Mrs. Harrington was purportedly staying. It seems these women have a way of getting tipped off that we're on our way. Let's see what the good captain knows about all of this."

As Archambaut started the engine, his phone rang. It was his secretary. He put it on speaker.

"Hello Teresa, what bad news do you have for me to make this day a total disaster?"

"Well sir, I don't know if it's good or bad but Captain René Bouvil is here to see you. He says it's very important he talk with you."

Archambaut and Dubois looked at each other in amazement.

"We're just leaving Brussels now. Can he come back at 7:00?"

After a pause. "Yes, he says he'll be here at seven."

31

Alexander was still having trouble believing what was happening to Tim Harrington. What was more troubling was that he could not even make an educated guess as to a diagnosis. His experience was that every case, without exception, has a pattern. While it may be difficult to discern, the pattern was there. It was always there. Using his vast knowledge and expertise, it was Alexander's responsibility to uncover the pattern that would lead to diagnosis and treatment. It was a responsibility that he welcomed and in fact relished.

Here in Tim's case, however, nothing fit together or made sense. Thus far, he relied exclusively on test results conducted or overseen by his son. While he had no reason to doubt the validity of the test results Phil had given him, he did not trust anybody else's work without verification. He had to do some investigation of his own.

When Alexander arrived at seven in the morning to check on Tim, he found him drenched in sweat. The sheets and blanket were so disheveled and strewn about that, if he had not known better, he would have sworn that intense sex had taken place in this bed. Alexander went to the console and printed out the records for the previous night. Tim's brain waves were all over the place. Something was going on in there, but what?

He had never seen anything like this. Tim seemed to be calm now but it was as if his brain had been fighting a titanic battle the night before. His body had appeared to join in as well. As far as Alexander knew, other than a convulsion or two, this was the first time Tim had exhibited any body movement whatsoever. He did not know whether this indicated progress or decline. Also, he was not sure if this latest development would delay the surgery schedule, or even if surgery was possible now. None of the pieces fit together. When Doctor Pritak arrived from Chicago, they could all confer and arrive at a suitable plan of action.

•   •   •

Dr. Manesh Pritak's plane had landed at Newark Airport remarkably on schedule at 3:00 PM. A car service was waiting for him at the airport. Rather than a hotel room, Dr. Pritak indicated that he would stay with relatives down in Edison, New Jersey. He had numerous relatives who were excited to see him. Alexander hoped that Dr. Pritak realized he was here for a purpose, that this was not a social visit. He had work to do and he had to do it quickly. Tim's window was closing.

He need not have worried about Dr. Pritak. He was energy, efficiency and purpose personified. Although he had participated in surgery in Chicago in the morning, gone to the airport, and taken a flight (he refused first class accommodations and flew coach), he ordered the limo driver to take him to Barton Medical Center.

Alexander was overseeing yet another battery of neurological tests when Dr. Pritak walked into the room. Dr. Frazier arrived shortly after that. Alexander looked around, hoping that Phil was with Frazier, but he was not.

After introductions, the three doctors discussed the case and examined Tim together. Initially, the two local doctors were not impressed with Dr. Pritak. He was rather gangly in appearance, standing at about six foot one and weighed maybe 140 pounds soaking wet. He had swarthy skin, a mustache and jet black hair slicked to the side. Being in an area of the country with a large, highly educated Indian population, the doctors worked with Indian doctors and nurses on a regular basis. Still, there was a level of prejudice and stereotypical images of Indians.

Their attitudes changed the instant Manesh Pritak started to speak. He asked probing questions in clipped, precise English about Tim's condition: his autonomic responses, his caloric intake, his brain wave measurements, everything under the sun. Pritak's professional demeanor, medical knowledge and insight were second to none.

After fifteen minutes, Dr. Pritak asked if he could meet Mrs. Harrington prior to the surgery. Dr. Frazier said he would arrange it but inquired if there was a special reason.

"I want to evaluate the psychic energy that I have at my disposal before we start," he replied.

Alexander and Frazier exchanged skeptical looks.

32

Anna was walking down the hall when she saw Doctors Frazier and Alexander Mordecai accompanied by an Indian man who she assumed to be Dr. Pritak emerge from Tim's room. She ducked back around the corner, waiting for them to leave. She just could not take yet another doctor giving her all the platitudes and assurances about "getting to the bottom of this" or asking her the same endless set of questions she had been asked a hundred times already. She wanted a few quiet moments with her husband, knowing there may be so few of them left.

Once the three doctors had departed, she entered the room, shocked yet again at the condition Tim was in. She went to sit beside his bed when her phone rang. Despite the fact that at this moment she had about the same use for telephones as she did for doctors, she looked at the number and answered.

"Hi René."

"Anna, I am happy I did reach you."

She looked at the clock. It was 10:00 AM. That made it 4:00 PM in Paris.

"René! I've been so worried about you. And guilty, too. Is everything okay?"

"Yes, I am fine but much has happened. How is Tim?"

"The same, which isn't good. What's happened?"

"Let me start with the good news."

Anna took a deep breathe, knowing that bad news was to follow.

"I did speak with Alexa Fontaine, who went by name Sophie Alain when the police questioned her after Monsieur LaFleur's murder. She is person that said you were there. She tell me full story. I meet with Inspector Archambaut to talk about this and clear you of murder. When I go to see him earlier, I was told he is in Brussels, so perhaps he speaks with her already."

René paused.

"Why do I think you are done with the good news?"

"Ms. Fontaine acted at the request of her uncle, a man named William Canford. He was the one who killed LaFleur. I verified that he is the same man at the restaurant and who followed us in the car. I checked with passport control and he has left the country. I have a call in to your FBI to see if he entered the US. I believe he is there now. I did some checking on Mr. Canford and he's had numerous charges filed against him by the police throughout Europe but he has never been convicted. It's unclear why he has not been.

"Be very careful. I think he is dangerous and is after you. He wants that coin you have."

"I hope that's all."

"No, I regret to say. When I come home from work, Marie, the novice from convent wait outside my door, for you, for me, for anybody. She is in tears. She spoke to you before you left?"

"Yes, she did."

"She also say she did give you some papers. A diary of Sister Catherine, correct?"

"Yes."

"Mother Superior knows you have diary. She contact her boss, Monsignor of Notre Dame de Paris who tells her Marie must be kicked out and maybe excommunicated for what she did. He also accuse you of stealing diary and coin. He claim coin and diary are priceless antiquities. He will contact the police to file complaint unless you return both coin and diary."

"Well, add that to the list of charges against me. They're not getting anything until I'm done with them. Is Marie okay?"

"Yes. She is very upset. They scare poor girl. She say Mother Angelique is kind but has not choice. She must send Marie away from convent. Mother gives Marie some money left from selling chest but Marie come here because she has nowhere to go. She stay as long as she wants."

"You are always such a dear, René. If you can help her get a passport and bring her to the airport, I will pay for a ticket for her to come stay with me. It is the least I can do."

"We discuss that later. I must get ready to meet with Archambaut. Marie is coming with me; her story has bearing. You take care of yourself, okay?"

"I will. Other than almost losing Tim numerous times and him being in a persistent vegetative state that have doctors baffled and not having slept a full night in three months and doing battle with the Catholic Church and being an internationally wanted criminal, I'm doing fine."

René laughed. "At least you do not lose sense of humor."

"If I didn't laugh, I'd cry twenty-four hours a day."

"Things will turn around, I feel it."

"I hope you're right. Thank you so much, René. Again, I can never repay you."

"A bottle of wine is always right answer."

Anna hung up and returned to her vigil at Tim's bedside. René was doing all he could on his side of the Atlantic but she needed to do more over here. She knew she was way out of her realm, though. She needed help but did not know where to turn. The most logical place to look for answers related to the thirty pieces of silver was the church. Her most recent foray into a church was a fiasco, but the Catholic Church had always been a source of comfort and strength throughout her youth. Her parents had ensured that she went through catechism and all the other proper Catholic training. Then they left it to her to decide how observant she would want to be once she reached adulthood. Her response has been not to be observant at all.

During her parents' divorce, Anna saw many of her parents' "friends" from church desert them. 'You shouldn't divorce,' they warned her mother. The church does not condone it. Instead of being there when they were needed most, one by one they stopped calling. Anna found this appalling. She would never forgive them, or by extension, the church. Her mother, on the other hand, went full circle. At first she was deeply hurt and also turned against the church. Then, like the divorce itself where she later went on to become close friends with her former husband, she returned to the Catholic fold. Since being diagnosed with multiple sclerosis, her fervent religion often bordered on fanaticism.

Anna did not trust the church. Given her recent experiences, this was natural, but once she discovered that it was Judas Iscariot with whom she was dealing, she was in way over her head. Now she needed the church for guidance.

She contemplated walking into the local parish, going up to the same priest who had spouted platitudes to her and handing him the coin, telling him it belonged to Judas. The shock value would be worth the price of admission but she dismissed this approach.

She decided it better to approach the church leaders back at her old church in Toronto. Her mother was still there and had become increasingly devoted to that parish over the past few years. Anna just hoped that she would be content with rosaries and daily masses, and would stop short of turning into Grandma. Anna could not bear it if her mother joined the ranks of professional mourners.

Her mother had vaguely mentioned that a new priest had started a short while ago but Anna could not recall her saying if any of the old ones were still at the parish. She would prefer to talk with someone who remembered her as a girl. Father Francis was always nice and understanding. He fit the mold of a priest, at least in her eyes. He would hopefully give her both the benefit of the doubt and wise counsel. She got the number for the parish rectory from information and dialed. A young man's voice said hello.

"Father Francis, please."

"Father Francis?"

"Yes, Francis Manses."

"Oh, Father Francis is no longer with us."

"Do you know where he can be reached?"

"What I mean," the young voice hesitated for a moment, "is that he passed away several years ago after fighting a long illness."

She did remember her mother mentioning something about his death. The news made little impression.

"I'm so sorry. He was such a nice, decent man."

"That's what I have heard. I never met him. My name is Father Mark Carew. I came to the parish last year. Can I help you?"

Anna hesitated. This was the last thing that she wanted. She despaired at telling her story to a complete stranger but there was hardly time to go priest shopping.

"I do need to talk to someone. My name is Anya Harrington." Anna could not quite figure out why she used Anya instead of Anna. Her mother never accepted or acknowledged the modest name change and, since she was back on her mother's turf, she subconsciously reverted. "Perhaps you know my mother, Elana Dubcek. She is a member of your congregation."

"Mrs. Dubcek? Of course, I know her very well. She has mentioned you many times. You're a nurse down in New York, right?"

"New Jersey, actually."

"Yes, yes. My geography of the States is woeful. How come I have never met you? Your mother is such a regular congregant and she occasionally brings your sister, Magda. I would have assumed that she would have dragged you along at some time or another."

Anna felt a little sheepish. On her visits back home, her mother had indeed made many attempts to bring her to church. Anna had a million and one excuses not to go. Sometimes it was a headache. Sometimes she would use the fact that Tim was a Protestant and would be uncomfortable at Mass as an excuse. (Tim did not care one way or the other but went along with his wife.) Through it all, Anna had stepped foot in a church a handful of times since she was a teenager.

"It just never seemed to happen," Anna responded noncommittally.

"Well, how can I help you?"

"This is going to sound insane but please hear me out."

Anna launched into the saga, omitting things here and there but by and large telling the entire story. Father Mark asked a few questions to clarify a few points but was mostly silent, letting Anna do the talking. When she reached the part where she realized that in her hands was one of the thirty silver pieces accepted by Judas for betraying Jesus Christ, there was an audible gasp and a muffled 'Oh my God' at the other end of the line. When she postulated that there was a magical, as well as sinister, power associated with the coin, there was no disagreement coming from the Father. She told him about Sister Catherine's diary, including the part about saying Kaddish.

When she concluded, there was complete silence. Anna was not even sure Father Mark was still there.

"Father Mark?"

"I am still here. I'm just in shock. I would bet you are expecting me to ask if you have had your head examined recently."

"That would be about the response I would expect, but I cannot tell you how serious I am about all this."

"I don't doubt your motives or your beliefs for a second, Mrs. Harrington. I just find it so incredible. I realize you've been under a great strain and may not be thinking clearly...or rationally."

"Are you saying you won't help me?"

"No, no. Not at all. I'm just trying to think this over. You have to admit it's not something one runs into everyday, even in my line of work where we're trained to believe in miracles. If by some stretch of the imagination you are correct, this would be the find of the millennium. Are you absolutely sure?"

"How can anyone be sure about this?"

"Let's take this from the top. Explain to me how you think this coin belonged to...to...I feel like I'm supposed to say: 'He who must not be named.' Just recap what you think you know one more time."

Anna took a deep breath. She was not sure whether she was wasting her time and giving the good priest a good story to tell his buddies over a glass of wine or whether she was making headway. In any case, she decided to plod on.

"Well, everything just seems to fit. I think the five people, or rather souls, including my husband, who are trapped in this dream world are the ones who had substantial contact with the coin over the years. The others, the ethereal spirits floating though are the ones who may have touched it over the centuries. I'll be joining them some day.

"I've thought about this an awful lot. Let me tell you what I think may have happened.

"Matthew 27:5 says that Judas threw the coins down in the temple, departed and went and hanged himself. I would doubt that he just let the silver pieces drop. Rather, he was distraught and angrily threw them to the floor. Possibly they spread out all over the place as they hit. It's possible that a Roman guard was in the temple when Judas threw the coins down. The Romans were all over

Jerusalem at that time. One could have rolled to his feet and he picked it up, pocketed it and walked away.

"Then, the coin would have worked its way down through history to us, sometimes in someone's possession, most of the time lost or locked away. The Turkish sailor could have gotten his hands on it as he was traversing the Mediterranean. Madame de la Tour's diary says that her husband picked it up in the City of Bari, which is on the eastern coast of Italy. When she received the coin as a gift, it already had the hole punched in it. She referred to it as a medallion. At some time or other it got a hole punched in it. Maybe someone thought it would make a good luck charm to hang around his neck. By wearing it around the neck it increased the contact with the wearer. I'm rambling, I'm sorry."

"You're doing fine. Please continue."

"After the sailor, it resurfaced when Guillaume de la Tour gave it to his wife, who later went on to become Sister Catherine. She seems to have been able to put some of the puzzle together. Perhaps because of her upbringing and background she was able to understand some of what the people in her dreams were telling her.

"I do find it interesting that the first thing she did after getting the coin was to change her life so that she did good for the poor and destitute. In the end, her aristocratic background caught up with her and got her killed. After that, the coin stayed locked up in the convent attic for two hundred years until my husband got his hands on it."

Anna could practically hear Father Mark thinking this over before he said anything.

"You entered this dream world and spoke to your husband?"

"Yes."

"And where were you?"

"Aceldama, the potter's field purchased by Judas's thirty pieces. Trust me, Aceldama is not a word I have ever even heard in my life before a couple of days ago, let alone have any clue what it means."

Again there was silence.

"You do realize how preposterous this all sounds, don't you?"

"I understand. In all probability I am going insane if I'm not a full loony tune already. But I also see that in some odd sort of way, it all fits together and makes some sort of sense. I'm not any kind of theologian; I don't even go to church. I do believe that there can be extreme power in faith and that unexplained miracles do happen. Something keeps egging me on, telling me that this is one of those cases."

"What do you plan on doing now?"

"That's what I am coming to you for. All I know is that I want my husband back. If it involves pleading to God for full absolution of Judas Iscariot's sins, I will do it. I just know that I am in way over my head and I need guidance and reassurance here. If you can't or won't help me, please tell me so I'll stop wasting my time; wasting Tim's time."

Anna's final words were choked with tears and trailed off into nothing.

"Please Mrs. Harrington. I understand and I'll try to help but, to be honest, this is way over my head, too. I'm a pretty bright guy but I just got out of seminary two years ago. May I talk with some other priests who have a little more experience and get back to you? I am aware of the urgency and will get back to you today. Would that be okay?"

"I...I guess so. As long as this will be kept strictly confidential. I am taking a great risk revealing this to you but it was a chance I had to take."

"Of course, this will be entirely confidential."

"Then yes, but please get back to me as soon as you can. Thank you so much, Father Mark. I look forward to speaking with you in a few hours. Good bye."

"Good bye."

•　　•　　•

When it got to be evening and Father Mark had not called, she got concerned. She tried telephoning him but got the answering machine. Evening extended into night and then into the next day. Still, she had no word. At 3:00 in the afternoon the phone rang. Instead of the youthful voice of Father Mark, Anna heard the voice of a much older, and much sterner, man. She anticipated trouble. She was correct.

"Mrs. Harrington?"

"Yes. This is Anna Harrington." She was not going to put on any pretenses or be anything less than herself with this man as she became Anna again, not Anya.

"This is Archbishop McAllister. I am the spiritual head of the Catholic Church for all of Ontario. I understand you had a conversation with Father Mark Carew regarding a coin that you claim to be one of Judas Iscariot's thirty pieces of silver. Is that correct?"

"Yes, it is." Anna felt as if she were up on the witness stand being cross-examined by a talented and ambitious district attorney.

"Father Mark explained your thought process in coming to the conclusion that the coin is what you say it is. I find this all very hard to believe."

The arrogant tone in his voice confirmed Anna's suspicions. "I find it hard to believe myself, Archbishop. I may very well be wrong. I am just going by intuition. If I'm wrong, so what? I'm just a raving lunatic. But if I'm correct..." Anna knew that no additional explanation was required.

"Let's for the moment say that you are correct. What exactly are you planning on doing?"

"That is partly why I came to you, to get guidance on what to do. I have an idea of what I want to do, but this is out of my league."

"Yes, it is out of your league. I think that the only possible course of action for you to take is that you must turn the coin over to the church so that it can be properly analyzed and possibly destroyed."

"What?"

"This power, if indeed it is a power, is far beyond what you or anybody can handle. You will return the coin."

"Return it? You never had it to begin with."

"It was the property of the Sisters of la Tour convent in Paris. It was improperly sold to you and now we demand it back."

Anna was astonished. The Catholic Church network was incredible. As soon as the Archbishop received this news, he must have notified the Vatican. The Mother Superior must have likewise contacted the Vatican. How else could this information have traveled this quickly? It also confirmed what René had told her: she was a marked woman and had to be very careful. What an idiot she was for calling the church. Still, she was not going to sit quietly in the face of threats.

"Demand? I don't know whether we got it properly or improperly and I don't care. We got it and it may be doing something to my husband. As long as there is the remotest possibility that this coin may hold the key to getting him back to me, I am holding tightly onto it. Nothing you or anybody says will tear it from me."

"You do not know what this coin can do. Nobody does. I sympathize for your husband, but we cannot let the life of one man jeopardize the souls of perhaps millions of others."

"What you are talking about?"

"The Apocalypse. This could be the first sign of the end of the earth and I am not going to be a party to that."

"You're crazy."

"That may be, but it is my responsibility to err on the side of extreme caution. I have discussed this with my superiors and, as we speak, Rome is researching the proper ritual that will be used to neutralize or destroy it. You have to turn the coin over."

Now Anna was mad. "I cannot. Your idle threats don't scare me."

"They are not so idle. For one thing, how would your mother and everyone else feel when they find out about the sinful way you earned your way through nursing school?"

"How..." Anna's voice trailed off. She had once believed that somehow her erotic dancing past could be used against her but, as time went on, she had dismissed the thought and moved on with her life. How would her mother and grandmother react? They would be devastated. She was sure that the Archbishop would not be above embellishing the story either, making her sound like a cheap whore.

"Believe me, this is important. We will not stop there either. I promise you that you will be excommunicated. I understand from Father Mark how important the Catholic Church is to your mother. Elana Dubcek would not take her daughter's excommunication lightly either. If we find out she knew anything about this or helped you in any way, she will be excommunicated, too. I am very sorry, but we have the capability to ruin you. Oh, did I mention that there are pictures? I have been advised that these are being express mailed to us today."

Anna could barely breathe. Her heart was beating a mile a minute.

"Judas would be proud of you," was all she could manage to say.

That comment made him pause, but just for a moment.

"We do not want to go this route. All you have to do is return the coin. Go to your local parish, explain the situation to the priest, give him the coin and have him call me at 416/555-1243. We will then consider this case closed. If I have not heard from the priest by this time tomorrow, we will carry through with the course of action I have described. Good-bye, Mrs. Harrington."

Anna hung up the phone without responding.

33

Anna thought back to her dancing days. It was a period in her life of which she was not proud, but neither was she ashamed. She started to do it for one simple reason: money. Working two jobs to get through college and nursing school made her constantly exhausted. One day, Magda confided in her.

"Anna, you look exhausted. Why are you doing this to yourself?"

"You know how much I've always wanted to be a nurse and live on my own. Mom and Dad don't have the money to help me out very much. I'm doing the best I can."

"Not quite. If I tell you something, will you promise not to tell anyone?"

Anna giggled and remarked that they were like two schoolgirls swapping stories about the boys in homeroom. Magda did not share in the laughter but stared soberly into her sister's eyes.

"Promise," she repeated.

"I promise."

"Haven't you ever wondered why I'm never hurting for cash? My secretarial job is okay but it's hardly enough to pay the bills, let alone allow for any luxuries. The reason I'm doing okay is that every Thursday night I dance nude in a bar down in Rochester. It's great money, most of which is under the table and in US dollars."

Anna stared at her older sister in astonishment. While Magda was not homely or unattractive, neither was she a stunner. She was always a free spirit but this was going way beyond anything Anna could imagine.

"I've been doing it for a couple of years now. It's kinda fun. I figure I'll do it for a couple more years and then give it up. You look stunned. Reactions?"

Anna did not say anything. She was a little depressed to hear that her sister, someone who was as close to her as anybody on earth including her mother, had been dancing for this long without telling her.

"I would have told you earlier but I didn't want you to be ashamed of me. I guess I wanted to remain that ideal older sister you look up to. I'm telling you now because I think you could do it, too. The schedule you're keeping now is killing you. This is such good easy money. It would solve many of your problems.

"In addition, much as I hate to admit it, you're much better looking than I am. You're beautiful. You'd have the guys eating out of your hand."

Anna surprised herself that she did not blurt out, "No, I could never do that. I'm shocked that you could even suggest such a thing!" Instead, when she mustered enough courage to reply, she meekly asked:

"What do you do?"

"Well, there's usually eight to ten girls working each night. There's a raised stage in the middle of the place and you get up there and strip. Some girls do an elaborate dance to accompany getting nude, others get right down to business and are naked in seconds. There are seats all around the stage and you go to each of them, show them what you got and they slip dollar bills between your boobs. You're up there for three songs and then another girl comes up.

"After you dance, you try to get guys to go into the lounge area and give them lap dances at 20 bucks for five minutes. Some of the popular girls have guys lined up waiting for them all night. Others have to settle for strolling around the bar giving mini-lap dances for dollar tips, hoping to entice one of them back to the lounge. I guess I'm kinda in the middle, not the most popular but I get my share of laps. The guys are pretty nice but you get an occasional sonovabitch. We have two bouncers to keep an eye on those types. Some nights, it's just a job but other nights it can be great fun. On occasion, you run into a guy who turns you on or who is real funny and you have a real good time."

Anna was having trouble believing what was coming out of her sister's mouth. A substantial part of her brain kept telling her that she could never do such a thing. In spite of this, the more she listened, the more intrigued, not to mention aroused, she found herself. The part of her psyche that said 'give it a try' was gradually winning over the part that wanted to tell Magda a flat out 'no way'.

"I wouldn't even know where to begin," was the best she could offer in rebuttal.

"I initially worked through an agent who did all the booking. He's a pretty nice guy, considering the line of work he's in. Some of the girls get hooked up with real dirtbags that fleece them for a lot of money. I'm sure my guy'd help you out. After the initial contacts are made, the rest becomes routine."

Anna agreed to give it a try.

She contacted Magda's agent and he arranged for her to do an audition. Anna insisted it be at a club far enough away from home that there was no chance anyone she knew would see her so they settled on Club Erotica in Meriden, Connecticut. Having worked with first timers on many occasions, the agent scheduled her audition for a Tuesday night when the club was not busy. A Friday or Saturday could be overwhelming if a dancer was not used to it.

Magda took Anna to the local mall the Saturday before her debut to select two outfits appropriate to the occasion. It was like when they were young and Magda would take her by the hand to go downtown to shop for candy. They decided on two outfits: frilly see-through lingerie with matching panties and a shiny gold bikini.

Early that Tuesday morning, Anna hopped into her car and sped off toward Connecticut. It was a beautiful autumn day, a great day for a drive. The foliage was in full splendor. Seven hours later, she pulled up to Club Erotica fifteen minutes before it was to open. She noticed that there were cars already in the parking lot with men ready to pounce as soon as the front door was unlocked. What was she getting herself into, she fretted to herself.

Because Club Erotica was located in a predominantly residential area, it studiously attempted to be as inconspicuous as possible. By and large, it was successful. The one-story windowless building was done up in a drab beige stucco. Other than a small—and, it might be added, rather artful—neon sign that hung over the front entrance and the curious lack of windows to the outside world, the structure could very well have housed either a doctor's office or a print shop.

She walked to the back door and knocked. The lock was released and a hulk of a bald man opened the door. He must be the bouncer. She introduced herself and the man, who naturally was known as Tiny, escorted her into the club. He walked her through the club to Frank, the owner/manager.

The inside of the club was both dingy and clean at the same time. Anna reckoned that it was decorated in about 1958 and had not been updated since then. A raised carpeted stage with an assortment of overhead neon lights and spotlights dominated the center of the club. Seats ran along each side of the stage. A bar encircled the stage, allowing room enough for the barmaids to scurry about, dispensing soft drinks and other non-alcoholic beverages to the patrons. State laws would not allow liquor to be dispensed in nude clubs. The inside walls were classic, with alternating panels of mirrors, carpeting (tastefully matching the carpeting on the stage) and walnut veneer.

Off to the side was a small room where the deejay played his tunes and kept track of the dancers' lap dances. Adjoining this room was the inappropriately named "VIP Lounge." This lounge was decorated in the same style as the rest of the bar except for five well-worn couches where the dancers gave their lap dances.

Even in the inadequate lighting of the club, Anna was gratified to see that it was kept clean. She would learn, and appreciate, that cleanliness was an obsession for manager/owner Frank. He demanded that spills (and other mishaps) be cleaned up immediately. The place was to be swept, mopped and scrubbed down each night after closing. Like her agent, she found him to be a relatively decent sort who always treated her fairly.

With a minimum of formality, he went over the club's ground rules.

"We run a clean, legal club here. Everything is strictly above board. If I hear about any extracurricular activities you girls are having on the side, out you go. I can't afford to get raided and closed down. Got it?"

Anna nodded. Of course, she later found out that plenty of "extracurriculars" went on, just none on-site. If you were one of Frank's favorites and a good money-maker for the club, this behavior was overlooked until it became too obvious or out-of-hand.

"We have five girls dancing tonight. Dusty called in sick at the last minute." Frank was more than a little disgusted with the unreliable Dusty. "I know you're a rookie so you'll go third. That way you can observe what the other girls do. You'll get a feel for what to do but you won't be standing around getting nervous. You'll go up on stage, do your dance and I'll see how the customers are with you. We'll take it from there. What name do you want to use?"

She had not given this any thought. Magda went by the stage name "Destiny". Anna had no intention of ever dancing where anyone would know her so she decided to go with her real name. Later, Tim would remark that he was impressed with her using her real name. She never let on that she did not make a conscious decision; it just happened that way.

What she observed was pretty much as Magda described it. The first girl, whose stage name was Misty, was a pretty good dancer. Lithe and pretty, this blonde got into her kicks and moves, peeling off one article of clothing after another. She'd get down on her back and spread her legs to give a patron a real good view, collect her dollar and move onto the next customer. She would stop to chat briefly with a regular but she made sure that every guy who was seated around the stage received personal attention.

After the three-song set was over, she was promptly replaced by a brunette with short hair and plenty of silicone. This girl, who went by the name Nadia, had a different approach. Very little dancing was involved. Anna was hard pressed to find any movement that anyone would classify as dancing. She undressed and moved down the line and lay on her back, kneeled or got in some other position that gave the clients a close look at her goods. For this privilege, they slipped a dollar into her cleavage, perhaps getting a feel of her breast in the bargain.

The guys seemed to like the first dancer but they were no less enamored with this one as well. This was true when she would get real close to a patron and drape her legs over the guy's shoulders. All he practically had to do was to lean over and he would have himself a free lunch, Anna mused.

By this time, two girls who were not dancing until later had made their way out into the bar area, working the men and hoping to entice them into the lounge for a lap dance. That was where the money was. All the women were obliged to dance on stage but you did not make much money up there. You did it and got off stage with the anticipation that lots men will find you appealing enough to want to spend lots of money on you as you gyrated in only a G-String on top of their crotches. You definitely did not want to spend the evening working the floor for single dollar bills. You wanted the twenties to roll in.

Anna tried watching the girls in the lounge area to get some lap-dancing pointers but stopped when it appeared she was leering at them. She would just have to wing it if she ever found her way over there.

Before she knew it, it was her turn to dance. As she strode up the stairs to the stage wearing the see-through lingerie, even she admitted she looked incredibly sexy. She decided that her act would be somewhere between the extremes, doing a little strip tease dance before getting down to business and stripping naked to give the gentlemen what they came to see. She plastered a frozen smile on her face to hide the nervousness. Once up there, she found that it was a lot easier than she anticipated but the whole thing was rather a blur. She vaguely recalled removing the upper part of the lingerie, walking around in just her panties. Next thing, she was crawling along the stage in nothing but high heels.

After the three songs were over, she covered herself up somewhat and went back over to Frank.

"Nervous up there, huh?"

"It showed that much?"

"Yeah, but our trusty patrons didn't seem to mind. The deejay tells me he's had ten guys come up to him to ask for a lap dance with you. Normally on an audition the girl just dances and we come to an agreement whether to continue or not. Then the next time out, it's full swing. Since you seem to be so popular and we're short-handed tonight, we can skip the formalities. You up for doing some laps tonight and then coming back on stage for a regular turn the rest of the night?"

"I guess so." Anna tried to sound noncommittal but in truth she was finding herself getting rather excited.

"Okay then. Go in back and freshen up. Come out when you're ready. We'll get you a couch and get you started."

There was no turning back now. Getting up on stage, taking your clothes off and exposing yourself to a bunch of strangers had brought it to one plateau. Now she was taking it to a whole new level. There were rules in the lap dance area. Many were observed; many were not. It was up to the girl to call the shots; she just had to be careful and discreet. In this particular club, contact was allowed. Men were allowed to touch the dancers anywhere except for the genitals, although some of the girls permitted touching even there. Even fondling of breasts was allowed. Anna was not aware of this when she first considered dancing. Now she was a little apprehensive.

Her first customer told her he was a lawyer. She was not sure whether he was telling the truth or not, but he seemed nice and somewhat articulate. She would come to discover that many of the men, and most of the women as well, exaggerated their importance and their professions. A lawyer often turned out to be a sales clerk, an accountant was a warehouse forklift operator and a nurse was a cashier. It was all part of the game.

Customer number one, who she somehow believed to be what he said he was, was in his upper 30s. He was courteous and overall a nice guy. They chatted some but he seemed intent primarily on the lap dance. His caresses, or more precisely fondlings, were tender and she admitted she was getting somewhat aroused. She calmed herself down if she hoped to make it through the evening. He was getting aroused as she sat on his lap. She was no virgin, having had several lovers, but this was a different experience as she felt his erection rising under her butt. He ended up staying a half hour with her. When he handed over $120 without batting an eye, she was in a state of amazement.

One after another the men came to her for a lap dance. Some of them stayed for one five-minute stint, others lingered longer. One guy poured out his life story over the course of an hour and fifteen minutes. When he readily forked over three hundred dollars, the state of amazement turned into a state of shock.

She happened to look down during one of her lap dances and saw a wet spot on the inside of one guy's trouser leg. She was so naive at the time that it never occurred to her that this would happen. She was embarrassed, he was embarrassed, and the dance ended rather awkwardly as he hurried to the exit. She could not even remember if he paid up for all the dances he had with her. She did not care. She just wanted a shower.

Anna made it through that first night. After giving the house and the deejay their respective cuts, she noticed that she cleared just over $1,000 in one night. That was incredible. She was exhausted. One girl warned her that she needed to pace herself a little. She would burn out otherwise. Anna knew she was right. The money would be less if she took breaks now and then but she would do quite all right.

She was also sore. Having a bunch of men grope you all over and squeeze your breasts for hours on end was quite an experience. It also leaves you feeling aches and pains all over. Her backside was rubbed raw from men who worn rough jeans. She noticed some of the girls using little towels to protect themselves. This also served to protect them in case the man had an "accident" during the course of a dance.

Despite the drawbacks, Anna decided this would be a perfect way to make good money in a relatively short period of time. She told Frank that she would like to dance on a regular basis. After awhile, as Magda had promised, the dancing did get routine. Anna settled on a schedule where she would dance three nights a month. Luckily, a close friend moved to New York City. It gave her a place to stay and it provided her with a built-in excuse for disappearing from town each month.

After she got her nursing certificate and was working in the pediatric ward of St. Vincent's Hospital, she continued to dance. In a large hospital, scheduling the days off was relatively easy. It became a bit more complicated when she started to work for a small clinic downtown. On more than one occasion her doctor bosses were upset with her as she disappeared for days at a time but because they were more or less lost without her, she could soothe things over with little difficulty.

Dancing became her little secret, a chance to display her wild side. Only her sister and a few select people knew about it. For awhile she took in a roommate, Cathy, who was also a dancer. It gave Anna someone to travel with and confide in. This arrangement was short-lived, however, as Cathy's drug and drinking problem became more and more apparent.

Anna danced a total of three years. For the most part, it was a good experience. Overall, the men were nice. Once in awhile she would run across someone who was a little too rough or crude or who stank, but there was never any incident for which the bouncer intervened. Like many of the dancers, she had a devoted coterie of fans, guys who would mark their calendars in eager anticipation for her next visit.

Men were infatuated with her, which she found more than a little pathetic. One guy proposed marriage in the middle of a lap dance. Anna started to laugh. When she saw that he was serious and how devastated he was at her reaction, she felt bad about it for a week. Luckily, when she returned the next month, there he was waiting in line for his dance. All had been forgotten and forgiven. She breathed a sigh of relief. She feared he might have done something drastic in the intervening period, he looked so crushed and defeated when she saw him last.

The first time she met Tim, he was seated at the stage. She came over to him like she did with any other customer. As she was going through her gyrations and writhings on the floor in front of him she noticed that he was looking into her eyes. Most of the men practically drool as they stare into nothing but genitals or breasts, but this guy would not take his eyes off of her face! Anna jokingly remarked to herself that he must be some kind of pervert.

An hour later, he was in the lounge to have a lap dance with her. He chatted a little but seemed rather quiet. It was almost as if he was choosing each word with extreme care so as to not say anything to put her off. Even as they were lap dancing, his primary attention was mostly on her eyes. It was starting to make her little uncomfortable, but at the same time there was something special about it.

Over the next four months, Tim became one of Anna's regulars. She cannot recall if she noticed him as a frequent visitor until after his third or fourth visit. If truth be known, she found many others of her regulars to be much more interesting and personable. Some of them would tell such stories and have her in stitches. Tim was always the more studious type. If he said anything, it was usually to get her to talk about herself, not to talk about himself. It was only after they started dating she discovered he was a full-time college student studying architecture. Still, there was something drawing her to him. She would have liked to get to know him but she knew full well the unwritten rule about dating the customers. A few of the girls did it. At least three of them ran a little business on the side with their clients but she was not going in that direction. These types of liaisons often led to disastrous consequences and were not worth pursuing.

Then Tim appeared at the pediatric clinic where she was working in Toronto. He was up visiting his sister when his nephew got an infection of some sort and he drove them to the clinic.

A young boy in the waiting room started to wail and did not want to see the doctor. The mother tried her best to quiet him down but he became louder and more agitated. After a few minutes, the mother apologized to the others in the waiting room and was about to leave with her son when the door to the offices opened and Anna emerged. She kneeled beside the boy and soon he not only stopped carrying on but was giggling. Anna took his hand to lead him in to see the doctor but, as she turned, she saw Tim, sitting there. They locked eyes and recognized each other.

Panic began to set in. If Tim had not been there with his sister and her sick son, she would have been suspicious that he was stalking her. Even if he was not stalking her, she was still ready to panic. She had thus far successfully kept her two worlds separate, but her secret could now be exposed.

The next time she emerged, this time to bring in Tim's nephew, Tim stood up.

"Could I interest you in dinner this evening?"

Fearing that if she said no he might vindictively tell everyone about her moonlighting job, she kept her calm and they went on their first date. She has thanked her lucky stars over the years that she stayed cool.

The date was traditional enough, dinner at one of Toronto's finest restaurants. Tim was more talkative here than he was at the club. His explanation was that at the club, with the music blaring and the atmosphere they were in, he did not find it conducive to conversation. She sensed that this was not true. There was also an innate shyness and reserve in him. She surprised herself that she found these traits very appealing. She was not attracted at all to bombasts and braggarts; there had been enough of those types in her life.

She also sensed that in many ways he was lost, looking for answers. Maybe that was why he frequented go-go clubs. She liked the fact that after one date, he was confident that she was the answer he was looking for. She could see that he needed her, perhaps even desperately needed her. She had been loved her whole life by a variety of people but she never sensed that she was needed by any particular person. She liked the idea very much.

Years later he confided in her how rudderless he had been until she came along. He was drifting without purpose or direction. When she came into his life, he made the commitment to focus himself, both professionally and personally, so that he could win and keep her.

She could see from their first date that Tim was the type of man who, once he found a woman he loved, would do anything and everything he possibly could to make her happy and fulfilled. He told her—although not in words but through actions—that she would come first in his life. Always. In comparison to most of the men she knew, including her own father, who loved others but whose first thought always seemed to be for themselves, this was not a bad situation to stumble into. It did not hurt that she liked him, and could even envision herself loving him, too.

On that first date, he demonstrated his sincere concern about her welfare. He warned her to be a little more careful with what she revealed to the men at the club, that she might be a little too open about herself. Many of the girls made up alternate lives for themselves during conversations with their customers. Mostly, it was done to impress. Other times, it was done to throw any potential crazies off the trail. In many cases, a dancer who had nothing in her life but dancing would say she was a college student or a dental assistant or a nurse. Usually, the men swallowed the story.

Tim had suspected that everything Anna told him in their little talks was nothing but the truth. Running into her in the clinic confirmed the fact. He was worried about her. He admitted that he had fallen for her but he was not a crazy nut. "Trust him on that count," he declared with a glint in his eye. Other men may not be so normal and he warned her that she should not be so open when she danced. She could get hurt.

To illustrate what he was talking about, he proceeded to recite back everything she had said about herself, much of it verbatim. Her being born in Czechoslovakia and immigrating when she was very young, her parents being divorced, her work in the hospital and now the small clinic and many more facts were included in the monologue. Anna was impressed with Tim's memory but, more to the point, she knew he was right; she should be more circumspect. If he knew this, so did dozens of other men with whom she had chatted. The guy who proposed marriage, for example, could use this information to stalk her if he got the inclination. She made a mental note to be a little less open and honest from that point forward. She also appreciated that Tim cared enough to give her this advice.

That first date went well enough. Anna half expected— and half wanted—Tim to attempt to make love to her at the end of the evening. When he drove her home, gave her a kiss and asked if he could see her again, she was a little miffed. He later explained that he very much wanted to make love to her but as soon as he saw her in the clinic, he knew he was in it for the long haul. To go after her right away would have been like he expected her to be easy because of her dancing. He did not want her that way. The best method to win her was to be as if they were starting from scratch. In retrospect, she agreed that his approach increased the respect they had for each other, although it did mean the loss of a night of fun.

She asked him later what he would have done if she had said, 'no, I don't want to see you again,' after that first date. He looked her in the eyes, "I knew there was no chance of that. You were as hooked as I was." She was not quite sure that that was the case, but she was not going to offer any comeback. Even if she weren't "irrevocably in love" with him, she still was interested enough to see what he future would hold, if in fact there was a future for the two of them. She was wise enough not to say anything in time that would disappoint him or alter his view of their world together. Whatever routes they each took in their relationship, they arrived at the same place to find irrevocable love.

After that first date, Tim had to get back to Connecticut for school but he traveled to Toronto the next three weekends in order to be with her. It was real sweet and quite chivalrous for him to drive up to twenty hours round trip to see her, but she also saw how bedraggled he was looking. She also imagined that this schedule must wreak havoc on his course work. While she loved the attention and found herself daydreaming during the week about Tim and the next time she would be able to see him, she knew he could not keep going on this way. She continued to dance and suggested that they get together when she came to Connecticut once a month. Tim reluctantly agreed and he would drive to the club and be there waiting outside at 2:00 AM to pick her up. They would go an all-night diner not too far from the club to eat something and talk.

She started to feel guilty about the life she was leading but the guilt was in no way due to Tim's demands. He was always understanding and solicitous. His preference was that she not continue dancing but he could not judge her or be angry. The money was real good and there were bills to pay. Also, if he condemned her for what she was doing, he would have to condemn himself for going there and meeting her in the first place. Instead, he would just see her when he could and wait patiently when he could not. The one thing he made crystal clear to her was that she was not going to get rid of him. She made it clear that she was not going to try.

Anna called Tim one day and said that she had quit dancing and wanted to look for a nursing job in Connecticut. He was thrilled with the news. When he told her he would start looking for an apartment for her, she asked if she could live with him. He responded that he already had a second key made.

Now that she was in love with Tim and could not imagine life without him, a new fear gripped her. She had to break the news to him that she was incapable of having children. When she was three she contracted a rare form of diphtheria. She survived but the disease rendered her ovaries useless. She was petrified that, once she broke the news to Tim, he would reject her. To her relief, his response was: 'Well, I'll never have to share you with anybody else, that is unless we adopt.' Two and a half years later they were married.

•　　•　　•

Her erotic dancing seemed so long ago, such ancient history. *How did the Church find out?* Maybe it was Cathy. Anna had lived with her for nine months when they were both dancing. They used the same booking agent. The two of them would drive down together from Canada. Anna would drop Cathy off at a club in Westchester County, New York and then continue on to Connecticut. Cathy was a sweet girl but she always had a bit of a drug problem. For all Anna knew, she was still dancing to support her habit. It was such a sad existence. It would not be too difficult to locate her and, for a price, get her to spill something.

The other possibility bothered her even more. There used to be another priest at her church when she was in nursing school. What was his name? John. Father John, that was it. She had just started to go with Tim and was sure she was in love with him, but was still stripping. Although Tim was fine with the arrangement, she was wrestling with guilt and all sorts of conflicting feelings. She needed to tell a priest about her moonlighting job. She preferred saying her confession to Father Francis, but John was the available priest on this particular day, so he took her confession. Could he have disclosed something that she said during confession? Could he have told the archbishop about her dancing? That is a mortal sin, isn't it? How could a priest betray her like that? Oh well. *This whole saga had revolved on betrayal. Why would it stop now?*

Anna had no doubt that the sleazy father of Frank, the go-go bar owner, would also be a prime suspect for supplying the pictures the Archbishop referred to. He was always hanging around the bar, leering at the girls, getting hugs so that he could get free feels whenever he could. He always made her and most of the other girls nervous when he was around. How he took pictures is anybody's guess but he was undoubtedly the one supplying them, for a handsome price she was sure.

She had gone through her dancing days without her mother, her grandmother, her employer or anybody else for whom it would have mattered being the wiser. Now, twelve years later, this secret would come crashing down around her because of an arrogant cleric. And it will crash. When the choice was between saving her reputation and the life of her husband, there was no choice.

Knowing the sanctimonious Dr. Richardson the way she did, she would most likely be fired. Not even the kindly Doctors Holt and Cohn could save her from this one. Richardson was the vengeful type who would smear her name all over New York and New Jersey. It would be impossible to get work doing the thing she loved most, working with and being around children.

If she worked in a cancer ward or with geriatric patients, she could outlast the uproar. Pediatrics, though, required doctors and nurses to be of the highest moral fiber, or at least to be perceived as such. She loved working with children; she had a gift for it. Since she was unable to conceive a child of her own, this was the best she could do. To deny this facet of her life would tear a piece out of her heart.

Tim was the biggest piece of her heart, though, and neither the Church nor Judas nor Richardson nor McAlister nor Jesus Christ himself would stand between them.

She had to act, and fast. She grabbed her car keys and headed to the hospital. She needed to be with Tim and get his reassurance once again.

34

René and Marie arrived at the Prefecture of Police at precisely seven in the evening. They were escorted in to Inspector Archambaut's office where he and Dubois were waiting.

René laid out all he knew about the case and about Anna's innocence. He had Marie relay to the Inspector all that she knew about the diary and the coin and then he finished his account. When he mentioned his meeting with Alexa Fontaine, Archambaut stopped him.

"So you were the man who was seen talking with Ms. Fontaine in the park."

René confirmed that he was the man.

"When we arrived, she had left town. We haven't been able to find her."

"After I spoke with her, I advised her to tell you everything she had just told me."

"Which was?"

"That she had never seen Anna Harrington. She came to you after having been ordered to do so by her uncle. Her uncle ordered her to break into Anna and Tim's apartment and get something that could be used to incriminate the Harringtons for LaFleur's murder. I believe you found a drinking glass with Anna's fingerprints at the scene. She did say that her uncle killed LaFleur by accident but that he could use the death to his advantage and he came up with this elaborate scheme to entrap the Harringtons. He is after something they have: a rare coin."

Archambaut was unimpressed with René's account.

"Nothing you have told me changes the evidence implicating Anna Harrington. I'm also considering bringing charges against you for hindering my investigation."

René was prepared for this.

"You have no evidence that I even knew of your investigation. Since I came to you voluntarily, you would be hard pressed to say in court that I was in any way hindering your investigation. Now, how about we put aside our traditional National Police – Gendarmerie animosity and work together on this case."

"But it is not your jurisdiction."

"True, but Anna Harrington is my friend who I am convinced is innocent. I am going to protect her, with or without you."

The two stared at each other until Archambaut burst out in laughter, surprising everyone.

"Fair enough, Captain. I agree with you that Mrs. Harrington is innocent and was being framed. I hoped that by continuing to press charges, we could draw out whoever was doing this to her. You did save me the trouble of having to track down Ms. Fontaine. I trust the summary of your interrogation to tell me there's nothing more to be gained from her. I could I suppose try and get her to arrest her for lying to the police, but the poor drug-addled girl has enough problems in her life. So, you say her uncle put her up to this? Did she mention a name for this uncle?"

"Yes, William Canford."

Both Archambaut and Dubois sat up straight at the mention of this name.

"Canford, you said?"

"Yes, you know him?"

"He's been a thorn in our side for a decade. Always involved in something illegal but we can never nail him for it. We can't even touch him."

"Why not?"

"Diplomatic immunity."

"Who gave him that?"

"The Vatican."

35

"Why don't you tell me about it? I strongly believe that unless we help each other, your husband may never return."

The words hit Anna like a thunderbolt. The Doctors Mordecai, Doctor Frazier and any other physician who had been associated with the case had always been positive and upbeat when they talked about Tim, even when they were dispensing bad news. She knew it was forced, but she appreciated the effort. This was the first time a physician or anybody hinted that there was a possibility they might not be able to save him. It floored her. However, she felt no qualms about telling the entire story, unvarnished and unabridged, to this man, this harbinger of doom. Maybe it was his curious use of the word "return" that intrigued her. She was not sure whether he would understand, but somehow she knew he would listen.

She watched him for a reaction, any reaction whatsoever, as the tale flowed from her mouth. There was none. She was not sure what she was saying, the words just spilled out. Even when she told about her entering Tim's dream world and the revelations that came to her about Judas Iscariot, he sat by impassively, waiting for her to conclude.

When she finished, everything all the way down to the threats she had received from the archbishop was revealed. She was exhausted. She also felt a catharsis. This was the first time she had shared everything with another person. She had never verbalized the entire sequence of events in one telling. Even with René she had withheld tidbits of information. Relating the entire saga in one session was therapeutic. She had spent so much energy working on the individual pieces of the story and trying to weld them together that she had not had a chance to step back and look at the totality of the situation. By losing focus for a few minutes, her mind was made clear. She was not sure whether Dr. Pritak had this effect or whether she had done it herself. It did not matter. She knew what her responsibility was and what actions to take.

"Do you believe any of this, doctor?"

He shrugged, not quite the reaction Anna anticipated. She had poured out her soul to this complete stranger and all she received was a shrug. Somehow, she had expected him to display profound knowledge and insight steeped in Eastern mysticism. A shrug was disappointing.

"I do not have any idea if this is truth or the product of a vivid imagination or multiple imaginations. I knew from the instant I met you that you were deeply troubled. I also knew that you had a deep, spiritual connection with the man lying here. Before I proceed with this procedure, I needed to make sure that your energy, the energy of the person most important in the world to Mr. Harrington, was channeled toward his recovery. It wasn't before. Now it is."

"Are you saying that I did not place my husband's welfare above all else? I have just told you what I've gone through over the past week. How can you say such a thing?" Anna was agitated at this stranger pretending to understand what she was going through or to know her intentions or affections. Dr. Pritak was unmoved.

"I did not say you were not concerned to the utmost, Mrs. Harrington. I said you were not channeled. I could see it in your eyes. I could feel it in your handshake. You were troubled and confused. Now, after relating the events as you understand them to me, I think you are still troubled but you are not confused. Am I correct in this assumption?"

"Yes, doctor. Yes, you are correct."

They stared into each other's eyes for a moment. The Rasputin parallel was getting stronger each second. Dr. Pritak broke the spell.

"I know that the doctors here are going to find it highly unusual and will protest, but I want you in the operating room when we perform the procedure. Would you agree?"

"Yes."

"You are strong enough to see your husband cut open and things done to his brain? He will twitch about and it will sometimes appear that we are losing him. Are you strong enough to sit there and let us do our jobs while you, in your own way, do yours?"

"I will be strong enough, doctor. When are you planning the surgery?"

"The day after tomorrow, on Saturday morning. Is Dr. Cohn all ready to accompany you to temple and assist you in the service?"

"Yes, he is."

"Good. I would like to see you again here on Friday night afterwards. Does that meet with your approval?"

"Of course."

"Till then."

With that, Dr. Pritak gave Anna a slight bow and left the room. After he left, it occured to her that she had no recollection of mentioning Dr. Cohn by name to him. She had not meant to withhold anything; it had not seemed important to tell his name. She wracked her brain to remember what she had said. Maybe she did identify him as the one who would be helping her with the Kaddish, although she was practically certain that she made a vague reference about a doctor at the clinic. She found herself staring at the door through which Dr. Manesh Pritak had departed, wondering about this odd man.

Anna had called Dr. Cohn earlier that day, advising him that Mrs. Kaplan, her fictitious neighbor, had passed away the previous night. He would be honored to accompany her to his synagogue, Temple Beth Shalom, for services that next evening, which was a Friday. Again, he told her that saying Kaddish for her friend was a mitzvah, a blessing. Anna's guilt engulfed her as she went deeper and deeper into her lie. She had no other choice. She hoped for it all to proceed without incident.

Dr. Cohn had suggested they meet at the coffee shop near the temple so he could fill her in on what to expect at the ceremony. He prepared a "cheat sheet" for her, a transliteration of the Kaddish. He was already seated at a booth when she arrived. She sat down and ordered a cup of coffee. He started right in.

"Kaddish will be toward the end of the ceremony. The rabbi will ask if anyone is mourning for a departed person. People who have lost someone will stand up. Sometimes, people near the mourner will also stand up so that the person is not standing there alone. It is a show of compassion and solidarity. I will be glad to stand up with you."

All Anna could muster was a wan smile.

"The customs vary from temple to temple. In our temple, it is customary for the mourner to recite the name of the deceased to the congregation."

"What?"

Dr. Cohn seemed startled at Anna's reaction.

"Yes, it's just a little tradition we have where the congregation becomes intimately involved in the bereavement process; they become one with the mourner. It is of greater comfort to the departed loved ones if they can share the name with others."

"Do...do you have to say the name?" Anna's plans were unraveling. She hoped to anonymously say Kaddish for Judas, pray that her act will be enough to free Tim from the hell or purgatory or limbo or wherever he was and let life go on. Her plan was to rush from the temple to the hospital and then, if Tim had regained consciousness, to St. Mary's Catholic Church, which was a block away and hand the coin to the priest. She had already called Archbishop McAllister to tell him that he could have the bloody coin. She was taking it to the church that evening. He advised her that she was being very wise in doing this. She hung up. It all seemed so simple.

Standing up and saying that Judas was the person whom she was mourning, however, had the potential to blow everything up in her face. At the least, she would be labeled as a complete idiot. More than that, word could get back to the Archbishop and he would follow through with his threats. She would put nothing past him.

Her actions would also be a slap in the face of Dr. Cohn and the rest of congregation. It would appear as if she was making a mockery of this sacred ritual. She did not want to do anything whatsoever that would show disrespect to the doctor or his fellow Jews. She felt backed into a corner. She was tempted to blurt out the truth to Dr. Cohn and hope he would be understanding and supportive. She also toyed with the ideas of either saying nothing or of saying the name "Naomi (she had gone so far in this charade to have even invented a first name for her fictitious neighbor) Kaplan" out loud but inwardly reciting Judas Iscariot. She dismissed this option. She could not run the risk of her embarrassment ruining the ritual; she had to proceed regardless of how mortifying it would be. She could not take any chances.

She would have preferred to go alone to a different temple, perhaps one where they did not ask for the name of the dead. She could recite his name in her heart and be done with it. She dismissed this as an option. She had no time—Tim did not have time—to go looking for another temple where she was a complete stranger to everyone. She was heading into a world that was foreign to her and she needed Dr. Cohn as a sponsor. His temple used a lot of Hebrew; she would be totally lost without his guidance.

"Our temple is Conservative, but over the years some Reformed touches have been added. We aren't quite to the point where we're having folk masses, although I wouldn't say that it's out of the question. Mentioning the name is one of the touches we have incorporated into the service that everyone seems to like. It's highly unusual in our temple not to say the departed's name. You don't have to be nervous. I will be there for you."

"Thank you, doctor, but please do not stand with me. It is something I need to do on my own."

"I understand, my dear."

No you don't. But I'm afraid that you will before too long. At least if you're sitting down, you will not share in the reproachful glares that your fellow congregants will be sending my way.

As the sun set, Anna and Dr. Cohn started their walk to the temple. Rather, Dr. Cohn walked, Anna trudged. She had an inkling how Sister Catherine must have felt as they led her from the *Conciergerie* to the cart that would transport her to the guillotine. The main difference was that at least Sister Catherine had a sense of finality about where she was going. Her faith even gave her certainty about her fate after the blade fell. Anna had nothing but question marks floating around her head.

The walk took a few minutes; Anna was hoping it could be made to last days. Dr. Cohn put his yarmulke on his head and prayer shawl around his shoulders as he headed into the temple. He ran into people he knew and introduced Anna to them. As he escorted her, more people came up to greet him before services began. Unfortunately, his usual seat was right in the middle of the auditorium. If they were at least in the back, maybe she would do her deed and then disappear through the doors without everyone staring at her. That was to be out of the question given where they were located.

Two things popped into her mind as she sat there dreading the upcoming ceremony. One almost made her laugh. She lamented why Jesus could not have been betrayed by someone named Bob Smith or Joe Johnson. If she got up and recited one of those names, no one would have been the wiser. Any one of a million other names would not have stood out, but it had to be Judas Iscariot. It was, as Sister Catherine's diary stated, the name of the most reviled man in history. Even Jews, who did not believe in Jesus as the Messiah, were familiar with the infamy of Judas Iscariot. She could not imagine a congregant leaning over to another and saying: 'Is that the Judas who used to live in Bayonne? I believe I read about his death in the paper the other day. I hear he left a wife and two kids. Poor guy.' It was a pretty good guess that everyone in the room will figure that there was only one Judas.

The other thing was that she wished Dr. Cohn had belonged to an ultra-orthodox instead of conservative temple. Often, the women sit separately from the men in those services. Given her ignorance of Judaism, it surprised her that she knew this fact. Maybe it came from watching *Fiddler on the Roof* all those times. Anyway, in an orthodox temple, Dr. Cohn could be a little more anonymous.

She looked at the dear, kind man and was sorry about the embarrassment he was about to endure. She hoped that once it was all over, he would allow her to explain herself. He had always been a friend in the office. She was not even sure that she would be able to work with him again. Despite his declarations that he was not religious, Judaism was important to him. The community and acceptance he experienced in the temple was a pleasure in his life. Her actions would be seen as a reflection on him, her sponsor for the evening. That was not right.

The evening services began. Anna heard bits and pieces. The cantor, she noted, had a beautiful voice, capable of lifting the entire congregation up to Heaven. Do Jews believe in Heaven, she wondered? It was impossible for her to maintain focus. Dr. Cohn must have detected her nervousness because he reached over to put his hand on her arm for comfort. This made her feel worse.

The Rabbi delivered a sermon on tolerance and acceptance. He warned the congregation that they should not rush to judgment. Often, the truth is buried below a veneer of falsehoods. Instead, he told them to wait until the facts were all presented and sorted out. Otherwise, hasty, ill-conceived opinions would be the result. His lesson was to be put to the test a lot sooner than anyone could have guessed.

After the public announcements were read, the rabbi announced that Kaddish would now be read. He asked anyone who was in mourning to please rise and after the recitation, they were invited to say the name of the deceased. From Dr. Cohn's description and the rabbi's tone, invited was translated to mean expected.

Dr. Cohn prodded Anna to stand. She rose along with seven other people in the pews. The cantor led the congregation in the reading. Anna read along using the transliteration provided by Dr. Cohn:

Yis'ga'dal v'yis'kadash sh'may ra'bbo b'omo dee'vro chir'usay v'yamlich malchu'say, b'chayaychon uv'yomay'chon uv'chayay d'chol bais Yisroel, ba'agolo u'viz'man koriv; v'imru Omein.

Y'hay shmay rabbo m'vorach l'olam ul'olmay olmayo.

Yisborach v'yishtabach v'yispoar v'yisromam v'yismasay, v'yishador v'yis'aleh v'yisalal, shmay d'kudsho, brich hu, l'aylo min kl birchoso v'sheeroso, tush'bechoso v'nechemoso, da, ameeran b'olmo; vimru Omein.

Y'hay shlomo rabbo min sh'mayo, v'chayim alaynu v'al kol Yisroel; vimru Omein.

Oseh sholom bimromov, hu ya'aseh sholom olaynu, v'al kol Yisroel; vimru Omein.

The temple was silent for a moment and then the first of the mourners spoke up: Morris Rivkin. The others followed at respectful intervals: Rebecca Fein; James Stern; Sol Cohen; Alex Goldhammer; Joseph Golokow; Abby Martz. Even though heads were bowed, Anna felt every eye in the place burning a hole in her as she hesitated. Dr. Cohn softy urged her to go ahead. She swallowed.

"Judas Iscariot."

The rustling and murmurs were audible. Dr. Cohn looked up at her in absolute bewilderment. Anna wished she could be absorbed into the pew as every eye was indeed burning into her. The air suddenly became unbearably stifling. After what seemed an eternity, she grabbed her purse, whispered that she was sorry to Dr. Cohn and bolted past the stunned people through the doors out into the open air. Tears streamed down her cheeks. Her consolation was that she had done it. Now rushed to the hospital to see if there had been any effect.

36

Phil sporadically returned to Tim Harrington's case since his father had appeared; he arrived at the hospital when he was sure Alexander would not be there. He would have dropped Tim as a patient but having Jen—he meant Anna—tell him to remain on the case was a strong incentive to put aside his ill feelings for his father and return to the hospital.

During this time, he was seeing a few of his other clients for psychoanalysis sessions, but it was obvious his mind was not focused on their problems. It was during one such session that his phone rang. Much to the consternation of the patient, Phil answered. It was the duty nurse from the trauma unit. She sounded panicked and asked that he hurry over to the hospital. Dr. Frazier was unavailable and Phil was still listed on the chart as a consulting physician. She explained that Tim Harrington was experiencing a seizure and the resident on duty, Dr. Suarez, was having trouble subduing him. Phil cut the session short, telling the nurse he would be there in ten minutes.

When Phil arrived, Tim was being restrained by the resident and three nurses. Even with all these people, Tim was able to put up a colossal struggle. Dr. Suarez had already given him a shot of thorazine and was about to give him another but he wanted to speak with the attending physician first. Phil looked at Tim, who was still unconscious but was straining to the utmost. Phil looked around but saw no signs of Anna. She would normally be here at this hour. Where was she?

A quick decision had to be made. "Yes, give him another shot."

The drugs kicked in and Tim's drenched body went limp. Even then, he gave an occasional involuntary twitch. *What is going on in there?*

Anna walked in. Phil could tell that she was expecting something to be different about her husband. She sank into a chair, crestfallen when she saw Tim lying there, unresponsive. It was obvious that he had been through something but that seemed to make no impression on her.

"Hi Jen, I mean Anna."

Anna sat down deflated. "I did exactly what Sister Catherine wanted me to do, but it didn't matter. It didn't matter at all."

"What are you talking about, Anna? Are you okay?"

"I said Kaddish; I said it for Jud." She stopped herself.

"I'm sure I have no idea what you're saying."

Phil left the room to go and gather a printout. Anna remained with Tim.

Tim lay there, immobile and asleep.

"What a goddamned fool I've been. Phil was right. It's voodoo. I'm insane and I've dragged others down as well. I doubt I can ever look Dr. Cohn in the eye again. Poor René is running around like a fool trying to get answers to totally idiotic questions and is in danger of being arrested, all because of me. If I got you back, I wouldn't care; but it didn't work. It didn't work."

Anna's tears could no longer be held back. She wept as she had never wept before.

Phil had re-entered and walked over to her but she refused his consolation.

He felt Anna's tears as much as she did. He looked on her and his mind saw the big sister who leveled the school bully with one punch. He saw the teenage girl walking him to school. He saw the woman who craved her father's approval and attention. He no longer saw Anna Harrington; the woman sobbing before him was now Jennifer Mordecai.

In all their life together, he had never seen her as upset as this. He could not conceive of anybody doing anything to hurt her in this way. She was the most loving and giving person in the world. Anyone who could hurt her so must have something intrinsically wrong with him.

Jennifer had always been there for him. He would not let her down; he would be there for her. No matter what it took, he would protect her.

Phil let Anna cry herself out and then he piled her into the car. He basically led her, or what was left of her, compliantly into the front seat like a lamb being taken to slaughter. The actions that he needed to take to protect her were beginning to crystallize in his mind.

It was about 9:30 PM when he walked her into the house. After being led to the bedroom, she crawled under the covers without undressing; she was asleep before her head hit the pillow. Phil tucked her in, gently kissed her cheek and turned to head out. At the door he could not help but turn around to look at her sleeping. How beautiful she was. His duty became clear. He turned on his heels and walked out the door.

• • •

Anna had been asleep no more than a half an hour when the phone jarred her awake. The call had already kicked to the voice mail before her wits returned enough for her to answer. She contemplated getting rid of the telephone once this was all over. For now, though, she had no choice but to answer it. She waited a few minutes to let the message get absorbed into the system and then picked up the receiver to call voice mail. Besides the recent missed call, there were two other messages waiting for her.

The first, as she half-expected, was Dr. Cohn. He was demanding an explanation (as was his rabbi), but his voice was not angry. Instead, it betrayed concern for her well-being. He wanted to talk with her. It was obvious to him that she was hurting and he knew her well enough that she must have a good explanation for her behavior. He was there to help her get through whatever it was that was bothering her.

She could not describe how much better his words made her feel. She punched in the next message. It was from a Bruce Friedman. He was a member of the Beth Shalom Temple and was there this evening. He was also a reporter for the *New York Herald*. He was planning on submitting a byline piece to the paper about her saying Kaddish for Judas and wanted to get a statement from her before he submitted it. He made it clear that he was sending it in whether he spoke with her or not, but he wanted to give her a chance to explain herself. He wanted to know if she was saying an earnest prayer for someone many people consider the vilest demon ever to have lived, whether it was a prank, like something someone does as an initiation to join a fraternity, or whether she was an anti-Semite and this was a novel way of defiling a most sacred ritual.

His tone, as opposed to Dr. Cohn's, was menacing and full of venom. She had no intention of returning the call. He would write whatever he wanted anyway. All she could do was to give him more ammunition.

She thought about the Archbishop. She had not yet returned the coin and it was past the time of his ultimatum. If he had not yet carried through on his threat, an article in a major newspaper would definitely provoke him. She was sure that, if the *Herald* agreed to print the article, word would get back to the Archbishop by tomorrow. The smear campaign would begin. If her acts had revived Tim, she could put up with all the rest, even the possibility of estrangement from her mother and excommunication from the church. With Tim still unconscious, the future looked bleak on all fronts. Dread enveloped her.

Reluctantly, she brought forth the third message. It was Dr. Manesh Pritak. His voice was anxious. It was urgent that he talk with her as soon as possible. He was on his way over to her house and would wait for her there. He was coming up from Edison and would arrive by 11:30. He hoped she was checking her messages and would be able to see him. He left his cell phone number in case she needed to reach him but he was on his way.

Great. The last thing Anna needed was a visitor. The way this was all going, she was sure he would break more bad news to her. There was nothing to do but wait, something she was not good at under the best of times. Now, it would be next to impossible.

Dr. Pritak arrived ten minutes earlier than he said he would. She could imagine how fast he drove up the New Jersey Turnpike. He walked into the house without even a hello. The level of excitement in his voice over the phone had not dissipated one bit.

"I spoke with Dr. Mordecai, the younger one, a little while ago. He described what happened and how dejected you were. I can't have this. I cannot have this at all. It just will not do. For the procedure to be a complete success, I need your utmost cooperation."

"Doctor, when I saw Tim, he was unresponsive, totally unconscious. I hoped...I prayed that today would be the day he would snap out of it."

"Why is that, my dear?"

"I did it. I went and recited Kaddish for Judas Iscariot. I believed maybe he would release his hold after I did this. It is what I have been building up to ever since Tim became unconscious...it didn't work."

"It didn't, did it?"

"No, you spoke with Dr. Mordecai yourself, didn't you?" Anna did not mean for the tone of her comment to come out so nasty but she was so frustrated and upset. Dr. Pritak did not seem to take offense.

"Let's review the situation for a moment. In the medical and scientific world, we like to have things controlled as we test one assumption at a time. You, on the other hand, have been basing your actions on many assumptions piled on top of each other. You have ventured into a world in which you have limited experience on the basis of dozens of guesses. Then, when you don't get the results you are looking for, you stop looking. I apologize if this sounds like I am lecturing you, given what you are going through. What I am saying is that instead of giving up, go back and review all of your assumptions. Look for mistakes or misinterpretations you may have made along the way and make adjustments. "

"I am just so tired, doctor. I don't know how much I have left."

"You have plenty left. Give it a chance. Tim needs your strength. He needs to tap into the bond that the two of you have for each other to give him strength."

Anna was not impressed. Since she last saw Tim, she was becoming increasingly convinced that it was strictly a medical condition he was experiencing. Maybe he had contracted some rare virus. All her thoughts about some mystical being holding him back were as ludicrous as they sounded. How could she be such a fool?

"Thank you doctor for everything you have done. I will be there for the procedure."

"Well, if you don't think that there is a strong connection between you and your husband, there is nothing more I can do here. I do have one question, though. Do you remember what time it was you said the Kaddish?"

"Around eight, I think."

"I believe that if you check Tim's records, you will find that, even though he never attained consciousness, it took three nurses, a doctor and two shots of thorazine to subdue him around that time. Could be just some chemical reaction in his body or maybe there was something else going on in there. I surely don't know, but I recommend that you think about it before tomorrow morning. Good night, madam."

Dr. Pritak left the house as quickly as he had arrived. What was it about this man? He seemed to believe and support her. He was even urging her on. When she had arrived at the hospital room, Tim was in fact covered with sweat but that had happened before. Phil did not mention needing three nurses and a doctor and drugs to restrain him. Why was that?

Anna was not feeling quite as despondent as she had before, but neither was she brimming with optimism. She wanted to go back to sleep but now her mind was racing. She might as well get her other duty call out of the way. She sighed as she picked up the phone.

"Hello."

"Hello, Dr. Cohn."

"If it isn't my little rabble rouser. How are you doing, my dear?"

"I'm so sorry, Dr. Cohn. I hope you can someday forgive me."

"It's already happened. At first, I must admit I was furious. I felt used and betrayed. Kind of a fitting feeling, considering it's Judas we're talking about. Then, as I looked around the temple, I realized that it was a shaking up we've needed for a long, long time. Like anything that you do for a while, things had gotten stale and routine. After the initial tumult died down, Rabbi Schecter led us in a discussion of the meaning of Kaddish. And it was a real discussion, not a sermon that we sit and endure. People who hadn't really thought about it were now asking insightful questions. Their questions induced other people to ask questions and so on. It turned into the most meaningful service I think I've ever been to. Thank you."

Anna was floored. "There is no need to thank me. The effect on the service was unintentional, I can assure you."

"Would you care to tell me now what this is all about? I think I have somewhat of a right to know why you have an affinity for the poor departed Mrs. Kaplan, I mean Mr. Iscariot."

The doctor's humor was having a miraculous effect on her mood.

"Yes, you do have that right but it's a long story that I would rather tell in person."

"Come right over. I'll put a pot of coffee on. You have my address, don't you?"

"Yes. Doctor, do you know a Bruce Friedman?"

"Yes, why?"

"When I got home, I found a message from him saying he was submitting a story to the newspaper about tonight's incident, although I do not think the part you just told me will find its way into the column."

"I've known Bruce since he was a kid. He's always been a little snot. He acts like such a big man around the temple, a *macher*, we would call him. Whenever I see him getting too full of himself, I ask him when he's going to work for a real paper. That gets under his skin. He's always trying to stir something up. Don't worry. Nothing will get in the paper. I'll give him a call right now."

"Will he listen to you?"

"Oh yes, especially after I remind him that I went to high school with his father who has a few skeletons that I don't think dear Mr. Friedman would like let out of the closet at a temple social hour. He'll listen."

"Thank you, doctor. I'm on my way over."

Anna arrived and Dr. Cohn became the second person to whom she related the entire tale. Like Dr. Pritak, he sat impassively and let her tell it in her own way, in her own time. When she finished, Anna looked to Dr. Cohn for reaction and reassurance.

"At first, I was a little hurt that you did not feel you could confide in me. Now, I can understand why you invented poor Mrs. Kaplan, may she rest in peace. I am not sure what I would have done if you had been up front with me. In all probability, I would have acted as you suspected. I would have tried to talk you out of it and suggested that you go see a shrink, which, by the way, is probably not such a bad idea even now. Be that as it may, I do understand what you are going through and why you feel you have to see this through to the end."

"You do? Please explain it to me because I am sure I do not understand it one bit."

"You remember how I was a few years ago when my wife, Rachel, passed away? I was a total wreck. I suspect that you and Tim have the same type of relationship we had. Anyway, when we first found out she had cancer, we did everything we could to battle it. You'll never know some of the off-the-wall treatments we were considering. In the end, the cancer won out. But I'll never regret that we tried everything even if it went against logic and my medical training. To this day if someone came to me and told me they had a, how did you put it, hare-brained way to get her back, I'd do it in a heartbeat."

"Are you telling me you think I'm right?"

"Not in the least. Medical school and fifty years in medicine did not prepare me to answer that question. One thing I can tell you is that your Indian doctor is correct. Tim needs your strength. You've followed your heart so far, and a damn good heart it is. So I say continue on to the end, whatever that end may be. You won't regret it."

"Doctor, there is one thing I haven't told you."

"And just when I thought I heard it all."

"The church is pressuring me to give the coin back to them. If I don't, they will smear my name all around."

"What can they say about you that's that bad?"

"I used to dance nude in a club. I was a stripper. I gave lap dances to men for lots of money. They say they have some pictures. They will make it sound a lot worse than it was but I won't be able to refute it with any credibility once the pictures are out. They have threatened to contact people who are important to me, my mother, you, and others in the office. They've also threatened to excommunicate me and my mother. Even though I'm not a practicing Catholic, the threat's hitting me very hard. That was why I was so concerned about Bruce Friedman's article. It would give them the green light to go ahead."

Dr. Cohn absorbed this for a few seconds and then asked a simple question.

"Do you still dance?"

"No, of course not."

"Damn. I missed my chance for a lapdance then, didn't I?"

"Yes you did, you dirty old man, although for you I would consider coming out of retirement."

"I greatly resent the old part. In terms of whatever happens, we'll address it when and if it happens. I want to assure you that you will have your job, even if it means paying you out of my own pocket. In terms of being excommunicated, you'd make a terrific Jew. I'd be honored to sponsor you...then again, after tonight's surprises, let me think that one over."

They both laughed as the tension was officially relieved.

"Your full concentration at the moment should be on that husband of yours. Don't get bogged down in all these other distractions. Now, it's getting late and I think we've said about everything that needs to be said. So off with you. Go home and get a good night's sleep. It's been one helluva day for all of us."

*   *   *

When she woke up the next morning, Anna was feeling a newfound optimism. Tim was no better off than he had been the previous morning but the difference was that they were going to fight. They would fight as hard as they ever had in their lives to defeat whatever this was that gripped him. Together they would not fail, she was confident now. The Church and Judas be damned. She hurried to get herself ready.

37

René and Archambaut sat in Monsignor Lachaille's anteroom, waiting for his current meeting to end. The receptionist explained to them that his eminence was booked for the day and would not be able to see them. They would wait.

After a half hour, the door opened and the Monsignor appeared as he was saying goodbye to his guest. He did not appear to notice the two officers until René stood up.

"Your Eminence, I'm Gendarmerie Captain Bouvil and this is Inspector Archambaut of the National Police. We'd like to ask you a few questions about William Canford."

At the mere mention of the name, Lachaille blanched. He turned to his receptionist.

"Alice, please reschedule my next appointment while I talk with these gentlemen."

He escorted them into his office and closed the door behind them.

"Mr. Canford does some work for us, usually as a kind of private investigator."

"Did you know," asked Archambaut, "that he may have been involved in the death of Mr. Etienne LaFleur, the man who assisted the Ordre de la Tour convent in selling some articles, including a rare coin that I understand you desperately want back?"

Lachaille blanched anew. "Death, you say?"

"Yes, he was killed and then it was staged so that it looked like a suicide and then steps were taken to implicate an American woman, Anna Harrington, who I understand currently possesses the coin."

Lachaille stood up and walked over to the window.

"I never realized a man was killed. I've always suspected that Mr. Canford operated in the gray areas of the law."

"And with his diplomatic immunity, sometimes in the black areas as well," interjected Archambaut."

"Yes, that is most likely true but because he produced results for us, we never asked too many questions, I'm afraid."

"What did you want him to do this time?"

"He was tasked to retrieve the coin Mrs. Harrington has in her possession. It is vital that the church get it back."

"Why?"

"You would not believe me if I told you."

"Try us." René responded. "I've seen some strange things over the past few weeks. One more would not surprise me."

The Monsignor decided to come out straight with it.

"The coin is one of the thirty pieces of silver given to Judas for his betrayal of Jesus Christ. There had always been rumors about its existence, and about its immense power. It's reputed to curse anyone who comes in contact with it."

Archambaut had had enough.

"I'm as spiritual as the next guy but if you expect me to believe this superstitious drivel about a cursed coin, you should get your head examined. No offense, your eminence."

Lachaille was about to respond but René cut him off.

"It's not drivel; it's all true. That's what Anna could not tell me. She thought I would believe her crazy, and I probably would have. But it all comes together. Tim's mysterious illness, him speaking to her in a dream, the nun, the Roman soldier, all of it. It all makes sense now."

"I'm glad you think so," was Archambaut's deadpan response.

"Where is Canford now?"

"He's in America, in New York."

"Do you think he's capable of hurting Anna?" René was getting increasingly concerned.

"Canford is the type of man who will do anything to accomplish his objective if he believes it to be a holy mission, which he will in this case."

"Knowing the kind of man he is, can you call him off?"

"I couldn't even if I knew how. This has worked its way up to the highest levels of the church. In any case, I have no way to get in touch with him. I know he's in the U.S. because he had us buy him airfare a few days ago."

"If he's that obsessed, why didn't he follow Mrs. Harrington to the States months ago when she first got the coin?"

Lachaille laughed.

"The bureaucracy of the church combined with the fact that he's very cheap. He's gotten burned a few times when we didn't properly reimburse him for his expenses so he makes us pay in advance. In this case his paperwork got lost and had to get multiple signatures before it could get approved."

René and Archambaut rose to leave.

"Thank you, Monsignor. You've been most helpful. May I suggest you do a better job of vetting the people who work for you from now on."

The Monsignor nodded but said nothing in return.

38

Alexander arrived at the hospital early in the morning, his custom whenever he had an operation to perform. As he took his first look at Tim, he knew something was definitely wrong. The outward signs were not obvious, but there was trouble. He asked the nurse if Tim Harrington's sugar level had been checked recently. She responded it was not included in the routine battery of tests. He gave no diabetic inclinations. Alexander ordered her to measure it for him.

At first, the young nurse was reluctant because the attending physician, Dr. Frazier, had not authorized any such procedure. Alexander was in no mood and advised her that he would do it himself if she did not move her backside. The nurse obeyed.

The results were as Alexander suspected. Tim Harrington's blood sugar level was so low that he was for all intents and purposes in insulin shock. Alexander reviewed the chart and found no record of Tim having been given insulin. Looking at the sugar level, he knew that if he did not act right now, the patient would be dead within a few hours. He and the nurse went into action, injecting adrenaline and high glucose solutions. Within ten minutes, his levels were back to near normal. Alexander knew that Tim Harrington was in no shape for surgery today, but why he was in this state was a complete mystery.

Dr. Pritak arrived soon after this episode, as did Anna.

"Dr. Pritak, could you please handle things here? There's something I need to check on."

As he was leaving the room, Anna intercepted him. "Alexander, thank you. You saved my husband's life. What happened?"

"I need to find Phil. I think he may be in some trouble."

"Did he have anything to do with this?"

"I can't talk. I just have to find him."

"You're too upset to drive. I'll drive you."

"Okay, let's go."

As they walked out of the hospital, a light but steady rain was falling. They drove to Phil's apartment and then to his office. Finding him in neither place, Anna suggested they follow her hunch. As they drove up, they saw him sitting on the front steps of her house. He was wet and disheveled, looking like he was waiting for someone to arrive. Alexander dreaded who that someone was. They stopped the car down the street so they would not startle or confuse him.

"Anna, let me go to him first, please."

"Of course."

Alexander walked up.

"Hi, Son."

"Hi, Dad."

"What are you doing here?

"Just waiting."

Alexander did not like the robotic responses he was receiving from his son but he did not have much choice. He had to coax Philip along.

"Mind if I wait with you?"

"No, maybe the two of you can talk when she gets back."

"Who, son?"

"Oh, Dad. You know very well that Jennifer is due home soon. I know she forgives you. I forgive you, too. She'll get back and we'll all have a good talk. I wish Mom were still around, she could join us, too. Jennifer makes real good coffee. She does everything very well. I wish you had gotten to know her better."

Alexander did do all he could to hold back his tears. Compassion for his son was mixed with profound guilt as Phil was indeed sowing the truth interspersed with his delusional babblings. He had to maintain his strength for himself and for Phil.

"Good. We'll have some coffee. You shouldn't be sitting out in the rain like this, should you?"

"I didn't even notice it was raining, to tell you the truth. I was so excited about seeing Jennifer again. I don't want to leave, though. I can't take a chance that I'll miss her."

"I'm excited, too, son. Of course you don't want to miss her. I'm parked over here. Why don't you come and sit in the car? You'll be able see her from there."

"That's a good idea, Dad."

As they started to walk to the car, Alexander casually asked his son: "Phil, were you at the hospital this morning?"

"Yes, I was. The man Jennifer is seeing is a patient there. He upsets Jen all the time. You should have seen her cry the other day. It would have broken your heart. Between you and me, he's not good enough for her. He's not doing real well. I gave him something to ease his pain."

"That was very thoughtful of you, son."

As they approached the car, a huge grin spread over Phil's face.

"Why you old fox you."

"What is it Phil?"

"She's sitting here in your car all along. You wanted to surprise me! I'll bet you and she had a nice long talk and patched everything up. This is wonderful."

They reached the car. Phil opened the door.

"Hi Jen!" he called out to his "sister."

Anna did not know how to respond until she looked at Alexander. Taking his cue, she played along.

"Did you and Dad have a good talk? Is everything okay now?"

"Everything is fine, Phil," she responded.

At Alexander's suggestion, they drove back to the hospital. Once there, they were able to convince Phil that he looked exhausted and needed a rest. While he said he was not tired, he agreed maybe some sleep would do him good. They found him a bed and gave him a sedative. Soon he was out cold.

Anna and Alexander sat down in the lounge.

"Doctor, are you okay?"

"Yes," he lied.

"Hopefully he'll be okay. The forced sleep will do him some good."

"I'm not so sure. There are many things that I've always passed off as eccentricities that I now realize may go deeper. We can't take any chances. I've put a call into Dr. James Cirillo. He's a psychiatrist who knows Phil. I want him to do a full evaluation."

"Do you think that's necessary? Maybe he's going through extreme nervous exhaustion. Heaven knows we've all been through enough stress to last a couple lifetimes."

"Anna, there's something I have to tell you. Phil tried to kill your husband this morning."

"What?"

"The low blood sugar levels resulted from a massive insulin injection Phil gave him just before I arrived this morning. If I had gotten there maybe a half hour later, Tim would be dead now. You have every right to press charges but I am begging you not to."

"Why shouldn't I?"

"I have two reasons. The first is I am convinced that he doesn't even know he did it. He did it to ease your husband's—or rather Jennifer's friend's—pain. He's doing whatever he can to protect her.

"The second reason is selfish. I've already lost one child due to neglect on my part. Losing a second would kill me."

The look on Alexander's face said it all.

"Nothing would be gained by pressing charges," she relented. "What happens next?"

"We'll have to put off the surgery at least a day. Tim's body and brain will need a while to recover strength. We still have to relieve the pressure on his brain, but it appears to be under control, at least for the moment. It is still a case of the sooner the better but I can't risk operating on him in this condition. Tomorrow we will know more. I need to sit down with Dr. Pritak a bit and replan our strategy."

He paused for a second and then felt that Anna needed some words of encouragement to hang onto.

"Things will turn around for the better. I have a good gut about these things."

"What was Jennifer like?"

Alexander stared into space a moment.

"Jennifer was a contradiction in so many ways. She could be brilliant one second and then make a boneheaded mistake the next. One moment she could be telling hilarious jokes and stories and then slip into deep melancholy. She was a tomboy who loved frilly dresses and perfume. The one thing that was consistent about her was how kind and caring she was with everyone she came in contact with.

"When she was born, I have to admit that I was depressed she was a girl. I have no idea where that attitude came from, but I felt it nonetheless. I think she sensed this, even though I loved her. I was working the longest hours of my life at that time. In short, I wasn't there for her when she needed me.

"I also think because of the contradictions I mentioned about her, she was a complex person. It was hard to know her. People like consistency; they like to know what to expect. People will take the easy way out. If it takes that much hard work just to get to know you, they'll move on to someone else. I know I didn't work hard enough at it.

"Phil, I think, was the only one she ever confided in wholeheartedly. When she died, he blamed me for all the things I've mentioned. We didn't speak to each other for over a decade, not until your husband drew us back together. Now, he seems to have transferred Jennifer to someone else: you. It appears we may be going through the cycle again."

"You'll get him back. You'll see."

"I hope so. God, I hope so."

Alexander went off to meet with Dr. Pritak. Anna hovered around Tim the rest of the day, filling him in on what was happening in the zoo they now called their lives. Maybe by repeating the entire tale with all its twists and turns out loud, some of it might begin to make sense. Of course, it did not work. Nothing made sense. At around five, she decided to head home and spend a quiet, undisturbed evening. Maybe rent an escapist movie to transport her mind as far away as possible from this mess.

Even though Dr. Cohn would keep all of this foolishness from reaching the newspapers, the wrath of the Catholic Church was looming out there. How could an Archbishop, a man of God, sound so menacing? Anna thought of her mother and then of how Phil and Alexander did not speak for years. She could not bear it if the Church carried through with its threat and told her mother everything, with embellishments. Anna would protest meekly but it would be her word against the Church and the pictures. She would have to depend on her mother's love, which was formidable. But her mother's love of God and Church was formidable, too. If the archbishop went so far as to excommunicate Anna, it could alter the special relationship she had always had with her mother.

The idea that she could be excommunicated hung heavily over her. When the archbishop mentioned it, she did not know how to take this threat. At first she almost laughed because it seemed such an antiquated concept that must have gone out of vogue in about the seventeenth century. The more she thought about it, however, the more distraught she became. On one level, she knew it was silly to be taking this threat seriously, but her subconscious kept tugging at her. There was always the comfort that she could return to the fold if and when she ever saw the need. Excommunication took away any opportunity to return if she felt the inclination. Even if no one else cared, she would always feel the stigma as an outcast that was placed on her. She knew she lacked the courage to be a Hester Prynne. It would eat at her heart from the inside out.

She could not let herself get mired in despair. She kept plugging along. Tim was her world and if that world no longer included her mother, so be it.

Even if Anna was a complete fool and an idiot to boot, this was no time to let a setback keep her from seeing this through to the end. If she was wrong in her belief that a coin can have powers, which any sane person would readily acknowledge it could not, the worse thing that could happen was that she remained a fool. On the other hand, if by some remote miracle she was fundamentally correct but had misread the signs, stopping now would be wrong.

The anger that was swelling in her was due to her conviction that she was positive she had read the signs correctly. By saying Kaddish, she had upheld her part of the bargain. The other party, namely Judas Iscariot, had reneged on his obligation. Although one would hardly expect anything different from Judas, it did not fit in with the way Anna lived her life. She had always proceeded on the assumption that people deserved the benefit of the doubt unless and until they proved otherwise. It was a philosophy that got her into trouble; she would get burned by people she had counted on but who, in the end, let her down. On the other hand, she found having an optimistic trust of people to be a much happier way to go through life than to start off with an automatic mistrust of them. She knew that this philosophy had rubbed off on Tim over the years and that he was a much better, and much happier, person for it.

But all bets were off. If you were to try and deal with Judas Iscariot, you had to go in knowing you were entering into a pact with the devil. She needed to confront Judas, and if necessary meet the devil himself head on, to get the answers she was looking for. Why didn't Kaddish work? Why didn't Judas stick to his end of the bargain? She was going back.

Anna was scared. Continued contact with the coin could suck her deeper into this dream world. Granted, she would spend eternity with Tim, but what kind of eternity would it be? Tim was not even Tim. He was a robot in his skin. She could end up the same. It was a risk she had to take.

She powered off both her phones; she did not want anything bothering her this evening. She slipped the chain around her neck and settled down. Sleep would not come easily as she was so keyed-up, but exhaustion overtook her.

39

After numerous fruitless calls to the FBI, New Jersey State Police and any other American law enforcement agency René and Archambaut could think of, René found himself on an Air France flight into Newark. They did not have enough evidence to convince anybody that Canford was a danger or, if they did believe he was a threat, that resources should be dedicated to track him down. 'The guy has Vatican clearance, for heaven's sake. How much of a threat can he be?' was the stock answer.

So, René contacted his "special friend" at Air France and was booked on the next flight to Newark. He hoped he was not too late.

He somewhat believed Alexa Fontaine: killing LaFleur had been an accident. But he also believed that Canford was not above making another accident happen, this time involving Anna, if she did not return the coin.

René felt as if he were chasing the Terminator, who was solely focused on achieving his task without letting anything or anyone get in his way. Canford's tunnel vision was so complete that the man had broken off all communications with the church until he completed his task.

Likewise, for some reason Anna had turned off her phones. René tried all the numbers he had to reach her and sent emails as well but got no response. As a result, he was on this plane, heading for Newark. He would arrive at around nine in the morning.

•　　•　　•

Light filtered through the bedroom curtains. Anna looked at the clock. It read 7:30. She had slept the whole night through. There were no dreams, no Tim, no Judas, nothing. She was practically in tears. It did not work. It was as simple as that. Why didn't she make the journey to Aceldama? Was there some reason she could not go back? Did Kaddish have some effect after all, just not the one she envisioned? Was Tim lost to her forever? Had she totally lost all semblance of sanity?

Her mood and optimism were plummeting. The emptiness she felt was as big as the ocean. Where could she turn? Turning to the church had backfired. She wanted to trust that the doctors knew what they were doing but, given the puzzled looks that they unsuccessfully tried their best to conceal, this option gave her little solace.

She pulled herself out of bed. There was no use lying there feeling sorry about her plight. Depending on his condition, they might operate on Tim today. As Dr. Pritak told her, she needed to be there for him. Tim could not afford for her to be despondent. Despite this latest setback, she was determined to move forward. She had no idea what other options were open to her but she could not be dissuaded. She could not give up.

As she was putting on her robe to head downstairs and put on some coffee, she heard a noise.

"Mags, is that you?"

She reached the landing and there he was, Canford, the man from the restaurant in Paris. He looked even more cadaverous than she remembered.

"Where is it?" he demanded. His voice had an English accent to it.

Anna shrunk back toward the stairs. "Where is what?" she responded, even though she knew what he was after.

"Let's not play games, Mrs. Harrington. You know what I'm after. It must be returned and destroyed."

Anna backed another couple of steps. As she did, her robe opened slightly and the coin revealed itself. Seeing it, the man lunged to yank it from between her breasts. She instinctively put both her hands up to halt his progress. He grabbed her right wrist with his left hand, reaching with his other hand for the coin.

Just then, Anna saw another man's hand reach around, grab Canford's arm and violently wrench it, turning him around, away from Anna. Once turned, a quick punch was delivered to Canford's solar plexus. He dropped to his knees whereupon his assailant wheeled to deliver a swift kick to the side of the head, but Canford had recovered enough to block the leg and to throw its owner momentarily off balance. This gave Canford enough time to get up to his feet and run out the door. The whole sequence took at most fifteen seconds.

Anna looked at Canford's back as he fled. When she looked back at the man who had saved her, she was shocked to see a priest.

"Black belt in karate. What can I say?"

Anna was still too flummoxed to say a word. The priest was a lot shorter than his voice let on. He was the type who would be described as small but wiry. He had a dark complexion, narrow set dark eyes and jet black hair. It was not yet eight in the morning and he had what appeared to be a permanent five o'clock shadow.

"Mrs. Harrington, I'm Father Mark Carew. We spoke on the phone."

"Thank you, Father. When did you learn karate?"

"My first parish when I was in seminary was in a rough inner city area. I was rather intimidated, so I took some karate lessons. Turns out I loved it and was a natural. A year and a half later, I was a black belt. Who was that?"

"William Canford. He works for you."

"For me?

"For the church; for the Vatican. He came to get this."

Anna showed Father Mark the coin, but at the same time realized she was somewhat exposing herself as she closed her robe around her. Father Mark smiled at her show of modesty.

"Should we call the police?" Father Mark inquired.

"No. No police. I have no idea what the legal status of this coin is. They may demand to hold it until that is sorted out. I can't let in out of my possession for a second."

"Fair enough."

"Would you like some coffee?"

"Yes, I believe I would. Thank you."

Anna set about making the coffee as the Father sat quietly at the kitchen table. She poured their cups and sat down opposite him.

"I hope this doesn't come out as rude—especially after you saved my life—but why are you here? Did the Archbishop not have confidence that Canford could do the job and sent you—a priest with a black belt—to get the coin from me?"

Father Mark took a sip of his coffee.

"I came to personally apologize to you for what has happened. I am ashamed that I played any role in what has turned into blackmail and physical threats. As a matter of fact, if it were not for my efforts, the blackmail never would have gone this far. You see, I believed—or rather believe—your story. I made an earnest pitch to my superiors to become involved. We needed to help you. At first, they thought I was a raving lunatic, much like many people I would assume are thinking about you."

He stopped to sip his coffee. Anna knew his last remark was not meant to be insulting. Rather, she sensed that his ramblings were a sort of confession. He was not only apologizing but going through the entire sequence for her so that she might understand and grant him absolution.

First, she took on the role of being Phil's therapist; now she was acting as a priest's confessor. She was tired and growing impatient. She wanted life to return to normal. She wanted to seek a professional's help rather than having it thrown back at her. If Father Mark wanted absolution, he would just have to find someone more qualified to give it.

Father Mark picked up where he left off.

"In the end, I guess I was so persuasive that Archbishop McAllister thought it was too risky to leave anything to chance. What happened next never should have happened. I'm here is to tell you that I think I can stop the blackmail."

Anna eyed the priest suspiciously.

"What could you possibly do to stop these wheels from turning?" Then she said, "I don't know what you could do to help. This all has seemed dictated by fate. There is nothing we can do."

"Well, I don't know much about fate but I do know a little about priests. As with many professions, the priesthood is a small, close-knit fraternity. After I spoke with you I went to my superior, Bishop Friend. I was rather persuasive and convinced him that we could not sit still. However, he was as befuddled as I was on what to do so he went to his superiors and it picked up steam the higher it went. I believe they called church officials in France. You know the rest. You're living the rest.

"I was ordered in no uncertain terms to stay out of it, but I just could not. After I found out what the Archbishop was threatening to do to you, I went where I should have from the start, my mentor Bishop Walker. I reported to him when I was just out of seminary and, if I ever had an idol, he is it. Bishop Walker is out in Manitoba now. That's why I did not go to him directly. Plus, chain of command and all that."

Anna was getting exasperated, wishing he would hasten the story.

"I phoned the Bishop yesterday to get his advice. He was livid when he heard what was happening. He agreed that, if what you say is true, the coin needs to be put in proper hands for study and, if necessary, destroyed. However, there was a right way to go about it and a wrong way. The Archbishop definitely chose the wrong way."

"I am so comforted that someone in the church has a smidgen of conscience. It is so assuring."

"Bishop Walker has a conscience and he has connections. The priesthood is a small, close-knit fraternity. It seems that Bishop Walker once apprenticed to Archbishop McAllister when the Archbishop was a Monsignor on his way up the ladder. Bishop Walker did not say as much, but I sensed that he knew some things about the Archbishop that could be embarrassing if they were made public. Of course you did not hear it here, but the Archbishop did not get propelled up the church hierarchy solely on the basis of his good works and faith. He is an able administrator who has many friends but, if truth be known, some of his actions were like the deal he offered you and may be viewed by some as rather unseemly. Even his high-placed friends may find it difficult to keep him where he is, heading a high-profile diocese like Toronto. I hear there may be a vacancy up in the Yukon Territory that he would be extremely qualified for."

Father Mark smiled. It was a mischievous but at the same time warm and comforting smile. It took a moment but Anna was getting Father Mark's drift. The blackmailer was being blackmailed. If it worked, her mother would not be contacted. There would be no scandal. There would be no excommunication. Dr. Richardson would not have his reason to fire her. Her reputation would remain intact.

"This will have to be done with finesse so that, to put it crudely, all of our backsides are covered. It may take a little while for you to receive absolute assurance that you will not be bothered, but it will happen. I assure you. Oh, and as far as I know, there are no pictures. Something the Archbishop made up to increase the pressure. A creative but evil touch, if you ask me.

"In regards to the coin, I do think it needs to be returned and studied," Father Mark held up his hand to hold off any protests Anna might make, "but I understand that you feel you need to work with it before you can let it out of your possession. Have you taken the actions you feel you need to?"

"I don't know." It was difficult for Anna to keep a tone of impatience out of her voice. "I went to temple and said Kaddish for Judas. Nothing happened. My husband is still in a coma. I have been so despondent since then. I was so sure that I had found the key but I was so silly to believe in such hocus-pocus. The doctors are recommending an experimental procedure that they believe may offer some hope. It may also kill him."

"I'm not here to judge whether what you are doing is "hocus-pocus" or not. It's my job to believe in miracles, so I can't tell you that you are wrong. But I did do some hard thinking. When in doubt, I tend to go to my primary reference book." With that Father Mark pulled a ragged old Bible out of his bag. "Of course, I'm familiar with the story of Judas and the thirty pieces. But since it's not usual sermon fare, I never focused on it in depth so I reread the passage.

"His betrayal is complete once he accepts the thirty pieces of silver but then he goes and compounds his sin by hanging himself. Suicide is frowned upon by most every religion. The Judeo-Christian tradition is no exception. A person who kills himself is taking away God's most precious gift from the world. In our beliefs he has committed a mortal sin and has endangered his soul. If you look at most of either the artistic or literary representations of Judas through the century, he is usually depicted as being in Hell or otherwise communing with the devil."

"Father, I hate to be rude but is your explanation going to land on a point in the not-too-distant future?"

"Yes, yes it is. I am sure he had somebody who mourned his passing but with the tumult of the period, they may have had to go underground. So Judas is dead and gone, forsaken by those closest to him. His is a soul that everyone always assumed was destined to go to Hell. What if his soul didn't go to Hell?"

"Why wouldn't it?"

"One simple sentence: 'Father, forgive them for they know not what they do.' That line has always touched me. Here Jesus was, in ultimate agony awaiting his death, and he forgave all of his tormentors. He did not say: 'Forgive everybody except Judas and the Pharisees and Pilate and maybe the crowds that turned against me.' It was a blanket request for everybody involved in this crime to receive forgiveness, and, to my way of thinking, that included Judas."

"So he wasn't damned to Hell?"

"I believe he was, but for the sake of argument and your dream scenario let's say he wasn't. Or let's say he was sentenced to a different version of hell than we're used to reading about. What did you call it, Aceldama? A rather exquisite form of punishment if you stop and think about it. The coin provides him an opportunity to gather disciples, somewhat the way Jesus did in life. It gives him an ongoing reminder in the afterlife of his treachery. To make it even worse, these disciples did not come to him willingly like they did to Jesus. Nor did they seem to follow him out of any higher calling. There were hundreds of other souls, floating through the ether. You theorized these were people who had simply come in contact with the coin. Further testament to Judas' treachery. If he had any conscience—which I think he did—this would further his torment as he knows he was responsible for the suffering of all these people. Altogether, this would make for a hell worthy of Sartre.

"But maybe, just maybe, while he was sentenced to this netherworld where he would be punished for his infamy, he was also provided a way out. All it would take is for someone to figure out how to turn the key to unlock the door."

Anna vividly recalled her foray into this dream world and the expressionless looks on Tim's and the others' faces. It was as if a drug or a spell had been employed to keep them in line and compliant. Luckily, Tim still had enough of a spark of independence left to provide her with a hint on how to break the spell, or at least she hoped he had.

"You mentioned a key to the door. What is the key, though? Don't ask me why, but I was positive that saying Kaddish for him was it. That did not work, though. What else can it be and how on earth do we find out? I've scoured Sister Catherine's diary dozens of times and no other clues have made themselves obvious. I even tried returning to Aceldama last night, but it was unsuccessful."

"I do think saying Kaddish may have been a piece of the puzzle but there may be another piece as well."

"Another piece?"

"Yes, a piece of silver. To continue with the story, Judas is gone but the money, the thirty pieces of silver, is still around. It's blood money, pure and simple. What if somehow the money itself got tainted?"

"Let me see if I get what you're saying here. Are you saying that the coins themselves were damned?"

"Even before this all happened with your husband, if I were to walk up to you and out of the blue say 'thirty pieces of silver' you'd know exactly what I was talking about, wouldn't you?"

"Why, yes."

"I would venture to say that most every Christian would also know the reference. A host of non-Christians as well. To paraphrase your President Roosevelt, it is an amount of money that will live in infamy."

"So this money is damned. Is this a curse that would go on forever?"

"Mind you, I'm making this up as I go along, but for argument's sake let's go a little further in the story. So far we have Judas throwing the pieces to the floor, departing and hanging himself. If you read further, you find subsequent verses telling us that the chief priests gathered up the coins but, because it was blood money, they could not put them into the Temple Treasury. Instead, they used this money to buy a potter's field, an Aceldama as it was known to the Jews of the day. In fact it was your use of 'Aceldama' that first gave me an inkling that maybe you weren't quite as crazy as you initially seemed. It's hardly an everyday word and, when you mentioned it, I became convinced that you might be telling the truth, or at least what you believed to be the truth. The coin was a shekel. Many historians have theorized that the Shekel of Tyre would most likely have been the coin used in the temple.

"So, anyway, even if this was blood money, at least it was going to some charitable purpose. It gave the poor a final resting place, albeit it a potter's field. By doing this act, the money itself would have been redeemed."

"I think you're losing me."

"What I'm saying is, suppose they missed one. Supposed they missed two. What if Judas threw the money to the floor and it scattered in every direction. The high priests would not lower themselves to scurrying around on their hands and knees searching for the coins. They would order their underlings go around and gather up the silver pieces. They would want it done as quickly and quietly as possible. Through the centuries, we have portrayed the high priests as evil men. They killed Christ after all, so they must be evil. Right? I personally don't think they were evil. They had their positions and jobs to do. Putting down a threat to Israel and Judaism was one of their jobs. I have trouble believing that they were totally unconcerned about killing Jesus. Even if he was a blasphemer in their eyes, he was still an innocent and holy man. It must have played at least somewhat on their consciences, although it's true that life was a little cheaper then. They still stoned women to death for adultery after all.

"Be that as it may, after Judas made his scene, they had some level of guilt and embarrassment. They would want to get rid of the money as expeditiously as possible. Who knows, in their hurry to get rid of it maybe they didn't take the time to count it all up. They might have relied on their assistant's count. Maybe somebody was passing by when Judas threw the money down and, when the coin rolled to his feet, they scooped it up. You mentioned a Roman soldier in the dreams; it could have been him. Or maybe the assistant pocketed a coin or two. Maybe he owed some money to the soldier and this was a simple way to pay it off. Who knows? Anyway, in the end, it could be that 28 or 29 coins went to buy the potter's field. Only 28 or 29 coins were redeemed. The other coin or coins, perhaps the one you have in your possession, never has been redeemed. It is still damned, still cursed."

Father Mark paused for effect. Anna could imagine that he gave a good homily.

"So, what can we do? Do we have to melt the coin down or something to destroy it?"

"For some reason, I don't believe destroying it is the answer. I don't think what you've done so far has been wasted except that you've done half the job. You redeemed and reconciled Judas, the man; now we must do something to redeem the money."

"I repeat: what can we do?"

"Exactly what the high priests did. Sell the coin and use the proceeds to help the poor, although I don't think there is much of a call for potter's fields these days. I think helping the poor while they're still alive would be just as effective."

"What are you proposing?"

"I'll buy it. I brought my checkbook with me."

"I have the receipt in my bag. It was 550 euros. That comes to about $700, I think."

"That's a lot cheaper than I thought it would have gone. I don't suppose the dealer had an inkling of what he had, did he?"

"He was pretty sure he had vastly undersold it. He had too much inventory and he wanted to move the coins so he was not as careful as he should have been. I somehow doubted it. He was a pretty shrewd businessman. You were saying?"

"I am prepared to offer you three times what you paid for it. I will then personally hold onto the coin until you say so. If our collective insanity is correct, there should be an improvement. Then, I, or rather the church, would keep the coin. Given that it would no longer be cursed or whatever, there should be no need to destroy it. It could be kept on as an historical relic, although verifying its authenticity would be nearly impossible. Do we have a deal?"

"This doesn't sound any crazier than the last two weeks have been. Yes, we have a deal. But I think we should amend this plan."

"How?"

"This whole concoction seems pretty intricately designed. For me to sell it to someone who can be seen as a willing accomplice, as someone who's in on the scheme, may be viewed as a, as a, what's the word I'm looking for.

"A subterfuge?"

"Yeah, something like that. God or whoever could see that selling you the coin—even though you could be viewed as *the* ultimate charitable organization—is us trying to game the system."

"What do you suggest?"

"Let me sell it to you but then you turn the proceeds over to an uninvolved third party. Whaddya think?"

"Works for me. Do you have anyone in mind who you can call on short notice?"

"A friend of mine works for the Center of Hope Charities. Her facility is about a half mile from here. If she's around, she'll be glad to come on short notice. I can only imagine her speed if she knows the Center will be getting over two thousand dollars."

"Sounds like a plan."

"I do have one condition."

"And that is?"

"That the entire transaction takes place at the hospital. Even if I've lost all my marbles, I can't turn back now. I have to play this all the way through. If Tim is a conduit, I want you and the representative of the charity both there."

"That sounds like a perfectly reasonable request."

"I'm beginning to wonder about you, Father, if you think any of this sounds reasonable. I do have one more request to make of you."

"Yes, I think you've earned as many requests as you want...within reason of course."

"Of course. Are you affiliated with a convent?"

"I don't know if affiliated is the right word but there is a convent not far from my church. The nuns help us out on a regular basis."

"So it is an order that does a great deal of work out in the community, not one that is withdrawn and totally devoted to contemplation and meditation?"

"Not in the least. They have their meditative side to be sure but they are very active in the church and in the community throughout the year. As a matter of fact, the Mother Superior is one heck of a softball pitcher. You haven't found religion all of a sudden and thinking of becoming a nun, are you?"

Anna smiled. Dr. Cohn mentioned about her becoming a Jew. Now Father Mark floated the idea of her becoming a nun. It was nice to be wanted, but if she ever got through this unscathed, she would be content with being what she was.

"Me. No, not at all. But there is a young woman I know who is. She is a young French woman who was kicked out of her convent because she helped me. The convent was not right for her anyway but she is destined to be a nun. She has too much to offer to the world to be shut away or to be shut out of her calling. I was wondering if your convent would offer her a position. She speaks English, by the way."

"Can the international paperwork can be worked out?"

Thinking of René and the fact that he invariably must have a "friend" down at the French State Department or whatever they call that agency, Anna responded, "I assure you that it can be arranged."

"Then let's get her over here. We don't have a surplus of young women knocking down our doors to be nuns these days. We could use some priests, too, if you happen to know of any guys with an urge to join the brotherhood."

"No, none at the moment," Anna responded with a laugh,

"It was worth a shot. Your French friend will be welcomed with open arms. Let me write down the name and number of the convent and the Mother Superior. Give me her name. You have your friend call and I'll tell the Mother to expect to hear from her shortly. She'll be so excited to get a new novice."

Anna envisioned Marie playing softball. She hoped that Marie played in her habit or some conservative dress. The hormonal-tinged ideas racing through the minds of the orphanage's teenage boys upon seeing her in a T-shirt and shorts would be quite frightening.

"Shall we head over to the hospital?"

"Okay."

They were about to leave when the phone rang. It was Dr. Pritak.

"Mrs. Harrington," he said in an fast, desperate voice, "Tim has suffered a brain aneurysm. They are rushing him to surgery. You need to get here right away."

"Get in my car. I'll drive." Father Mark volunteered.

40

Father Mark broke every traffic law in the book driving to the hospital, but Anna was not going to ask him to slow down. He got to the hospital in less than six minutes. Pulling up on the curb, he grabbed a card that read "Clergy—Emergency" and threw it on the dashboard. He gently helped Anna, who was a wreck, out of the front seat and walked her into the main lobby.

An elderly volunteer manning the front desk showed great agility in punching the keys on the computer and directed Anna and Father Mark to the surgery waiting room.

They rushed to the fifth floor. Father Mark picked up the phone and dialed in. He was advised that Tim Harrington was in the operating room. No word had come out about his condition or prognosis. There was nothing more the nurse could tell him at this time. All they could do was to sit tight and wait. Father Mark sat down beside Anna to wait.

"Anna, do you have the name and number of your friend down at the Center of Hope?"

"Wha?" It was the first utterance of any kind she had made in over a half hour. Not much, but it was something.

"I need the name of the person you know down at the Center of Hope Charities."

Anna's mind had no focus, but she was at least somewhat more coherent as the minutes passed. She pulled out her phone, went to Favorites, hit the Center's number and handed the phone to the Father.

"Ask for Elly. If she's not there, they can have her paged."

"Hello." A young female voice responded. It was a teenage volunteer. Father Mark silently blessed her for her service.

"Hello. I'd like to speak to Elly please."

"Just a moment. She's around here somewhere. Can I tell her who's calling?"

"My name is Father Mark Carew. I'm calling for Anna Harrington, a friend of hers."

"Hold on."

A minute later a voice came on at the other end. "Hello, this is Elly Fitzgerald."

There was a pause.

"Yes, that's my real name and I do a mean 'April in Paris.'"

"Hello, my name is Father Mark Carew. I'm a friend of Anna Harrington."

"Yes, how's Anna? How's her husband?"

"Not well, I'm afraid. He's in surgery right now for an emergency operation."

"Oh my God. Is there anything I can do?"

"Can you come down to the Barton Medical Center as soon as possible? It's rather important."

"Of course."

"We're on the fifth floor in the waiting room right off the elevator."

Elly was in the waiting room fifteen minutes later. When she walked into the room, she exhibited such an air of confidence that it appeared that she was walking into her own home or office.

By the time Elly arrived, Anna had recovered somewhat. She had gotten her color back and was looking like a human being again. Elly gave her a big hug and then introduced herself to Father Mark. The Father got right down to business.

"Ms. Fitzgerald..."

"It's Mrs., but please call me Elly."

"Okay. Elly, you may find the timing of this to be a bit odd but the reason we asked you to come down here is to make a donation to the Center of Hope Charities."

Elly indeed appeared perplexed but she still gave the Father a broad smile. "It does strike me as a little out of the ordinary given the situation but we stand ready to accept gifts of charity in any and all places. You of all people should know that God works in mysterious ways."

"Yes indeed He — or She — does."

His political correctness brought a quick smile to Elly's lips. Anna had by this time approached the land of the living enough that she could warm up to his comment as well.

"Elly, I need a solemn pledge from you that every cent of this particular donation will go to help those in need. Not a cent of it is to go to buy as much as a pencil. Can you promise me that?"

"Usually, our donations are deposited into a general account that covers all of our expenditures but we do have a special discretionary fund account that gets used for direct aid projects. The money can be deposited there. So yes, I can assure you that every cent will go to the poor. May I ask why it is so important? We have low overhead and I'm proud to say that even the lowliest pencil gets used in helping the poor and destitute."

"You will just have to trust Anna and me. Someday, I hope, we can sit down over a cup of coffee and explain the whole thing to you."

"That's good enough for me. Yes, you have my solemn word."

With that, Father Mark reached into his coat pocket and pulled out his checkbook. "Should I make the check out to Center of Hope Charities?"

"Yes, that will be fine," Elly responded, "but Anna, shouldn't you write the check? That way you can take it off taxes."

"No, that wouldn't be right," Anna responded in a monotone. "This money must have no strings attached or any hint of anything beyond a straight cash transaction."

As Father Mark finished making out the check, Anna handed the coin over to him. In turn, Anna gave the check to Elly.

"Eighteen hundred dollars, that's very generous. That money will help a good number of people."

"I hope so," Father Mark responded. "I chose eighteen hundred because it's a multiple of eighteen, the Jewish symbol for life. Let's trust that its meaning is fulfilled."

"It is appreciated. I have to get back to get ready for the noon meal. Anna, give me a call after Tim comes out of surgery and let me know how it went. If there is anything I can do for you, please don't hesitate to call."

"Thank you so much for coming, Elly. Someday we will get

together for lunch so I can explain what happened here."

"I'd like that. The Center and I thank you. Father, Anna." With that she left.

Anna and Father Mark settled down for the long siege, waiting for news from the operating room. An hour stretched into two and then into three. Occasionally, one of them would get up to go to the bathroom. Father Mark went downstairs and returned with two cups of coffee. Very few words were spoken.

"Elly sure is a dynamic, dedicated woman," Father Mark noted.

"The best I know."

"From where I sit, she has stiff competition."

"Thank you, Father, I appreciate that. I also apologize for my behavior earlier."

"You were fine. If I were in your shoes, I would have been much worse."

The conversation hit a lull as the clock pushed five hours.

"Can I tell you something in complete confidence, Anna? And I mean complete."

"Of course you can."

"I ask you that because what I am about to tell you is something revealed to me during confession. I could be defrocked—not to mention having my soul eternally damned—but I think that by telling you will help your life, and your mother's as well. I also figure that since it wasn't a confession about herself but something that was told to me during that time, I can argue a technicality."

"My mother?"

"Yes. You have been panicked about the Archbishop revealing your secret. You shouldn't have been."

"Why not?"

"Because, for one thing you are selling your mother far too short. She loves you so much that I don't think anything would shake her feeling for you."

"I know she wouldn't love me any less. I just don't want a change in our relationship. She, my sister and I are good friends. We've always been extremely close. I don't want a cloud hanging over that relationship."

"Well, the other thing that you should be aware of is that she knows."

Even though Anna knew what the Father was saying, she still had to play the game and hear it all.

"Knows what?"

"That you were a stripper, gave lap dances, all that."

"How did she find out?"

"I have no idea. Could just be a mother's way of knowing these things. I can never pull the wool over my mother's eyes. It came out in confession. She was in the middle of reciting all the "atrocities" she had committed over the past week when out of nowhere she asked me if you were in any danger of being damned. Then she told me what you had done for over three years some time ago. I assure you, her question came out of concern and love for you. There was no recrimination whatsoever."

"She even knew how long I did it? She never said a word letting on that she knew."

Anna paused, and then added, "So, what was your answer? Am I damned?"

"Some Vietnam vets have a saying that they know they're going to Heaven because they've already been through hell. After the last couple of months, you can say the same thing. You've already had your glimpse of hell. The question now is, will you be saved?"

Anna grimaced and silently acknowledged that he was right. *Mothers are incredible.* She sadly noted that she would never be able to enjoy the feeling of being a mother. Once Tim got better, she vowed, they would adopt a child.

After five hours, Anna could no longer remain in her seat. She started to pace and fidget. Was it a good sign or a bad one that it was taking so long? Was it a mistake that she had let the coin out of her possession, even for a moment? Did the coin have any significance at all, for that matter? While she believed she could trust Father Mark, she did not know him from Adam. Maybe he was a consummate con artist. Maybe he was in league with the Archbishop. Or with Canford.

She got her answer ten seconds later as the door burst open and Canford barged in, a gun in his hand. He aimed it at the priest.

"You stay over there."

He swung his aim over to Anna, but kept an eye on Father Mark.

"I don't want to hurt anyone, but I will if I don't get what I want right now."

As these words were leaving his lips, the door opened once again. Canford whirled around to find Alexander standing there in his scrubs, a horrified look on his face as he stared into the pistol's barrel. Canford, in full panic now, squeezed the trigger but as he did Alexander was abruptly pushed aside. He lost his balance and ended up sitting on the floor in an undignified manner as René catapulted through the door.

The gun blast filled the room but René was undeterred as he rushed in, driving his shoulder into Canford's gut. René's momentum carried then both five feet as Canford's crashed into a bookcase, hitting the back of his head hard on the top shelf. He went out like a light as both he and René settled to the floor.

If Anna had not been so in shock, she would have screamed. Instead she looked around at the scene, which surrealistically appeared frozen in time for a few seconds.

Alexander, in his blood-stained scrubs, was reaching for his sore backside as he sat on the floor. Father Mark had assumed a karate stance but had no one to fight. René lay on top of an unconscious Canford.

The frozen spell did not last long as everyone except Canford began to move. Anna went over to help Alexander up.

"I was coming in to tell you that Tim is going to be alright. He made it through surgery and is already showing signs of a recovery."

Anna felt a joy and relief she had not felt in months. She was about to hug the surgeon in appreciation when she looked over to see Father Mark helping René roll off of Canford. Blood oozed from between René's fingers as he held his chest.

"Oh my God! René!"

She rushed over to his side and cradled his head in her lap.

Despite the great pain he was feeling as he looked up at her, he smiled when he looked up into her face.

"Like I say, I am party in your hands, Anna."

With that he grimaced, his eyes closed and his head sagged to his chest.

"No!" she screamed. "Dear God! Please no. Please no."

Her voice trailed off as shock set in and she sat there mumbling incoherently.

41

Two hours later, Anna woke up to find Alexander and Father Mark looking down on her. For the briefest of moments she forgot where she was or what had transpired as she remarked to the two of them.

"I don't know whether to be flattered or nervous that I have a priest and a surgeon standing over me. Or maybe it's just the start of a joke."

Then her reality came crashing back down on her as she sat up straight.

"Tim! René!"

Alexander gently pushed her back down onto the cot.

"There, there. Stay calm. Tim's in recovery. That was what I was coming to tell you when all hell broke loose. There was an aneurysm on a blood vessel that was exerting pressure on his brain. That would explain all the weird thoughts he's been experiencing over the past few months. I've seen aneurysms like this be misdiagnosed for schizophrenia in the past. In any case, Tim made it through surgery. Now it's wait and see."

"Can I go to him?"

"He's going to be out for a few more hours. It's best for you to rest up yourself. You've been through quite a trauma."

"And René?"

Father Mark interjected himself.

"He's in surgery, Anna. You should have seen this good doctor spring into action. It was a sight to behold. He was barking orders to all of us. Until he showed up here again, the last I saw of him was accompanying the gurney to the operating room as he was pinching a blood vessel closed to keep René from bleeding to death."

"You were no slouch yourself, Father," Alexander commented. "The bullet penetrated one of Officer Bouvil's lungs. Dr. Frazier is working on him right now. He's the best thoracic trauma surgeon there is. It's wait and see."

Anna looked around.

"Where am I?"

"You're on one of the cots the doctors use to catch a few z's between shifts. You've been here for a few hours. I had the nurse give you a mild sedative to help you get some sleep."

"And Canford?"

"Yet another person in surgery. When your friend René tackled him, he hit the back of his head so hard that there was immediate swelling that was impinging on his spinal column. We had to go in to relieve that pressure. Otherwise, he could end up paralyzed for life."

"What will happen to him?"

Father Mark responded.

"He'll go to jail, for what he tried to do here and for the killing of Etienne LaFleur back in France. My superiors advised me that the Vatican had very quietly lifted his diplomatic immunity and is now pretending that Mr. Canford never existed or at least that they never had any dealings with him. From what I can gather, he has been very useful in cleaning up various messes over the years but the church always turned a blind eye to how he operated. This time, however, Canford crossed a line they could not overlook or gloss over.

"Why don't you get a bit more rest. I'll come back for you once there is any news about Tim or René."

"Thank you Father. And you too Doctor."

An hour later, Father Mark stuck his head back in.

"Anna, I got word that Tim's coming to. You want to go see him?"

Without responding, Anna sprung off of the cot and strode out into the hallway with the Father.

"By the way, Anna, you look terrible."

Anna paused to glance at her reflection in a window as they proceeded down the hall. He was correct. Her hair was stringy and dirty. Despite the recent sleep, the bags under her eyes were grotesque. Her clothes were disheveled and looked as if she'd been sleeping in them, which she had. Normally, if she had ever seen the image of herself that she was now looking at her initial reaction would be, 'How could you let yourself out of the house looking like this?' Instead, she had no second thought about venturing out looking like this.

"You're a priest. What do you know about how a woman should look?"

"Just because I can't buy doesn't mean I can't window shop. I know terrible when I see terrible and you fit the bill. I'm just saying. I don't want Tim's first sight to be something that'll make him say: 'Send me back to Aceldama!' "

Anna burst out in laughter. "Well, this will be a true test of how strong our marriage really is, won't it? By the way, it's Sunday, isn't it? Who's conducting your service today?"

"Before I left, I arranged for another priest to fill in for me. He'll perform the sacraments and let some of the congregants participate in a sort of a layman Sunday. My parish has more than its share of strutting peacocks who would love to get up and mouth platitudes to the congregation."

"They're called *machers*," Anna, the brand-new expert on Judaism, advised him.

"Yes, I believe they are. In any case, everything's in good hands...I think."

They reached Tim's room.

"I'll leave you here."

"No, please come in with me. I'm hoping for the best, but I'm still nervous. I don't know which Tim will be there for me and I may need you once again."

"As you wish."

Dr. Pritak, who had assisted in the surgery, was at Tim's bedside listening to his heartbeat with a stethoscope. When the door opened, he turned to greet Anna.

"It does not appear that you will require my full services after all, Mrs. Harrington. Your husband is going to be fine. He will drift in and out but the coma is over. I will stay here for two more days to monitor him. My New Jersey relatives that were so anxious for me to visit are now sick of me and ready for me to go back to Chicago."

"Thank you, doctor."

"You must be Father Mark Carew. I am Dr. Manesh Pritak." As they shook hands, Anna puzzled over the doctor's powers yet again.

She did not recall ever mentioning the priest to him. Maybe someone at the hospital told him. None of that mattered as her eyes zeroed in on Tim. She sat gently by his side. As soon as she sat, he partially opened his eyes.

He could not speak as tubes blocked his mouth and throat. Gauze bandages enveloped his head. He was still substantially under the anesthesia. To anyone else, this was a sick man. To Anna, he looked beautiful. Even half-closed, his eyes told her everything she needed to know. They were alive and penetrating. They sought her out and, once they found her, would not let her go until sleep forced them shut. He attempted to smile and to say something. She shushed him. He should rest. She knew all she needed to know; he would be all right. There would be plenty of time for chatter.

Anna did not even notice the doctor and priest departing the room. She sat, holding Tim's hand while he drifted in and out of sleep. Not a word was spoken for over two hours; none was needed. After the nurse came in to give him pain medication that would knock him out for the night, Anna decided to head home. She gave Tim a kiss on the cheek, confident that the worst was over. She could leave with full assurance that over the next few days and weeks he would recover totally.

42

"Hi, hon. What took you so long?"

"Oh, I had some errands to run. Then Magda called. You know how it is."

Both Tim and Anna smiled. His recovery had been miraculous. A little over one day after the operation he was breathing on his own. Another day later, he was speaking again, albeit in a raspy, halting manner.

"Yeah, I know how it is," he croaked. "I know even more that I love you so much. How long was I out anyway?"

"It was about two weeks. There were times we almost lost you. I don't think the doctors have any clue how you survived. They say the pressure on your brain induced your unconsciousness. When the vessel burst, they were able to pinpoint the problem and correct it, even though it almost killed you."

The official diagnosis attributed his condition to circulatory problems that put pressure on his brain, causing him to lose consciousness. Once repaired, Tim's condition improved. The medical professionals were totally perplexed as to why none of the MRIs, CAT Scans or any of the hundreds of other tests that were administered detected the problem.

While Alexander was in no way condoning his son's actions, he did note that the attempt Phil made on Tim's life perhaps saved it. Tim's reaction to the insulin made the aneurysm more prominent and easier to detect and treat. Anna took this explanation as a devoted father seeing good in even the vilest actions taken by his offspring.

"While I was out I had a dream," Tim said. "Know what it was about?"

Anna knew full well but was afraid to mention it for fear that the dream would recur. By voicing it, she may be forced to realize that it was not a dream after all, like in a horror movie when everyone thinks the evil creature has been eliminated but subsequently discover that it had one last curtain call left. She responded with a simple, "No, what was it about?"

"It was your face. That's all. It got dim for awhile; I was losing you, but it was always there. I kept trying to reach out and touch it, but it was always out of reach."

Anna leaned down to him. With a still weak arm he reached up and stroked the smooth skin of her cheek.

"Eventually, you came closer and became clearer than ever," he said as he was still holding her, staring into her eyes. "That's when I woke up. Know what? You're even better looking in real life."

"I bet you say that to all the nurses."

"Yeah, especially Julio. He's my day nurse who gives me all sorts of wonderful drugs. As a matter of fact, he just gave me some and I'm starting to drift away into oblivion."

"Get your sleep my love. We'll talk later."

"Goodnight, darling." Then, from somewhere deep in his drug-induced stupor he mumbled, "Anna, thank you. We all thank and bless you. What you have done is a *mizvah*. You have freed him, freed us."

Tim drifted off into a deep sleep.

43

Within a week, the doctors announced that Tim was well enough to be discharged. They patted themselves on the back for a job well done, although Anna could tell that they would be perplexed by both his illness and his subsequent recovery. They could not figure why Tim was showing minimal after-effects. Several of the hospital's neurologists pestered Tim after his release to get him to submit to some follow-up tests. Sensing he was to be a lab rat, he politely refused.

Anna did not care what the reason for his recovery was. She knew she would be driving her husband home the next morning. Let the doctors believe whatever they wanted; she had gotten her love back from the abyss. She appreciated that Alexander acknowledged her perseverance and steadfast devotion as a contributing factor to his recovery. She knew that her efforts consisted of far more than moral support but the lack of credit did not bother her in the least. She did not want credit; she wanted Tim. As far as she was concerned, the last two weeks had been a nightmare that could now return to the netherworld where dreams exist.

.   .   .

When the morning arrived for Anna to take Tim home from the hospital, she could scarcely control her excitement. Magda was back in town to help out. That coming weekend, Father Mark was driving Elana down from Toronto for a visit. They would all be together.

Tim steadily grew stronger. Within three weeks he was able to start working on a limited basis. He soon had more clients than he could handle. Within six months, the Harringtons' lives returned to their natural suburban rhythms. Gradually, the dreams became what they were, dreams.

Anna found it interesting what Tim remembered about the whole ordeal and what he did not. On occasion, like when he was drifting away after the operation, he would come out with a comment that could only have been dredged up from his dream world. But then, after making a comment such as this, he would return to the present with little or no recollection of the words he had just spoken. If Anna asked him to repeat what he said, his response would be a blank stare. The doctors attributed this to being a natural part of his recovery process. The brain, they would say, can often act unpredictably after a serious trauma like he experienced. Time would be the greatest healer in this case. Sometimes after a head trauma, people's behavior can often be erratic and unpredictable.

Although his memories of the entire ordeal were sketchy at best, he realized how much he owed his lovely wife. Many men dramatically claim that their wives saved their souls; Tim knew it to be a fact. Somehow, even with a burgeoning business practice, he always found time to be attentive to Anna. Their passion seemed to grow daily.

Anna went back to the clinic shortly after Tim came home and loved it. Working with children again fulfilled her. She and Tim started to talk seriously with adoption agencies.

Even Dr. Richardson did not bother her now. Whenever he became cantankerous, Dr. Cohn's line about 'not discovering the difference between his ass and his elbow until his third year of medical school' would pop into her mind. It became difficult to take him too seriously after that.

As for Dr. Cohn, he went on as if nothing had ever happened. He could have very easily held the entire episode over her head but not once did he ever bring up Judas or lap dancing or any of it. Instead, he was his joking, lovable, jovial self who treated her as a colleague and as a friend. It was very much appreciated.

Anna arranged the lunch with Elly as she had promised. She could not bring herself to tell her friend about Judas, the coin, Sister Catherine, or any of the saga. It was just too ludicrous. As time passed, Anna herself was having difficulty believing that the whole nightmare was anything more than the product of her vivid imagination. Instead, she told Elly that the scene she witnessed in the hospital waiting room was generated by an old Czech superstition her grandmother had related to her many years ago. If someone was dying and that person's loved ones knew in their hearts that his or her time had not yet come, they should sell something that the dying person loves and give the money to charity. The act of charity would soften the anger of the evil spirits and they would loosen their control over the ailing person.

Elly seemed to buy the explanation, although she was a little baffled as to why a priest would partake in a ritual like this. Anna was rather proud of herself for being so creative.

Anna was worried about Phil and whether he would ever fully recover. She visited him on a monthly basis. Often, Alexander would accompany her; sometimes she would go alone or with Tim. Unfailingly, Phil would be pleasant and appear to be content. He was well provided for. Alexander paid out of his own pocket to ensure that all his needs were met. He even covered the cost for a satellite dish to be installed at the sanitarium so that Phil could have access to the baseball package.

Anna would want a fuller life for herself, but Phil appeared to be adjusting very well to his present circumstances. In his own mind anyway, he had regained something he loved dearly that had been tragically taken away from him. Maybe he was suffering before and this was his version of fulfillment. Anna sighed and was there for him.

Anna noticed a gradual improvement in Phil but never to the point where he could be declared fit to go home and resume a normal life. On one visit, he said, "Hi, Anna." It was the first time he had not called her Jennifer since being hospitalized. While it filled them with hope, Anna and Alexander knew full well that he would revert the very next time they saw him. Still, they were ecstatic.

As she had feared, Alexander was now profoundly alone. When she invited him to dinner, he accepted without hesitation. After that, he was a regular guest at the Harringtons, becoming a part of their family. One day, Alexander looked at Anna and said, "You know, I can understand how Phil's mind made the transference. Jennifer shared qualities that you have: kindness, consideration, an innate goodness."

"Why thank you, Alexander. It's always nice to hear such compliments."

"Well-deserved ones, my dear."

René made a full recovery from the surgery, although he did have to give up playing rugby because a part of his left lung had been removed. Anna and Tim were shocked when they received a letter telling them to set aside a date the following year for his marriage. They could never conceive that he would ever date one woman let alone settle down and get married. Her name was Nathalie. Anna was not sure which of René's "special friends" she was, but she thought she might be the one from Air France who helped her out. In any case, they advised René that they would be happy to return to Paris for the wedding. Tim promised to stay away from coin dealers while he was there. To emphasize the point, he gave his entire collection to Elly's nephew as a gift.

René advised them that Oncle Pierre was writing a book on the life of Sister Catherine. He had struck a deal with the convent for the rights to the diary. He was able to get the Mother Superior to agree to an interview about her beheaded predecessor. In return, Pierre would donate a portion of the royalties to the convent to help keep it going.

Anna kept in close contact with Marie, who was thoroughly enjoying her new home at the convent in Toronto. The paperwork had been worked out and she was settling in nicely with the convent. The Mother Superior spoke very highly of Marie, saying that she had dived right in at the orphanage. The kids loved her and she was a hit with everybody. Because of the time she had put in as a novice in France, they reduced the requirement at this convent and made her a full nun in short order.

By the tone of his reports, Anna could sense that Father Mark was taken with Sister Marie. Now, that would be a great couple if they ever decided to abandon their calling.

Anna remembered the twinge of jealousy she felt in Marie's presence. Despite men looking right past her to gaze on Marie's beautiful features, the two of them had hit a chord somehow. She sensed a long-term friendship being built up, even though they were from different worlds. If ever there was a beautiful soul, it was Marie.

Anna felt proud of herself that she could be of help to Marie, even though she knew it was a byproduct of her quest to find a way to cure Tim. She liked to think that she would have done the same under other circumstances as well.

Because of the international intricacies, it would take some time for Canford's final disposition to be worked out, but he definitely was heading to prison. Anna gave depositions to both American and French authorities. She did not want to testify; she would rather the whole episode be put behind her. But if she did, so be it.

For her part, Anna became somewhat of an amateur theological historian. She and Father Mark had hour-long conversations, on the phone no less, discussing the nuances of Judas, the coin and other relevant topics. Father Mark was the one who came up with the idea about redeeming the coin itself. She started to come up with some theories of her own.

Her theory was that Judas Iscariot, after he committed suicide, was sentenced to a sort of purgatory where he would be left in limbo. God furnished him with a window to look upon the living world: the coin. In some ways, this was worse than Hell. The access back to the world gave him continual reminders that the Christian world considered him the most reviled and hated person in history.

The souls of the people who came in closest contact with the coin served to reinforce this Hell. Tim reckoned that it was the people who wore the coin on their chests, close to the heart. These souls were provided to Judas as his disciples. Recreating a condemned world in the image of the living world he had departed two thousand years ago would increase his suffering. The Roman guard, the Turkish sailor, Sister Catherine, Tim and even for a brief interval, Anna herself, were all victims. To Anna, these people, or rather their souls, were innocent bystanders in a supernatural drive-by-shooting.

The two original gentlemen were sucked into this world entirely. They had no clue as to how to get out. While she was still alive but under the coin's influence, Sister Catherine began to see the signs and made the initial steps to unravel the mystery. Ultimately, however, it led to her downfall. Tim was well on his way to becoming the next permanent resident of Aceldama.

The hundreds of people who had superficial contact with the

shekel over the centuries were the ones who floated through Aceldama. Anna imagined that after he died, Etienne LaFleur entered the miasma.

Anna, in concert with Marie, Father Mark, René and others, used Sister Catherine's work as a base and finished the redemption process. Now, whether it was an act of Judas, Jesus or some other power, Tim was released from that other world. Hopefully, all the unwitting participants in this little drama were also now being compensated and rewarded.

Anna liked to believe that Sister Catherine, who in life had found the path to her true happiness and fulfillment through Judas and the coin, was being allowed to return to it through Sister Marie. For both of these Sisters, the greatest joy was in helping others. Now, Sister Marie would continue that effort. Anna built on the efforts of Sister Catherine to unlock the mystery; Marie was building on the life of Sister Catherine to do good deeds.

Anna found it interesting how the coin impacted Sister Catherine in a different way than it did Tim. She could only guess how it influenced Marcus and Atticus. Tim was terrified by the dreams, afraid that somehow the death of his father was coming back to haunt him. Tim could wear the medallion for a few short months before it consumed him. Sister Catherine, on the other hand, used the coin to make her life better. She wore it for fifteen years. She saw her dreams as a blessing and a revelation that caused her to change her life, devoting it to help others in need.

Over the coming years, Anna would often discuss and refine her theories with Father Mark. Now that she had her life and Tim back, she could enjoy the luxury of idle speculation and theological discussions. Father Mark would offer his own embellishments and throw in some profound theological implications. Tim would throw in some historical tidbits that he had picked up.

One time when they were in Toronto staying with her mother, Anna had an anxious moment about Tim. They, along with Sister Marie, were visiting with Father Mark at the rectory. Tim asked the Father if he still had the silver piece. Father Mark cautiously glanced at Anna, and then replied that he did. For all the urgency that the church leaders had expressed about destroying the coin, the wheels of the ecclesiastical bureaucracy churned slowly. Father Mark had had it in his possession for months and had requested instruction, but none was forthcoming.

Father Mark was wary about handing it over to Tim. For all their theological speculation and theories, Anna and the Father knew that for all intents and purposes they were in total darkness regarding any supposed powers it may possess. It was a fun mental exercise developing all of their intricate theories, but it was also pure guesswork. They liked to think that their actions helped Tim to recover, but they had no idea whatsoever as to the truth. In addition, even if by some stretch of the imagination they were correct and the coin did in fact have some mystical powers, they had no idea whether the actions they took had any effect in neutralizing those powers. For all they knew, the piece of silver could be as potent as ever. Maybe Tim's recovery was due to removing it from around his neck in the nick of time. Exposure to it once again could restart the cycle. Still, Father Mark felt he had no right to refuse the request.

Tim took it in his hands and studied it intently. He ran his fingers over the profile of Melqart, whom he had since learned was a Phoenician god of the sun and re-vegetation. Nobody said a word. After a few moments that seemed like an eternity to Anna, he handed it back to the Father, 'A lot of fuss over a cold piece of silver, isn't it?' Collective sighs of relief were expelled as they returned to their discussion as if there had been no interruption.

Sometimes, Anna would think about the Father in the same way that perhaps Sister Marie was carrying on Sister Catherine's good works. She never believed that somehow the souls of either Marcus Carolis, the Roman sentry who had the errant coin in the first place, or Atticus Tiompk, the Anatolian sailor who made it into a medallion centuries later, could be lodged somewhere in this good priest. They were too brutish for that but she liked to think that there was some metaphysical connection that brought Father Mark into her life. She would never know. Anna found comfort in the fact that she got to know the father and that that Marcus and Atticus, regardless of what they did in their lives, were at last finding the peace and contentment they had been denied for so long.

Against all her upbringing and ingrained training, she also found herself feeling concern for Judas and his fate. She could never determine his role, or whether he played one at all. Maybe he was a victim as much as anyone, caught up in a vortex in death, just as he had been during his life. Maybe he was not evil incarnate but someone who was clumsily searching for peace, like so many people are. Going against everything she had been taught her whole life, she wished Judas well and said an occasional prayer on his behalf.

Or maybe her husband had had a circulatory problem in his brain. Maybe it took modern science and medicine and the great skills of Dr. Alexander Mordecai to detect and treat the problem.

In reality, Anna Harrington did not care what the truth was. No, she did not care one bit.